CAUGHT UP IN YOU
CARDINAL SPRINGS

LAUREN MORRILL

To all the messy girls…
You're not messy
You're abstract fucking art

AUTHOR'S NOTE

In *Caught Up In You*, one of the characters is struggling with anxiety, and panic attacks are depicted on-page. If that means this book isn't for you right now, please set it aside. It will always be here when the time is right.

CHAPTER 1

WYATT

October 14

"Wyatt!"

My sister's voice wakes me from sleep like the whistle of a train: loud, then trailing off as she races past my bedroom door. The bathroom light floods the hallway, and I squint.

"Hazel? You okay?" I croak as I pry myself into reality. I sleep like the dead, and it usually takes half an hour and two cups of coffee before I'm able to put words in the right order.

But then I remember two things:

1. My baby sister is pregnant.
2. She's due in four days.

I sit straight up in bed.

"Hazel? What's going on?"

"Well, here's the thing," she calls from the bathroom. "I might be in labor?"

I trip out of bed and reach for a pair of sweatpants that's lying in a heap on my floor, then join the heap when my big toe gets caught on the hem and I go down like a bag of hammers. "What do you mean, *might be*?"

"Well, either my water just broke or I peed myself. But nothing is happening. No, like, contractions or anything. So maybe it's just pee? I have no idea, this being my first rodeo," she says. I can't get over how remarkably calm she sounds. Like there isn't a whole person about to emerge from her body. "Actually, there's a puddle on the floor next to my bed. It's either pee or amniotic fluid. If my water broke, I have to be at the hospital within an hour even if I'm not feeling any contractions. So I need to figure this out. Can you go smell it for me?"

"What?" I am not awake enough for this conversation. My brain is swimming in questions and the *really* good dream I was having about eighties-era Bruce Springsteen. It was all white T-shirt and biceps and an ass that wouldn't quit and *the Boss*. You know how it is.

But finally, with great effort, I land on one question. Just one.

"What does amniotic fluid even smell like?"

"Uh, not like pee!" she yells back. "I'm going to stay here on the toilet because when I stand, more…uh…liquid…comes out?"

"Right," I mutter. I take a deep breath and try to feel every part of my body in this moment. This is not a dream, no matter how much I want to keep caressing Bruce's ass in those jeans. Hazel is pregnant, and there might be a baby coming *right now*. And all that stands between me and a screaming ride to the hospital is me smelling a mysterious puddle.

"Please?" Hazel begs.

I sigh. "You better make me that baby's godmother," I tell her as I pad down the hallway and into Hazel's room. Thankfully the floors are wood, so whatever greets me will be easy to clean up. It's about the only thing that'll be easy to clean up in my sister's room, which is stuffed with teetering stacks of textbooks and hardcovers and overflowing with potted plants, each healthier and hardier than the last. "It's like the Rainforest Café in here," I mutter, stepping over a pothos vine.

"Who else would be the godmother?"

"Maybe that little bitch from high school? McTinsleigh?"

"Ryleigh. And you're just mad that I loaned her your leather jacket and she threw up coconut rum on the lining."

"You bet your ass I'm still mad about that," I reply, locating the puddle. "I found that jacket at a flea market in Orlando, and it *still* smells like a spring break mistake."

I take another deep, centering breath and remind myself that this is probably just one in a long list of disgusting tasks that awaits me as a future live-in auntie. Because there is going to be a whole-ass *baby* living in my house. And anyway, Hazel is my little sister, and there's not a thing I wouldn't do for her, including smelling a mysterious bodily fluid. My love for Hazel is why I'm here in Cardinal Springs to begin with, and that has turned out not to be such a bad thing. Hazel has given me all the best things in my life, and she's about to give me my niece.

The puddle is roughly the size of a serving platter with a Jackson Pollack–esque spatter pattern radiating outward. It's clear, as far as I can tell. I've been working in bars for more than a decade, so I've dealt with many a mysterious puddle. But I've never had to smell one.

"Let's fucking go," I whisper, squaring my shoulders. Then I drop to my knees, get as close to the puddle as I can tolerate, and sniff.

"Well?" Hazel shouts.

"Saddle up, cowboy!" I yell back. "We're having a baby!"

———

"You look like you just returned from 'Nam," my sister says to me, her voice a dreamy whisper as she dips her chin to nuzzle the downy soft head of Eden Wyatt Hart. Yes, her middle name is mine, and frankly that's the least I deserve after watching my sister's vagina turn into a portal to hell.

"Well, you woke me in the middle of the night to smell a

puddle, and the next thing I knew I had a front-row seat to what a placenta looks like, so it's going to take me some time to recover," I reply.

Though to be honest, I'm already starting to forget. Eden is only an hour old, but already her little pink lips, chunky cheeks, and fuzzy red head are turning the memory hazy. I carefully slide into the sliver of bed beside my sister, resting my head on her shoulder as we both stare at Eden. "So, red hair, huh?"

That was a surprise. Hazel and I are true brunettes, though we've both experimented with different hair colors over the years. Mine currently has hot-pink highlights, and Hazel's growing out a copper balayage. But Eden? She came out looking like the love child of Pippi Longstocking and Carrot Top.

"Her dad," Hazel whispers, her eyes going watery.

I hold my breath. In all these months since Hazel arrived home from college with her surprise belly, she's barely mentioned Eden's father except to say they spent only one night together and she has no idea how to find him. And I haven't pushed her. She's had a lot on her plate, what with trying to figure out her online classes for the spring so she won't get too far behind and can finish her landscape design degree at Cornell, to say nothing of all the prep involved in becoming a mother. My book nerd little sister has approached it all with the same tenacity she applied to prepping for her SATs. I've always figured she'd tell me about the baby's father when she was ready.

Which is now.

"It was winter break. I stayed at school to work in the botany lab, remember?" Her eyes never leave her daughter as she talks.

Her *daughter*. God, it's simultaneously shocking and absolutely right.

Hazel takes a deep breath, and I give a quiet nod, not wanting to interrupt, to break the spell. Laying eyes on her daughter for the first time has cracked something open in Hazel, and it's my job to catch whatever falls out.

"It was the first week of January and bitterly cold, but it hadn't snowed. If it's going to be that cold, it really should snow," she laughs, like it's the first bit of wisdom she's instilling in her daughter. "Otherwise it's just miserable. But one night I left the lab late, and as I crossed campus, the first flakes began to fall. And there he was: tall, lanky, with this thick, wavy red hair. I could see the snowflakes landing on it. He was staring at his phone, lost. I asked him if he needed help. His name was Alex, and he was passing through on his way from Toronto to New York, where he had an audition for something. A play, I think? He was in line in front of me at the Botanist and we just started…talking. About coffee and plants and life. I honestly don't even remember how it started, but it was incredible. I'd never had so much to say in my life."

I can barely picture this, but I know how big of a deal it must have been. My shy, quiet sister was always more interested in the book in her lap than the people around her when we were growing up. It took her six weeks of living with me before she said more than six words in a row. There must have been something really magical about this meeting…about *him*.

"One thing led to another, and he said he had time to kill so he didn't get to New York too early. He didn't have a place to stay there, couldn't afford a hotel. Anyway, I invited him back to my apartment, and we had this incredible night." She blushes. "Anyway, when I woke up, he was gone. To be honest, I was crushed. It seemed like we'd really connected. I didn't think he'd ghost, but…there you have it. Same old story."

She laughs softly to herself, then leans down and places a kiss on the top of Eden's head. "But he left you behind, baby girl, and how can I be mad about that?"

I let out a long breath, turning the story over in my head. "You didn't get his last name?"

She looks up and meets my eyes, her lips quirked into a grin. "Adams. Alex Adams. Can you believe that? Might as well be John Smith."

"We could hire a PI, maybe. Or send Eden's DNA to one of

those ancestry places. Maybe one of his relatives will turn up." I'm quickly slipping into fix-it mode, which is my standard operating procedure.

Hazel shakes her head. "We'll find him. Someday, I know we will," she says, then yawns. "If he's meant to be found, we'll find him."

A nurse pops her head in. "Morning, Mama! How goes life with your new little miracle?"

I have to stifle a snort. Look, having just witnessed it, childbirth is indeed a miracle, and I will fight anyone who has something less than stellar to say about the wonder that is Eden. But all of the women on this ward talk like Precious Moments figurines come to life.

"Good," Hazel replies. "Tired."

"Why don't you try to get some sleep. It's vital for a healing body," the nurse says, and that I can get on board with. "We can take her to the nursery, or we can pass her off to your sister."

Hazel looks momentarily panicked at the thought of Eden leaving her arms, but I give her an encouraging nod. "I can take her, Haze. You've got to sleep."

"You're tired too," she says, letting out another leonine yawn.

"Yeah, that's what coffee's for," I say. "Grace and Carson are about to drop off provisions. So you sleep, I'll hold Eden, and when you wake up, there will be muffins from Crimson 'n' Cream waiting for you."

"Oh, that sounds like heaven," Hazel says as I take the sleeping baby, wrapped up tight like a burrito, from her arms. When I've got Eden nestled in the crook of my elbow, Hazel rolls over gingerly. As her eyes start to flutter shut, she whispers, "I wish we could call Mom."

An ache rockets through my chest, because of course that's the one thing I can't give her. We'll have to wait until Mom has time at one of the obscenely expensive pay phones at the prison where she's being held. We'll have to wait for the fuzzy, disembodied voice alerting us that we have a collect call. That's when my mom will get the news of Eden's birth.

Until then, we're just a little family of three.

I don't fall asleep, but at some point during the next hour or so, my brain definitely goes into hibernation. I alternate between staring at Eden, who's sleeping in my arms, and the monitors beside Hazel's bed. Now that the adrenaline from the birth has worn off, I don't know if I've ever been this tired in my life. If I think too hard about all the ways my life is about to change, a wave of panic swells inside me. But I swallow it down, because panic won't help me now.

I need to pull it together, just like I did eight years ago when the social worker called, letting me know that my mother had been arrested. That she wouldn't be making bail. That Hazel was staying with a friend for the night, but if I couldn't get to Cardinal Springs in the next day or so, my sister would be placed in foster care.

I packed that very day. Called to quit my job at the bar when I was already headed north, Nashville and all my mistakes in the rearview mirror.

Libby Hart—my mother, if you can call her that—had once again made a stupid decision because of a man. Only instead of stealing her car or slapping her around or breaking her heart, this man had loaded her Corolla with a duffel bag full of meth and told her to drive it to Chicago. Libby wasn't even a drug user. She should have known better, shouldn't have put Hazel in danger like that.

But as angry as I was—and still am—I can't deny that coming to Cardinal Springs and taking responsibility for Hazel was exactly what I needed.

I sigh, thinking about letting Libby into this little cocoon. I'll have to pretend that I'm not furious, so angry I can't see straight, because Hazel, with her good nature, has forgiven Libby.

Hazel still calls her Mom.

Libby hasn't been Mom to me for decades.

"Oh my god, he's *so* hot."

Whispered voices outside the cracked door of the hospital room jerk me out of my inner monologue. Under slept and overwhelmed is the perfect state for eavesdropping on hospital gossip.

"Seriously, he's like the Midwestern Henry Cavill."

"I would take him to an on-call room in heartbeat. Hell, I'd do him in the third-floor janitor's closet. The one with the leaky ceiling tile?"

"Is he single?"

"As far as I know. I mean, he's always working, so maybe a hospital hookup would be perfect."

"Susie down in radiology went to prom with him. She says he's an amazing kisser."

"God, if he was good in high school, imagine what he could do with that tongue now."

A half moan, half groan seeps through the door, and then the conversation dies, replaced by a shuffle of feet. Then one of the voices says, louder and brighter, "Good afternoon, Dr. McBride!"

"Hi," the good doctor replies, his voice deep and friendly, the audio equivalent of a cozy flannel blanket on a cold winter's day.

Then the door opens and his tall, broad-shouldered frame is filling the tiny room. Six foot something and dark haired, his blue eyes filled with a kind, yet steady warmth. He's wearing a pair of khaki pants that makes him look sexy and not at all like a youth pastor. He's also got on a navy shawl collar sweater with a white lab coat over it, a stethoscope around his neck.

I still don't know exactly how I feel about Owen McBride, pediatrician and Cardinal Springs golden boy. I've lived here long enough to have heard tales of his baseball triumphs in high school and college, of the stray animals he's rescued and the old ladies he's led across the street. He's basically the floor model of a *good guy*. A person like that would normally cause me to roll my eyes, but Owen McBride is also my best friend's older brother. He really *is* that nice.

And he's so fucking hot that sometimes it hurts to look at him.

Now the conversation in the hall makes sense.

"Hey," he says, his voice low to avoid disturbing Hazel. But she's already stirring, as if she senses the brute force of his hotness in the room. "How are we doing?"

"Good," I say, dragging my focus down to the baby in my arms. "She seems to be doing all the baby things just right."

"Hey, Dr. McBride," Hazel says as she pulls herself up to sitting, wincing only slightly as she settles onto a maxi pad the size of a Subway sandwich tucked into a pair of mesh undies.

"Hi, Hazel, it's good to see you," he says. He holds his giant hand underneath the sanitizer dispenser, then rubs it into his palms in a way that absolutely should not be sexy but somehow is.

Jesus Christ, I need to get laid if I'm lusting after a man applying industrial foam hand sanitizer.

He crosses the floor and holds out those clean, capable hands, and thank god I don't have to answer any questions, because I'm not sure I have the power of speech at the moment. I may be attracted to Owen McBride, but I think I kind of hate the affect he has on me. This level of attraction can only lead to disaster.

I watch as Owen takes Eden to the little bassinet beside Hazel's bed and unwraps her blanket. That rouses the baby, who promptly squinches her eyes shut and opens her mouth, letting out an ear-splitting protest.

"Good lungs," he says with a chuckle, then warms his stethoscope before placing it gently on her tiny chest and belly. A little V appears between this thick, dark brows as he listens. When he's done, he wraps her back up like he's doing origami, and as soon as Eden is snuggled back into her blanket, she quiets. Then he lifts her, and I let out the most embarrassing involuntary whimper at the sight of this giant man holding this tiny baby. He hands Eden to Hazel, then smiles his golden boy smile.

"She's perfect," he says, like he's offering a benediction.

"She is?" Hazel's voice betrays all the hope and terror that I imagine comes with being a new parent, but another smile and a gentle pat on the shoulder from Owen seems to relax her.

"Absolutely. You did great, Mom," he says, and I tear up at the new title for my baby sister. "Don't hesitate to call with any questions, and you'll get a text from my office about your first appointment. We want to see her in three to five days to make sure she's eating and gaining weight like she should, but right now I have no concerns."

I didn't realize that *I* was holding my breath, waiting to hear the verdict from Eden's doctor. Eden looks good to me, and she's eating and sleeping, and Hazel and I have fumbled our way through our first diaper change (bless the kind nurse who refrained from laughing as she guided us through the motions). But what do I know about babies? So I'm grateful for his reassurance.

And then, with a final smile, he's gone.

"Put your tongue back in your mouth, Wyatt," Hazel says with a smirk. "Or ask him out."

"The man wears khakis, Hazel," I reply, settling back into the plastic recliner that's become my temporary home. "He owns *multiple pairs* of khakis. Owen McBride is not for me. And besides, I have other things going on right now."

And then, as if to remind us that she is now the boss, Eden lets out a wail that could wake the dead.

CHAPTER 2
WYATT

Three months later
Friday, January 13

"Have you seen this forecast? They say we're supposed to get, like, a thoroughly apocalyptic ice storm this weekend," Hazel calls from the living room. But I can't focus too hard on the weather. I'm too busy enjoying the fact that for once I can actually hear her voice.

Over the past three months, I've fallen deeply in love with my adorable little ginger niece. I've watched her sparkling blue eyes focus more and more on the world around her. I've watched her start to figure out her hands, attempting to grab for things but most often winding up with her tiny fingers tangled in my hair. I've watched her get stronger, holding her head up even as she stubbornly protests tummy time.

And I've *heard* the little bugger screaming her lungs out. Every day, starting at about five p.m. and continuing for a solid three hours until she wears herself out, then again for four or five shorter stints during the night to express her displeasure at, I don't know, life? The dark? The fact that she's not yet old enough to enjoy the wonder and beauty that is the hot Cheeto?

Colic is a motherfucker, let me tell you.

But a couple of weeks ago, the screaming slowly began to subside. The jags got shorter, the wake-ups less frequent. She's still not sleeping through the night by any means—god, that's the dream—but at least she doesn't audition for the Metropolitan Opera after each of her late-night feedings. And today when the witching hour hit, she seemed too focused on her rainbow baby gym to lodge her usual protest.

Thank. Fucking. God.

"Wyatt, did you hear me? An ice storm. They're saying tomorrow afternoon." I poke my head out of the kitchen and see my sister refilling the diaper changing station she has set up in the corner of the living room. "We've got plenty of diapers and wipes, but do we need anything else?"

I check the fridge. We're stocked with eggs and milk, and there's plenty of bread on the counter. "We can make French toast for an army if this thing actually hits," I say, because Central Indiana weather forecasting is always a bit of a guessing game.

"Good," Hazel says, then gives Eden's belly a playful rub. The baby's eyes go wide, and for a second I think we're in for a grade-A protest, but then her little lips pull into a baby grin, her dimples deepening. Hazel and I pause to smile down at her, my stomach doing that warm, gooey evolutionary thing that makes me want to get my IUD removed.

I tell you, when the kid started smiling, it really took the edge off all that screaming.

Hazel glances up at me. "What are your plans for tonight?"

"Uh, let's see. Ernie is tending bar tonight, so I'm off. Which means I'm on duty at my part-time job: being Lady Eden's handmaiden."

Hazel scoffs. "You should go out."

"Nah." *Going out* has thoroughly left my vocabulary. Hazel may be the mom, but the two of us are a team. On nights I work at the bar, I take the after-midnight shift at home, pulling an all-nighter because I can sleep during the day. Then I wake up and tag in so Hazel can get ready for her spring online classes.

My whole life is Eden and Hazel.

"Come on, why not? She's doing so much better, and if this storm is coming, we're all going to be trapped in here. For days, potentially. You haven't been out in—" Hazel pauses to do math, but I've got the answer ready. I haven't been out since this kid was born. Taking care of a baby is a full-time job, and I've been too tired to even *think* about dragging myself out of our little brick rancher to find some fun.

"It's fine. I don't feel trapped here with the little princess," I say, bending down to nuzzle her soft cheek.

"Okay, but maybe I feel a little trapped here with *you*," Hazel says.

I jerk up to stare at her. "Hey!"

Hazel shrugs. "I know I'm being impolite here, because you have been Wonder Sister ever since I showed up pregnant. You are, bar none, the greatest auntie in the history of aunties. But you and I are both dangling from the frayed ends of our nerves. If this kid is finally calming down, then all I want in the whole world is to put her to bed, lie on the couch, and watch the trashiest television Bravo has to offer in a *silent* fucking house."

I scoff. "And why do I need to leave for that to happen?"

"Because you walk like a herd of Clydesdales, and you can't watch the housewives without pacing," Hazel says.

"Those bitches stress me out," I grumble.

"Wyatt, I love you more than anyone in the world other than this little peanut," she says, nodding down at the baby, who is swiping at a dangling stuffed lion. "But it's time for us to exit survival mode. Real life is waiting. *Your* real life is waiting. You're not the one who had a baby. So please, go out and have fun before I die of guilt over this whole situation."

An ache settles deep in my chest. "You don't need to feel guilty. You know I'd do anything for you, Haze."

She gives me a gentle smile. "I do know that. You've shown me time and time again. So what you can do for me now is get out of this house and take the old Wyatt out on the town."

Which is how I wind up alone in my rattling old pickup truck, cruising down the highway toward my favorite dive bar. Alone, because I called my two best friends only to find out that Grace is up in Chicago, where her studly new boyfriend's hockey team is playing a doubleheader, and Carson is home with the flu. I'm all by myself for the first time in I don't know how long.

I'm not mad about it.

I dig into the center console, pull out a cassette, and pop it into the tape player. My wine-colored Toyota Tacoma was born in 1999 and is so bare-bones it doesn't even have a CD player. I long ago decided to embrace the Stone Age technology, and I love to scour thrift stores and garage sales for tapes, which means that most of my music falls on the vintage end of the spectrum.

Now, Heart wails out of the staticky speakers, and I wail right along with them. As soon as I leave downtown Cardinal Springs and turn onto the highway, I press the gas pedal—*hard*—and let my voice soar right along with Anne Wilson's. I grip the steering wheel and feel myself coming back online, my back melting into the old driver's seat.

I've lived in the little brick ranch house on Mulberry Street for nine years, but my Tacoma is probably the closest thing I have to a home. The minute I was old enough to babysit, I started saving cash, squirreling it away where my mother couldn't dip into it to cover utilities or buy movie tickets. I bagged groceries, I waited tables, I weeded and mowed and shoveled mulch. I did any job I could find until I could afford my truck.

I was sixteen when I bought it. It was already eleven years old, and I got a pretty good deal on it because the tires were bald, the brakes needed replacing, and the windshield had a spidery crack from one side clear to the other. But I didn't care. It was *mine*, and the truck meant I was *free*.

So when I turned eighteen and my mom decided she was

going to follow some biker from Orlando up to Indianapolis and that she only had room for one kid, I was content to load my meager belongings into that truck bed and set off to make a life for myself in Nashville.

My only regret was that Hazel had to go with Libby and not with me.

But then the phone call came five years later, and I loaded up this truck again to move back to Indiana. To clean up yet another one of Libby's messes. To get my little sister back.

I've thought about upgrading the truck. At this point it's a quarter century old. But the thought of parting with it makes my breath catch in my chest. So I keep it.

Besides, at this point I know how to fix basically every part of the damn thing myself. I can't imagine owning a new car that would put me at the mercy of an honest-to-god mechanic. I'd rather change my own oil, thanks. Hazel demands that if I drive Eden around I use her Subaru, with its back seat and airbags, and I've got no problem with that. But for just me?

This truck is my homegirl.

My destination, Sorry Charlie's, is only thirty minutes away, located on a quiet stretch of highway halfway between Cardinal Springs and Indianapolis. I met Glenn, the owner, years ago at a tattoo shop in Bloomington. The motto of Cardinal Springs seems to be "What's your business is my business," and when it comes to my business, I don't like to share. So when I need to unwind, to find a hookup, to drown my sorrows (or all of the above), I head to Sorry Charlie's.

I'm just about to flip the tape in the deck when the dim lights of the Sorry Charlie's parking lot come into view. I bounce the truck over the gravel and park. It's Friday, so the bar is buzzing, which is good, because that means I have a chance of meeting someone. Going out isn't the only thing that fell by the wayside when Eden came along.

My drawer full of vibrators are as exhausted as I am.

The interior of Charlie's is dark and smoky, even though

people haven't been allowed to smoke inside for more than a decade. The stale memory of cigarettes lives in every crack and crevice. Most of the light in the room comes from a collection of flickering neon beer signs and a glowing jukebox in the corner, which is playing John Mellencamp. As soon as my worn motorcycle boots hit the sticky wood floor, I feel at home. I certainly spent more time in dive bars growing up than whatever trailer or cheap apartment Libby had us in.

"Wyatt! Long time," Luke calls from behind the bar. His honey-blond hair is curling out the bottom of a ratty Colts cap that I know from experience smells like Budweiser and weed. He grins that crooked grin I like, and I slide onto the barstool in front of him. "Where ya been?"

"Family stuff," I reply. "Can I get an Upland?"

"Sure thing," he says, winking, and I'm just about to start psyching myself up to go home with him again—he's sweet and a giver, but my clit is about a quarter inch north of where he thinks it is, and last time I tweaked my back trying to gently nudge him in the right direction. But when he slides the beer bottle in front of me, I notice some fresh ink on his forearm. CAMILLE, it says in dark, swooping script covered in a layer of Saran Wrap.

"You got a new girlfriend, Luke?" I tip my bottle at his new tattoo.

He gazes down at his forearm like there's a golden retriever puppy there. "Yeah, we met Christmas Eve. Karaoke at the VFW. She brought down the house with 'Gloria' by Laura Branigan. She's amazing."

"Congrats, man." I try to smile through the twinge of disappointment. I've been kind of fine with these last three months of celibacy—or at least too tired and distracted to care much. But coming to Sorry Charlie's has broken the seal, and now I need to get *laid*. Luke would have been a gimme, but now I'm going to actually have to do some work.

Ugh, I'm so tired.

I glance around at the motley collection of jokers hanging off barstools, crammed into booths, and—god help me—playing darts in the corner. And unfortunately, I think I spot a couple of repeats in the crowd. Guys I *definitely* don't want to deal with again, either because of their futons or their lack of bath towels or, in the case of the guy currently lining up a dart, his mother.

I'm sizing up a strapping farm boy who looks like he was bred to play Indiana basketball and drive a tractor when the kitchen door swings open and a barrel-chested, grizzled older man steps behind the bar.

"Oh my god, I thought you'd skipped town," he says, his voice a nicotine growl. He leans across the bar and grabs me by the shoulders. "Get over here, girl."

And before I know it, I've been lifted off my feet, wrapped in a bear hug from Glenn Fielding, the bar's owner.

"My sister had a baby," I tell him once I've settled back on my stool. "And let me tell you, that shit is no joke."

"I've got four sisters, and all of them reproduced like they need kids to work the farm," he says with a laugh, slinging a dishrag over his shoulder. "Trust me, I know from babies."

"Well, this is my first night out in months, but I'm not sure if it's going to be, uh…" I glance at the sad collection of subpar dick.

"Fruitful?" He follows my gaze around the bar. Most everybody either came with someone or is old enough to be well outside a fun age gap. "There's a Pacers game, a Grinders game, *and* an impending ice storm. I think this is about what you're gonna get tonight."

He glances up as a gust of cold air whips through the open door of the bar. "Or maybe I spoke too soon…" Glenn waggles his eyebrows, pretending to pant like a dog.

"Glenn! I'm gonna tell Michael on you," I say, laughing, but the sound catches in my throat when I spin on my barstool and spot the figure standing just inside the door, his glossy dark hair lit by the red Budweiser sign over his head. He's looking down, and when the phone in his hand lights up, it illuminates the dark scruff on his face.

I gasp.

Owen McBride has ditched the khakis tonight. Instead he's wearing a pair of dark jeans, a wine-colored Henley stretched across his chest. His caramel-colored Carhartt jacket is open, a navy scarf loose around his neck. He pauses on the mat just inside the door, and though I can't hear it over the music, I can practically feel the stomp of his heavy leather boots somewhere deep in my belly.

I turn back to the bar, where Glenn is smirking at me. "Looks like tonight might be your lucky night after all. You know him?"

"Only well enough to know he's not for me."

He scoffs. "And why's that, now, sugar?"

"That guy is the golden boy of my town. Perfect in every way and very much not my speed," I reply. "I bet Owen McBride is a perfectly sweet and giving boyfriend, but you know that's not what I'm looking for, Glenn."

I take one last peek over my shoulder and watch Owen settle at an open two-top, his nose still buried in his phone. When he sits, his muscled thighs test the seams of his jeans. It's a shame he's too buttoned up for me. That body looks like an adult playground.

"Sometimes the nice ones..." Glenn trails off, and I know his eyes are tracking Owen. Glenn's been with his husband for thirty years, but he still appreciates a fine specimen. "Gentleman in the streets, something else entirely in the sheets."

I snort. "Only in my wildest fantasies, Glenn."

CHAPTER 3

OWEN

I'm already stepping through the door of this middle-of-nowhere bar when Francie's text lights up my phone.

I groan. This is the first time in weeks that I haven't had to worry about calls from patients, and I drove for damn near an hour under threat of an impending ice storm just so I could wind up in a dive bar by myself.

Fan-fucking-tastic.

Of course, I've got no right to be mad. Last time I was supposed to meet up with Francie, my ex-girlfriend turned best friend, I had to cancel because of a pink eye outbreak. And the time before that an entire fourth-grade class came down with COVID.

But just before Christmas, when a third bout of pink eye ripped through the elementary school population of Cardinal

Springs, I finally broke down and hired another pediatrician for the practice. Dr. Fatima Adebayo just finished her residency at the Children's Hospital of Atlanta. She's smart and conscientious, and after training her on our office protocols for two weeks, I'm letting her take shifts on the after-hours phone.

But I'm only marginally relaxed about it, and the flickering neon lights in this place are already putting me even more on edge. The jukebox in the corner finishes playing the last clanging guitar riff of John Mellencamp's "Hurts So Good" and launches into the clanging guitar riff of…John Mellencamp's "Hurts So Good."

"Dylan, I told you if you don't cut that shit out, I'm tossing you out on your ass," calls a grizzled old bartender with a gray beard long enough to braid. A young guy in a trucker hat surrounded by other young guys in trucker hats dissolves into the most undignified giggles I've ever seen.

I sigh.

OWEN

How did you even find this place?

FRANCIE

It's halfway between you and Indy and the photos online looked delightfully sketchy

How is it? You're not gonna get Deliveranced, are you?

If you hear banjos, RUN

I gaze around the dim bar that's somehow smoky even though no one is smoking. But I spot a Pride flag hanging behind the bar next to a photo of a young Senator Obama shaking hands with a younger version of the grizzled bartender. I snap a photo and send it to Francie, then settle into a chair at an open table.

FRANCIE

Oh good! Promise me you'll stay and have a
beer? I know your instinct is to go all introvert
and bolt, but you've been working nonstop for
too long. Stay and relax

OWEN

Says the woman who just blew me off for a shift
in the ER

FRANCIE

Rude

But fair

Anyway I wanted to tell you in person but the
medical gods keep conspiring against us, so…

A photo pops up of her left hand, her deep brown skin glistening in a golden hour sunbeam and a shockingly large diamond on her ring finger.

OWEN

Holy shit! He did it! Congrats!

FRANCIE

Thank you! You'll be one of my bridesmen?

OWEN

You don't want me on Josh's side?

FRANCIE

Absolutely not. You'll be wearing salmon pink
with my sisters, you brat

OWEN

Whatever the bride wants

FRANCIE

Yay! Okay, now stop staring at your phone. Talk to a stranger! Get in some trouble! Have a one-night stand! Do something you'll regret!

OWEN

I'll get right on that, Frank

FRANCIE

Sarcasm is unbecoming, O-Town

"Whatcha drinking tonight, Doc?"

A low, sultry voice yanks my attention away from my phone. The first thing I notice is the pink streaks in her hair. Then my eyes drift to the tattered V-neck of her T-shirt and the swirling black ink rising out of her cleavage before landing on the devilish curve of her pouty pink lips.

Wyatt Hart. As if Francie conjured her. Because trouble?

Wyatt Hart is it.

Troublemaker, trouble-finder, just plain *trouble*.

She both turns me on and terrifies me.

"You work here?" I say, blinking like a fool and trying to reconcile the appearance of my sister's tiny punk-rock best friend, bartender at the Half Pint, all the way out here at this place so remote I'm not sure it even has a name.

Wyatt rolls her eyes. "Yeah, Doc. I work full-time slinging drinks in Cardinal Springs, and in my spare time I drive thirty miles north to freelance at this shithole."

"Watch your mouth, girlie," the bartender calls, but he's smiling.

Wyatt salutes him with her beer bottle. "I'm out drinking, just like you," she says to me. "That is, if you pull your nose out of your phone and actually order a drink."

I glance back down at the phone in my hand. When I walked in here, I was exhausted, the kind of tired that leaves you both heavy and jittery, somehow. I feel the absence of the on-call phone, which has spent the last couple of years living in my back pocket, interrupting every moment with its trilling ring.

But suddenly that exhaustion, that anticipation of disaster, all melts away. Francie's directive to get in some trouble? Well, trouble is standing right in front of me with a devilish grin, an acid tone, and shit-kicking boots.

She looks like she gets into trouble on the professional circuit.

And I'm interested in getting into some too tonight.

"I was supposed to meet someone, but she just texted that she can't make it," I say, finally managing to talk to her like a grown-ass man and not some stressed-out puddle of exhaustion.

"*She?*" Wyatt asks, cocking an eyebrow. "You got yourself a secret girlfriend, Doc?"

"No," I say, liking the nickname on her lips a little too much. "Francie's just a friend. I mean, we used to date back in med school, but it didn't work out, and we've been friends ever since."

Wyatt lets out an exaggerated groan and melts down onto the open barstool next to me. "Are you seriously telling me you're such a good guy that you're actually friends with your ex?"

"She's my *best* friend," I add, even though I know this fact is going to wind up on the wrong side of whatever balance sheet Wyatt keeps about me in her head.

She takes a long swig from her beer bottle, smiling into the glass. I have to force myself not to stare at the elegant line of her neck. "God, Doc. They should study you in a lab. Figure out a way to clone you or something. Replace all the absolute dillholes masquerading as men."

"Sorry you've had such bad luck," I tell her, meaning it.

She shrugs, but I see the way her eyes flick over to the guys at the dartboard like they've all personally wronged her.

"So, what, you staying or going?" she asks.

I should go. If I'm not going to meet Francie, I should get in my truck and drive straight back to Cardinal Springs and crawl into bed, catch up on all the sleep I've missed since…well, since medical school. And there's an ice storm coming and a flu going around. I'm willing to bet that the after-hours line at the practice is going to start ringing off the hook right around midnight. If I go home now, I can help Fatima out with calls. This is her first night on duty, after all.

But even as my brain is bullet-pointing all the reasons I should walk out of this bar, my eyes won't stop drifting down to the flowers inked on Wyatt's milky-white skin—what are they, roses? My fingers twitch with the urge to reach out and trace the lines, maybe dip beneath the black lace of her bra, visible at the neckline of her shirt.

"I'll stay."

She winks. "Good." Then she turns over her shoulder. "Glenn, get this man a beer, would ya? He needs to unwind."

My beer—a bottle of whatever she's drinking—arrives quickly, and I'm glad to have something to do with my hands. Also something to do with my mouth that isn't saying something stupid in front of this woman. I give myself till the count of five—plus three long sips—to formulate something cool, or even just *normal*, to say to her.

"So I came here because this place is halfway between Cardinal Springs and Indianapolis," I finally say. "What brings *you* all the way out here?"

"Well, Eden's colic has finally subsided, so Hazel booted me out of the house to get laid."

I choke on a mouthful of beer, and Wyatt laughs. I have the sense that she gets off on making me nervous. Always has.

It makes me tempted to discover all the other ways I could get her off.

"Oh man, that's fun," she says, raising her beer bottle along with her eyebrows.

"What is?"

"Making you blush."

"You're pretty good at it," I admit, feeling the heat in my cheeks.

She grins.

She's playing with me. And inviting me to play with her. It's giving me that familiar flare of adrenaline I used to feel when I'd stand on the pitcher's mound back in high school, the thrill of hearing the thud of the ball hitting the catcher's glove. It's been a long time since I've felt that zing of adrenaline, the kind that doesn't come from panic or stress. The kind that comes with a delicious release.

Wyatt Hart is playing with me.

And suddenly, I want to play too.

CHAPTER 4

WYATT

"So, I'm guessing that since you're sitting here with me, you haven't had any luck?" Owen asks. He runs a hand through that shiny, thick hair of his and raises his beer bottle to his pillowy lips. He's easily the best-looking man in this bar, if not the entire county, and the fact that he's sitting next to me just goes to show I've got no luck at all.

Because the hottest guy in the bar?

Yeah, he's of absolutely no use to me.

Hooking up with Dr. Golden Boy would be fun, I bet, but he comes with a cargo hold's worth of baggage. My best friend's brother? Check. Beloved member of the community? Check. Such a relationship guy that he's best friends with his ex-girlfriend? Motherfucking *check*.

That doesn't mean I'm going to stop playing with him, though. It's not like I have any other plans for tonight.

"See that guy over there?" I point to a classic Indiana dirtbag farm boy with a huge belt buckle and a dirt-stained trucker hat. He's currently trying to give his buddy a wedgie. "Back in March he walked up to me—stone-cold sober, I'm pretty sure—and said,

'I wish you were my pinkie toe so I could bang you on every piece of furniture in my house.'"

Owen chokes on his beer. "He did not."

"He did! And he said it with his whole chest!" I chuckle at the memory. "Frankly, the audacity was *almost* a turn-on. But it was thoroughly overpowered by the cringe."

Owen shakes his head. "I cannot imagine saying that to a stranger. Honestly, I can't imagine saying that to anyone I know, either."

I cock an eyebrow at him. "Not into flirting?"

"I didn't say that." The tops of his ears go red, and I want to chase that blush like a high.

"Okay, then flirt with me," I say, scooting my chair closer to him until my knees brush his. I lean in so that we're face-to-face and cross my arms over my chest. I'm rewarded when his gaze drifts down to the swell of my breasts.

Fuck, this is fun.

He pauses, his dark brows furrowed in confusion. "What?"

I let a cocky grin spread across my lips. "Seriously. Flirt with me. Right now."

He rolls his eyes, trying to play it off, but his cheeks flush the most glorious scarlet. "That's…not how it works."

But now I'm revved up. I cannot stop. I am horny and have no prospects in this bar beyond this blushing man I cannot have. I've had two whole beers after not drinking for three months. Hell, I'm drunk on being out of the house, listening to a jukebox play "Hurts So Good" for the fourth time. I'm just thrilled to pieces to hear a sound other than a baby crying.

If I can't get laid, making Owen McBride blush is maybe the next best thing.

And so I give him my best devilish grin.

"How *what* works? Your moves?" I ask. I level my gaze at his gorgeous baby blues, pinning him to the chair with hooded eyes. "Owen, are you telling me you have actual *moves*? And you won't show me? How dare you allude to moves and refuse to demonstrate them! Come on, please? Pretty please? I promise never to tell anyone about your moves or use them against you. I'm just asking to see them, Owen. Please?"

I bat my eyelashes and rattle on like a schoolyard bully, desperate to make his cheeks flush again. Instead, his jaw ticks like he's thinking hard or trying not to smile. Then his beer bottle hits the table with a heavy thud.

He leans forward until I can feel the heat coming off him, his long legs caging mine between his knees. He rests his warm, heavy hands on my thighs. He gives the slightest flex of his fingers, just the barest hint of a squeeze, and it sends an electric shock directly up my legs and into my panties.

But it's nothing—*nothing*—compared to the way his ice-blue eyes go dark, practically navy, one heavy brow rising.

"You done being a brat, Wyatt? Or do you really want to play?" His voice is the most delicious deep growl of warning. The sound reverberates through my body, and it's all I can do not to shiver.

All my words evaporate in my mouth. Only a tiny huff of a sigh escapes, my lips parted in half shock, half arousal. And every one of those reasons why Owen McBride isn't for me?

They run straight for the hills.

Then he releases me, leans back in his chair like a Roman emperor, and reaches for his beer. Like nothing ever happened. Like he didn't touch me, didn't growl at me, didn't turn me the fuck on with that little stunt.

But when that beer bottle meets his lips again, I don't miss the quirk of a smile.

"Holy shit, McBride," I say, and swat at his biceps, trying to erase the heat coursing through my body like an electric current.

He shrugs, the corners of his lips tugging up farther. "You asked to see my moves."

"It's always the nice ones," I say, shaking my head. I turn and rest my elbows on the tabletop before I do something stupid, like climb into his lap and try to taste the beer on his lips.

Owen laughs. "Yeah, I think you've said that to me a time or two."

I reach for my own beer and find the bottle empty. I want to order another, but if I have a third beer on a night like tonight, lord knows what I might do. I set the bottle back down on the table and laugh.

"I don't even know if I have anything to say back to that."

"Wyatt Hart at a loss for words? There's a first." Owen's grin spreads wide now, the kind you see in toothpaste commercials. The kind that winds up on the front page of the local newspaper after he rescues a baby from a well or whatever Boy Scouts like Owen McBride get up to in their spare time.

I hate how much I like it.

"Where'd you learn to talk like that, from Archer?"

Owen scoffs. "You seriously think that of all my brothers, *Archer* is the biggest flirt? Archer has all the finesse of a third grader selling Girl Scout cookies."

I roll my eyes. "Luckily, much like Archer, Girl Scout cookies sell themselves."

He laughs. "Got a thing for my big brother, eh?"

I shake my head. "Not my type. But anyone can see you McBride boys are genetically blessed. You're all built like Paul Bunyan and have that thick wavy hair that should be in shampoo commercials. To say nothing of the blue eyes on you people, my god."

There's that damn grin again. "Dang, Wyatt. If you want me so bad, just speak up."

Maybe it's the two beers, or maybe it's that I don't like feeling like he's got the upper hand, but either way, I lean in and say loudly and clearly into his ear, "*I want you.*"

The grin drops from his face, his blue eyes going wide. I've got him, and what I said even has the benefit of being true. But then I drop back onto my stool. "Unfortunately, you're not for me."

He scoffs. "And why is that?"

"Because I'm here to get laid, and you're here to have drinks with your ex-girlfriend, who is now your best friend."

"So?"

Oh, this sweet summer child. He actually looks puzzled.

"So you're a relationship guy," I explain. "And I'm not a relationship girl. I'm the kind of girl who likes to work out her frustrations and fulfill her needs with a willing and talented partner, but I'm not looking for dinner and dancing."

Owen stares at me for a long beat, those dark brows furrowing. That studious gaze sends heat into my cheeks, and just like that, I'm back off my game.

Then he smirks. He *smirks*. I didn't even know Owen McBride could do that.

"That's a shame," he says. "Because I'm a *great* dancer."

Fuck. This is not how I imagined this conversation going.

I try to get my feet back under me. Because even if he is turning out to be a grade A flirt, it doesn't change the fact that I am absolute not, under any circumstances, going to hook up with Owen McBride. No matter how much my fingers itch to know what the planes of his muscular chest feel like, no matter how much I want to sink my teeth into his full lower lip and then soothe that bite with my tongue, no matter how much I want to feel those big, strong, warm hands all over my body...I am absolutely not hooking up with Owen McBride. It would be like bringing a puppy home from the pound and then taking him back the next morning.

I nod. "Oh, I believe that. I also bet you have a preferred florist for sending ostentatious bouquets to your lady love." I dig my chipped nail into the corner of the label on the beer bottle. "Flowers make me sneeze, Owen."

He nods like he's filing that away. So studious, this one.

"So fuck buddy, yes, flowers, no," he says, and there go my hormones again. Jesus Christ, Glenn needs to turn down the heat in this bar before I start sweating.

I paste on my best unimpressed grin, because the only thing I want less than a relationship guy is to lose this verbal jousting match.

"You kiss kids' boo-boos with that mouth?"

"I have a handheld fan shaped like a butterfly," he says with a lazy shrug. "Big hit with the toddler set."

Why does *that* turn me on?

Within seconds, there's a pile of beer bottle label shreds on the table. Owen's eyes track my fingers like he knows he's got me. That little pile is proof of the tatters of my control.

"You know, it's possible you're wrong about me," he says, his voice so low that it almost disappears beneath the noise of the jukebox. Which is playing "Hurts So Good" *again*, like John Mellencamp himself is trying to convince me to fuck Owen McBride. And there's no doubt it would be, as the Coug says, *a little bit of fun.* I let my eyes roam over his tall, muscular frame, confident and relaxed on that wooden barstool. Oh yeah, sing it again, Johnny Cougar, because lord knows there *are* things we could do.

"I'm not wrong," I say, but my voice cracks.

Owen reaches for my hand, stilling my fingers on the beer bottle.

"I *am* a boyfriend guy. A really fucking good one," he says. "I listen and send flowers and apologize sincerely. I *like* spending time with a woman, learning her body like a textbook, high-lighting all the best parts."

My mouth has gone dry, and I can hear the whoosh of my blood in my eardrums.

"But I haven't really had time for all that lately, and anyway, sometimes a little trouble is fun," he says. And I'm pretty sure my heart skids to a halt.

Owen tips the last of his beer into his mouth, then sets the bottle on the table. He pulls out his wallet and drops a twenty next to it—of course he's an extravagant tipper—then rises from his stool. My gaze follows him, my head tipping back. Fuck, he's tall. And his shoulders are capped with the most delicious muscles that strain at his Henley.

"I think I'm done here," he says, shrugging on his coat. He turns to me, those ice-blue eyes capturing mine. "I'm going to head out to my truck. I'd love it if you came with me."

His eyes are smoldering in a way that's usually reserved for guys who've broken hearts or seen the inside of a county jail. That is *not* Owen McBride.

Where did *this* guy come from? Am I actually wrong about him?

And then, as if he's on a mission to scramble my brain and my lady parts in one go, he leans down, his lips just barely brushing my ear.

"Come with me, Wyatt," he says, his voice like a shot straight to my clit. It takes everything I have not to leap off this stool, bolt out to the parking lot, strip off all my clothes, and wait for him, splayed out on the hood of his truck.

But I do have *some* semblance of self-control, and I'm not about to surrender all of it. So I reach up and grab a fistful of that shirt, relishing the softness of it in my grip. I tug on the fabric until he bends down.

Now it's *my* lips against *his* ear.

"You sure about that, Doc? No take-backs."

And then I dart the tip of my tongue out, flicking the soft skin just beneath his ear. The groan he lets out comes with the kind of electric current that should blow every fuse in this place.

He grabs my hand, tugging me off my stool. I let myself be pulled, let my body fall into his. The hard planes of muscle I imagined are under my palms. I may be about to make a colossal mistake, but hey, I'm really fucking good at those. At least *that's* in my wheelhouse.

"Let's go," he says. The commanding tone is unfamiliar but so, *so* good. I want to strip off all my clothes and bathe in the heat of it.

CHAPTER 5
WYATT

I let Owen pull me through the bar, my hand tucked into his. I have no idea what's going to happen next. If he were any other guy I had picked up in a bar, I'd think we were going to go fuck in his truck in the parking lot. But surely that can't be what's about to happen. I mean, this is Owen McBride. If he's had sex anywhere other than a sensibly firm mattress with memory foam pillows and freshly laundered sheets, I'll eat my boot. And if he's acting out because of me, he's going to wake up tomorrow with nothing but regret.

And the thought of Owen McBride regretting me feels like an anvil to the chest.

I'm three steps from talking myself out of this whole thing when my back hits the driver's side door of his truck, a shiny, dark gray beauty, hulking and tall, just like him. His hands grasp my jaw, and then his lips are on mine.

And Owen McBride does *not* kiss like a boyfriend guy.

Owen McBride kisses like he's left a trail of broken hearts from here to the Canadian border and back again. He kisses like he's looking for the secret to eternal life in my mouth. He kisses like a starving man who can be sustained only by me.

Oh, this is the best kind of bad idea.

Owen's tongue slides along the seam of my lips, and I part them for him, swallowing the greedy sound he makes when I lick him back, letting my teeth scrape over his full bottom lip. He presses me against the cold steel of his truck, but he mitigates the chill with his warm body. His feet part, his boots framing mine, and the evidence of his desire presses into my belly. God, he feels incredible, and I give my hips a roll of appreciation.

In answer, his hands slide to the nape of my neck, his fingers tangling in my curls. Never taking his lips off mine, he grips and pulls.

Owen McBride *pulls my hair.*

And oh my god, I did not think my scalp was an erogenous zone, but the moan I let out says otherwise.

"Get in the truck, Wyatt," he growls.

God, I want to. But this isn't just some random hookup. This is Owen. Grace's brother. I see him all the time. If this goes bad, there's no escaping him. Fuck, if this goes *well*, there's no escaping him. This is why I drive nearly an hour out of town when I need to get laid. I don't want to get tangled up in *anyone*, least of all my best friend's older brother.

Owen pulls back slightly, but it's only to capture my earlobe between his teeth. My pussy clenches at the sensation.

"I can feel you thinking, Wyatt," he says, his tongue tracing a line from my ear down to my collarbone, where he laps at the sensitive skin. "This is not a moment for thinking." His hand snakes me behind me, giving my ass a squeeze before reaching for the door handle. "It can just be fun. What do you say?"

Can it?

Fun is my specialty, but my head is spinning, and so is my control. But Owen's got me in the palm of his hand. It feels like I may be losing it, but he's found me.

And that…*that* scares me.

As if he can see every thought scrolling across my forehead like a Times Square stock ticker, he captures my mouth with a deep kiss that burns every fear and hesitation right out of my mind. My hands rake down his chest and slide around his hips, my thumb pressing into that little valley that leads to an impressive erection. I tug him closer, wanting to feel him like a relief map, not wanting to miss a single sensation.

"More," I groan, ignoring my second thoughts, sprinting away from them without a backward glance.

Owen grasps my hips and lifts me, shifting me so he can pull the driver's side door open. The leather seat is wide and pushed back to accommodate its very tall driver.

If you had told me this morning that I'd end my day dripping wet and about to crawl into Owen McBride's truck for a one-timer, I would have said you were writing some pretty fantastical fanfic about the world's sweetest man.

But then the world's sweetest man yanks me toward him by my belt loops, covering my lips with his once again. And while he works over my mouth, he grasps my wrist and pulls my hand to his cock, hard and straining against his jeans.

"Fuck," he mutters against my lips, and it's the sexiest combination of sound and feeling of my life. His lips move to my neck, then nip at my collarbone.

"Do you have a condom?" I ask, leaning my head back against the cold metal.

"In the truck," he says, tipping my head back down so he can capture my gaze again. "Get in the fucking truck, Wyatt."

His phone buzzes first, a gentle vibration in his pocket that I instinctively thrust toward. But then mine goes off, an air horn of an alert that sends my heart into my throat.

"What the fuck," I say, reaching for my phone in my back pocket. My intention is to silence the damn thing and then get to work on the button of Owen's jeans. I'm anxious to see what I've been feeling against me. I'm already thinking about dropping to my knees right here in the gravel, imagining what it would feel like to hold that impressive control in my hand, to take it from him, to watch him fall apart.

But Owen gets his phone out first, and his brow furrows. A matching alert is on my own screen: a weather warning. The temperature is dropping faster than anticipated, a fact I hadn't noticed because Owen has me so hot I'm practically sweating. I watch my breath fog up my screen as I realize that the ice storm is coming sooner than the forecast said.

"Shit," Owen mutters into the glow of his phone.

"Yeah," I reply. My first thought is Hazel and Eden, alone in our house. We don't have a generator, and if the electricity goes out it'll get cold fast. "I should get back."

"Yeah. I need to make sure the generator kicks on at the practice if we lose power," he says. He scrubs a hand down his face.

"So much for the moment," I quip, trying to mask the misery I feel. If blue balls were a real phenomenon, I'd have it right now.

"It doesn't have to be," he says, somehow both sweet and filthy.

"It does," I say gently. This was always going to be a one-time thing. And frankly, it probably shouldn't even have been that. Now that the frigid air is cooling me down, I can see how carried away I was getting. I was seriously ready to suck Owen McBride's cock in a parking lot. Jesus Christ, *what was I thinking?*

And while he doesn't know about all the dirty thoughts I had, it was obvious from the feel of him that he had plenty of his own. Thoughts I'll never know, because I'm watching them fade right in front of me.

"Yeah," he says, half groan, half sigh.

"Well, you did convince me," I tell him.

"What?" Goddammit, his face looks almost hopeful.

"I was wrong about you," I say. "You *are* a little bit of trouble."

And at that, he blushes. He *blushes*, and I damn near dive into his truck, ice storm be damned. I can still feel the ghost of his firm grip, those hands that surely know all kinds of ways to make me scream. My lips feel swollen and achy from his attention.

I *want* him.

Which is the surest sign that I should not—*cannot*—have him.

"Give me your phone," he says.

I look up at him, and there's a ghost of that commanding stare on his face. "What?"

"Give me your phone," he repeats, and he's still got that heated tone, the one that would have ordered me to do all manner of delightful things. And so I slip my phone out of my back pocket and pass it to him. He taps the screen, then holds it up to my face until it unlocks. He taps furiously, then passes it back. On the screen is an open text message from me to a number I don't recognize.

> Owen, I'm going to text you when I'm home safe.
> And if I need anything during the storm, you'll be
> my first call.

I swallow a groan. This man is a test from the devil; now I know for sure. The devil is absolutely tempting me to make a fat stack of bad decisions. But then another text pops up on my screen.

> HAZEL
>
> You okay out there? I just got the weather alert

I sigh. "Party's over," I mutter.

"I'm serious, Wyatt. You need to text me when you're home safe," he says, his voice stern.

I roll my eyes, the spell broken. "Yes, *Dad*," I say, but Owen captures my chin between his thumb and forefinger, leveling me with a look.

"Not my kink," he says, and the flame of desire in my belly lights anew.

He grabs my hand and pulls me across the parking lot to my truck. He reaches into my back pocket with one of his big hands, extracts my car keys, and unlocks the door. It creaks open under his tug, and he stands there until I'm settled in the driver's seat. Then he shuts the door firmly and leans toward the window.

"Drive safe," he says, and this isn't a platitude, it's a *command*.

I did not take Owen McBride for bossy, but I like it.

It'll be a nice memory for when I'm home and picking a toy from the drawer in my bedside table.

Because that's all this can be.

A memory.

———

Owen's headlights are in my rearview mirror for most of the drive back to Cardinal Springs. Just as we reach the town line, he flashes his brights before turning to head to his office. And that's when I'm finally able to take a full, deep breath.

For the last thirty miles, I've been on pins and needles, replaying that kiss. The feel of the cold metal of his truck against my back, the warmth of his body covering me. The feel of his lips and tongue and teeth, his hands as they explored my body. The way my skin heated every place he touched and the way it still burns with desire now.

I hope that the longer I drive, the more that heat will fade, but it doesn't. When I pull into my driveway, stopping beside Hazel's battered Subaru, I'm still vibrating from our encounter.

The air is frigid, and it smells like snow. Any minute now the ice will start to fall. I should go inside. But instead I sit there, holding my phone.

"I'm not going to text him," I mutter, flipping it over in my hands. Ghosting Owen seems like the quickest way to exorcise our encounter from my mind.

But of course there's no ghosting Owen McBride. He's part of my life whether I acknowledge what happened between us or not.

And the worried way his brow creased when he shut my truck

door…I don't want him worrying about me. That'll just prolong the misery, right?

So I unlock my phone, navigate to the text message he sent, and type.

Made it home

There. That's all. I did what I promised I'd do.

But I don't stop typing.

Everything okay at the office?

The little bouncing dots appear almost instantly, accompanied by a fizzy feeling in my stomach.

OWEN

Yup. Just wanted to double-check that the generator had fuel. Need to be ready to do X-rays when a kid I won't name because of HIPAA regulations inevitably tries to snowboard down the icy hill behind his house on a sheet pan

WYATT

Gotta make sure the lights are on for when someone eats yellow snow

OWEN

You laugh, but someone's mom is going to call me about that first thing tomorrow

WYATT

What do you do for yellow snow?

OWEN

Drink plenty of water and watch for nausea and
vomiting

Don't eat yellow snow, Wyatt

WYATT

Thanks Doc

OWEN

You're welcome

Let me know if you need anything else

I tell myself he means medical information or help deicing my driveway, not a string of explosive orgasms.

I think after what I witnessed Owen McBride doing tonight, I'm lying to myself. But I'm just going to have to keep lying until it becomes true.

WYATT

Good night Doc

I'm still smiling down at my phone when I hear a car pull up to the curb behind me. It's a white taxi, dinged and rusty and in serious need of some engine work and a new muffler. The rear passenger door creaks when it opens, and I blink at the figure stepping out. Her hair is longer and grayer, no longer dyed her signature cherry-cola red. She's missing her uniform of winged eyeliner and deep red lipstick, and her brows aren't tweezed within an inch of their lives.

But when she smiles, the crinkles at the corners of her eyes are as familiar to me as my own face. I remember how she'd smile like that when she told me we were having ramen noodles for dinner for the fourth night in a row, or that she'd forgotten to move the laundry from the washer to the dryer so I should just turn my underpants inside out, or that we were being evicted *again*. Always trying to make her personal disasters seem like fun adventures. It's the same smile she gave me as she was being led out of the courtroom, when she told me to take good care of Hazel, that everything would be fine.

It's just ten years, Wyatt. It won't last forever.

No, ten years didn't last forever. It didn't even last ten years, apparently.

"Hey, honey bun," Libby Hart says, heaving the small duffel over her shoulder. "Aren't you gonna welcome your mama home?"

CHAPTER 6
OWEN

February 14

"Jackson Evans is positive for strep," Dr. Fatima Adebayo says, leaning against my office doorframe, arms crossed, her long box braids gathered over one shoulder.

I scrub a hand over my face and groan. "How many is that this week?"

"Fourteen," she replies.

"And his sisters are probably going to be fifteen, sixteen, and seventeen before the week's out."

Fatima shrugs. "That time of year."

"Better strep than the flu," I say, knocking on my desk for luck and sending up a prayer of thanks to Alexander Fleming for his rad discovery of antibiotics.

"Or norovirus," Fatima adds.

I narrow my eyes at her. "Do *not* speak that into the universe."

She arches a sculpted eyebrow. "Dr. McBride, are you superstitious?"

I grimace. I'm a scientist. I know better than to believe in all that shit. But I'm also a pediatrician, and at this time of year, I'll take any help I can get. If the universe is offering, I'm not going to roll my eyes at manifesting or vision boarding or whatever.

"I'm at least a little 'stitious," I tell her, and she laughs.

Fatima sheds her lab coat and folds it over her arm. It's six o'clock on a Tuesday, and our day is finally over. We've been going nonstop since eight this morning, when we opened to a flood of walk-ins, all with sore throats and fevers.

"Norovirus is coming whether I mention it or not," she says.

She's right, of course. One of the things that impressed me when I was interviewing her was how no-nonsense she is. With adults, anyway. With kids, she has endless patience. It's the perfected combination for a pediatrician.

"Let's just hope we get a little breather between strep and the onslaught of spring allergies," she continues.

"We won't," I reply. This is only my third year in private practice, but that's long enough to know the rhythms of small-town pediatrics. "Not unless we get another snowstorm in March."

Fatima lets out a long sigh. "Tell me again why I moved to Indiana?" She grew up in Miami, went to undergrad and med school at the University of Florida, and did her residency at the Children's Hospital of Atlanta. Her first Indiana winter has been a harsh wake-up call.

"Because you interviewed the weekend of the state fair and were swayed by the wonder that is the pork tenderloin sandwich?" I offer.

"That deep-fried piece of heaven seemed like enough, but then the temperature dropped below zero and I discovered a new kind of cold," she says.

"Welcome to the Midwest!"

"My people are from Nigeria. We are not made for this," she says, giving me the stink eye. She can complain all she wants—I heard her shrieks of delight as she sledded down the hill behind our office back in January. And again in February. Twice. "I'm heading out. Daphne's making me some fancy three-day lasagna she saw on YouTube. You have any Valentine's Day plans?"

I shake my head. "Sleeping," I say, feeling the oncoming yawn creep into my jaw. "Amelia Harper's mother called me twice during the night to update me on the state of her daughter's stool."

"Did she finally pass that battery?" Fatima asks.

"At four seventeen a.m." The yawn overtakes me. "I couldn't get back to sleep after that."

She grimaces. "What the hell did you do all morning?"

"I rode my Peloton until I couldn't feel my legs."

"You're a freak," she says. "And you need a date."

"What I need is a nap."

Fatima crosses my tiny office and leans toward me across the desk, both palms flat against the wood. "I'm here now, Owen. That means you have time to do both."

Then she winks, turns, and struts out of my office like a woman with some very good Valentine's Day plans.

I pull out my phone, and after a few taps, the familiar screen appears. Immediately, my phone feels warm, the brief text exchange with Wyatt Hart like a worry stone in my palm. Her messages to me are a month old now. The last one was sent at almost midnight on Friday, January 13.

And every day since then, I've imagined texting her again. I've imagined kissing her again. I've imagined pushing her into my truck and seeing if her needy pussy was as wet as I imagined.

I don't know if it's because our night was interrupted or if it's something more, but I cannot get this woman out of my head.

Which is a problem, because Wyatt is *everywhere*. She's behind the bar where I meet my brothers after work. She's tagging along with my sister to family dinners. She's even in my office, sitting beside her sister while I perform her niece's well-child exams.

And every time I see her, she acts like nothing happened. Nothing on her face ever betrays that we kissed, that I touched her, that I was minutes away from dragging her into my truck, peeling down those jeans, and burying myself inside her.

Get in some trouble.

Thanks a fucking lot, Francie. I was supposed to have a one-night stand, and we didn't even get the one night. All I have is this text exchange. Otherwise I could maybe convince myself I made the whole thing up.

But I guess the fact that I've been hopelessly pining for this woman for the last month is a sign that a one-night stand was never going to work for me. I tried to be something I'm not, and this is what I get: a month-long erection and a collection of filthy yet unsatisfying dreams.

My phone vibrates, and my heart leaps into my throat. But it's not Wyatt. Why would it be?

It's my twin brother.

FELIX

Finished at the site. Headed to the Half Pint. You coming?

My first instinct is to say no. I even type it. I'm exhausted, work is only going to get harder this week, and drinking with my brother is not how I want to spend Valentine's Day.

But then I picture the little pink-haired spitfire behind the bar.

OWEN

See you in a few

CHAPTER 7
WYATT

The Half Pint is packed.

Never in my life did I think I'd find a packed bar on Valentine's Day to be a respite, but that's what happens when your formerly quiet, empty house suddenly contains a baby and a mother who's newly free from prison and driving you crazy.

Honestly, to put any of this on Eden is unfair. That angel baby is a goddamn delight these days, what with the smiling and the giggling.

It's my mother who's driving me out of my ever-loving mind.

"If we don't get some more men in here, and quick, this whole event is going to be a bust," Mrs. Eberle says, gazing around the bar with a furrowed brow.

And it's true. The Half Pint is pretty devoid of dick tonight, which is unusual. But Mrs. Eberle is hosting a speed dating event to benefit the Women's Auxiliary, and the men of Cardinal Springs seem to have gotten the message and stayed home.

So far the bar is mostly filled with women ranging in age from their early twenties (my friend Carson, looking nervous in jeans and a loose pink sweater) to their late eighties (Mrs. Tingle, wearing a floral caftan and raring to go). But there's only a handful of men, and most of them look like they came straight off a shift and had no idea there was anything other than drinking happening here tonight. They're all holding hot-pink index cards, though, hand-printed name tags on their chests. Mrs. Eberle isn't letting anyone out of here without participating.

Except for me, thank god, because I'm working.

"Well, you can always just mix it up and have everyone meet everyone else. Less heteronormative that way," I say.

Mrs. Eberle pointedly ignores me and turns to Grace. "Where are your brothers?" she asks, wringing her hands.

Grace looks up from her perch at the end of the bar, where she's hunched over her phone, watching the Grinders game. Her boyfriend, hockey god Decker Brooks, is playing the Vipers tonight, and she's just hoping her man stays out of the box.

"Felix said he was coming," Grace says, her eyes back on the phone, her brow furrowed as she follows the action. "He said he'd text the others."

This is the only way I get to see her these days, since she spends most of her time either at the bookstore she opened a few months ago or watching hockey. She assures us that once the season is over, she'll return to the land of the living. If I didn't know just how perfect those two are for each other, I'd wretch. I don't believe in love generally, but I make an exception for Grace and Decker, because I watched them both stumble ass-backward into happiness. That man would walk through fire for her. Hell, he's leaving the NHL for her (well, for his broken body *and* for her). He's one of the very rare good ones.

And even so, I keep my eye on him. I know all too well how someone can seem like the perfect guy, and then one day you wake up and he's pinning your best friend to your couch with his tongue and calling it "songwriting."

But what did I expect? It's not like I've ever had good role models for love or relationships. Maybe if I'd seen Grace and Decker together earlier in my life, I might be a believer. I might have been able to spot a snake in the grass when he slithered up to me. But I didn't know sparkle from spit back then, and now I have to change the radio station several times a day just to avoid hearing the evidence of my worst choices climbing the country charts.

"Hey, hon! How's your night going?"

Speaking of bad examples of love and relationships, in walks my mother, her hair dyed back to her favorite cherry-cola red. She's also found the boxes of her clothes that I shoved in the attic and reclaimed her favorite jeans, the ones with the holes in the thighs and rhinestone butterflies on the ass. She looks like Shein Paris Hilton. I try to be pretty nonjudgmental about shit like age-appropriateness, but the woman is in her early fifties. Would it kill her to dress less like an early-aughts disgraced heiress?

And she apparently didn't stop her exploring in the attic.

"That's my shirt," I say through gritted teeth, eyeing the vintage Stevie Nicks *Bella Donna* T-shirt she's wearing.

My mother grins like we're thick as thieves. "Yeah, but who introduced you to Stevie Nicks? If it wasn't for me, you wouldn't even have this shirt."

Yep, that sounds just like the Libby Hart I know and barely tolerate. Always making everything about her. She'll probably get a stain on it, then leave it on the bathroom floor. Just another one of her messes for me to clean up.

"Are you even allowed to be in a bar?" I ask.

"I'm not drinking, hon," she says, and she has the gall to look annoyed. But I've learned to keep a close eye on her. I don't mind if she makes bad choices for herself, but I'll be damned if I let her decisions affect Hazel and Eden. I don't even want her staying with us, but the house is still technically in her name. And a condition of her parole is that she has a stable place to live. As much as I'd love to tell her to kick rocks, I'm not in the mood to do battle with the State of Indiana.

I did, however, banish her to the basement. I'm not about to give up the primary bedroom to her. Not when I'm the one who has paid the mortgage these last nine years. Not when I'm the one who had the furnace replaced last winter and the new garage door opener installed last month. Her name may be on the deed, but that is *my* house. It's the only long-term home Hazel has ever known. It's where Eden will grow up safe and happy for as long as Hazel wants to raise her there.

And Libby Hart will not fuck that up. Not like she fucked up so much of my childhood.

"If you're not drinking, then what are you doing here?" I ask.

"Speed dating," she says with a wink and a saucy grin.

Jesus fucking Christ. Because what Libby Hart needs in this season of her life is a *man*.

Mrs. Eberle, who's been stone still, listening to every single word like she's trying to commit it to memory, finally leans forward to extend one of those stupid index cards.

"I thought you had too many women," I say.

"Oh, it's fine, there's always room for more!" Mrs. Eberle says, but I'm pretty sure what she means is *I need only two things in life: Jesus and gossip.*

My mother hands over a ten-dollar bill, then carries her name tag and index card to an empty two-top. Which at least means I'm done talking to her.

The door to the bar flies open, and Archer McBride stomps in, his jaw set, his lips pressed into a thin line. He's wearing a Cardinal Springs High School Hockey hoodie and a frown. Felix McBride comes in behind him, rolling his eyes at his big brother and scratching at the stubble along his jaw as he scans the bar. I find myself holding my breath, watching the door behind him, but Owen's not with them. I exhale and try to decide if that's a good thing or a bad thing.

"Welcome, boys! Here you go." Mrs. Eberle thrusts a name tag and a hot-pink index card at each of them.

"What's this for?" Archer asks.

"I told you—speed dating," Felix says. When Archer opens his mouth to protest, Felix cuts him off. "It's for charity. You're doing it. Sit down."

Archer's jaw tightens again, but he takes the card and the name tag and stomps toward an empty table.

"What's his problem?" Grace asks.

Felix shrugs. "He won't say, but I think it has something to do with the BMW parked in Madeline's driveway."

Madeline is the single mom who moved in next door to Archer last summer. The two of them have become good friends, though anyone with eyes can see that Archer's feelings are bigger than that. Well, anyone except Madeline, who seems blissfully ignorant that the hulking ex–hockey player next door is made of Jell-O when it comes to her. "I think Betsy's dad showed up for a surprise visit?"

"More *importantly*, where's Owen?" Mrs. Eberle asks. I can see her silently counting heads. Owen's arrival would make the numbers slightly closer to even.

"He said he was coming," Felix replies, slapping his name tag onto his broad chest. He glances out at the crowd and spots Keeley Wentworth, a teller at the bank with wide brown eyes and a penchant for low-cut tops. He grins and heads in her direction.

"We're not starting yet!" Mrs. Eberle calls, but Felix ignores her and slides into the chair across from Keeley.

I, however, am still stuck on the fact that Owen is coming.

Over the last month, I've had plenty of practice being face-to-face with Owen McBride. I've served him beers and sat across from him at McBride family dinners. I even sat practically shoulder to shoulder with him in a tiny candy-colored exam room while he balanced Eden on his knee, his stethoscope pressed to her chest. I tried not to stare at the little V that always formed between his brows when he was listening to her heartbeat or the way his face lit up when she giggled at his silly faces.

I did not realize how many pediatrician visits a baby has in the first four months of her life.

And each time I saw him, my mind replayed our parking lot encounter like my own personal porn film. Anytime I was near Owen McBride, I wound up pressing my thighs together, simultaneously trying to stem the tide of arousal and chasing the feeling toward the cliff.

I really wish we had just fucked in the parking lot that night. Then I'd have this out of my system.

I feel like the ghost of Owen McBride has been edging me for weeks.

Ernie, the owner, pushes through the swinging door from the back and drops a box of limes on the bar. His gray hair is shaggy and curls at the ends, and he shakes it out of his eyes, the neon beer signs reflecting off the silver hoop in his ear.

"Ernie, will you step in if—" Mrs. Eberle begins, but Ernie cuts her off with a snort.

"I've been married twice already," he says, shaking his head. "I'm out of the game."

"C'mon, third time's the charm," I say with a wink.

Ernie rolls his eyes. "How about you shut your smart mouth and go grab us another keg of that cherry IPA. We're almost out, and this crowd is gonna want it," he grumbles, but his eyes are glittering. He's always sort of been my surrogate father, and even though he's got all the warmth of a dying cactus, he's always been there for me when I needed it. I've worked at the Half Pint since I moved back to Cardinal Springs eight and a half years ago. Ernie's second ex-wife, Margo, used to sit with Hazel when I worked nights. Every year on my birthday, Ernie makes sure there's a strawberry cupcake waiting for me on the bar with one lit candle for me to blow out.

He's remembered far more of my birthdays than my mother.

About six months ago, Ernie dislocated his shoulder trying to heft a keg, no small feat for a man in his late sixties. He's been going to physical therapy entirely against his will, and I've taken over keg duty. Not an easy task. I like to think of myself as small and mighty, but a full keg weighs more than 160 pounds. Luckily, I've got a system.

I head through the kitchen and into the back storage room where the full kegs wait. There's a rusty old red wagon waiting beside it that Ernie found at Goodwill, and I drag the keg off the shelf inch by inch until it lands in the bed of the wagon with a riotous clatter. Then I head out the back door, because there are a few wonky steps and tight turns in the kitchen, and the wagon does better bumping through the alley and in the front door of the bar.

Unfortunately, the safety light in the alley is out, and I don't see the pothole I usually navigate around with ease. The front wheel of the wagon disappears into it, the bed tipping and the keg rolling out onto the ground.

"Fucking great," I mutter. I stare down at the silver behemoth. I have no chance of lifting it back into the wagon, which means I'll have to resort to rolling it down the alley and through the front door like a rogue pirate.

I bend over, feeling the cold February air on the bare skin above the waistband of my jeans, and wish I'd thrown my coat on over the cropped T-shirt I'm wearing. I assumed I'd have this damn thing inside in no time, but as I struggle to turn the keg on the asphalt, I realize this is going to be a slightly longer journey than I anticipated.

"Come on, you stupid beast," I say to the keg, which has no response other than a metallic scrape as I wrestle it into position.

"Wyatt? You okay?"

I jerk to a standing position and spot Owen at the end of the alley. As if his presence carries an actual electric current, the alley light buzzes and flickers on.

The man looks like he's bathed in heavenly light, an actual angel in powder-blue scrubs, his tan Carhartt jacket over top. He's tall and solid, and he looks *warm*.

I shiver.

"I thought you weren't supposed to wear those out of the office," I say, nodding at his scrubs. I say it to keep inside the sloppy moan that wants out at the sight of him.

He glances down and chuckles. "They're clean. A patient

tossed her cookies all over me about an hour ago, so it was this or go naked," he says.

Oh. Fuck. Me.

And that shitty lamplight is just enough to show off the blush flooding his cheeks.

"No shirt, no shoes, no service," I croak.

He laughs, then drops his eyes to the keg at my feet. "Need help?"

"No, I'm just going to roll it—" I start, but before I can even get the words out, he has walked over, gripped the handles with those strong, sure hands, and lifted the keg into the wagon. He doesn't even grunt.

It makes me wonder about all the ways he could throw *me* around.

He takes the handle of the wagon and says, "In the front?"

All I can do is nod and follow after him and the squeaky wagon like a lost puppy.

Inside the bar, Mrs. Eberle actually squeals at the sight of Owen before handing him an index card and a name tag. I watch his face closely as he listens to her explain the rules of speed dating, and the slight furrow of his brow tells me this is not what he had in mind for tonight. But Owen's too good of a guy to make any trouble. He nods and smiles and agrees to whatever Mrs. Eberle wants. He even gives her a twenty-dollar bill and tells her to keep the change.

Everything he does makes me want him, and everything he does reminds me why that is a terrible idea.

But nothing makes that more clear than the tight fist of irritation in my gut as I take my place behind the bar and watch Owen sit down with Felix and Keeley Wentworth. That's when I realize that I'm going to have to stand here for two hours and watch Owen flirt with a bunch of women.

And I'm *jealous*.

CHAPTER 8
OWEN

"Hey there, cowboy, I don't believe we've met." Wyatt's mother slides into the seat across from me. Like Wyatt, she's short, with round pink cheeks and a mischievous grin. Her hair is dyed a shade of red that definitely doesn't occur in nature.

I reach a hand across the table for a shake. "I'm Owen," I say. "Nice to meet you."

"Such a gentleman," she purrs, grinning. "Tell me a little bit about yourself."

I glance over her shoulder and spot Wyatt, who looks like she's considering hurdling the bar and dragging her mother out of the Half Pint by her dyed hair.

I give her a little shrug, and she actually bares her teeth at me.

Libby spins in her seat and catches Wyatt staring daggers. She turns back to me, rolling her eyes. "That girl can be a bit prickly," she says, then leans across the table like she's sharing a secret. "It's because she's had to take on so much."

"She is very good at taking care of her people," I say. "She's been a great friend to my little sister."

"Oh, Wyatt is a good friend to all. All but me, but I guess I have to earn that right back," she says with a one-shoulder shrug.

She picks at a cocktail napkin on the table, carefully shredding it into little bits.

Behind her, Wyatt huffs and spins on her heel, pushing through the door into the kitchen.

"She should be out here, not me," Libby says. "She deserves some happiness. A little something good, if she'll just let herself have it."

"Oh?" I ask. I know Wyatt would sooner die than let me learn anything about her from her mother, but I'm desperate for Wyatt Hart lore. Absolutely starving for it.

Libby sees my obvious interest and smiles, abandoning her cocktail napkin. She leans toward me on her elbows. "You ever heard of that marshmallow test? Where the kids were offered a marshmallow but if they didn't eat it right away, they got two?"

It's a staple of freshman psych and often misinterpreted, but I know it. I nod.

"Well, Wyatt would wait for the second marshmallow and then give both to someone hungrier than her," she says. I can tell she's simultaneously proud and dismayed. "She'll never put herself first, but she needs to. Not that she'd ever take my advice." Libby leans back in her chair hard, huffing out a little breath. "And she probably shouldn't, because what do I know about life?"

"Switch!" Mrs. Eberle calls.

"It was nice talking to you, Ms. Hart," I say, still turning over this bit of information.

"Oh, please, call me Libby," she says, then glances over at the bar, where Wyatt is back at the register, closing out a tab. "And good luck, honey."

Before I can say anything else, Jasper Francis from the body shop is shuffling me to the next table so he can take my spot in front of Libby. I move down to the last chair, across from Delilah Perkins, who waits tables at Pete's Diner. I've known her since we were kids. We graduated from CS High a year apart but spent a semester in the same gym class. She's always been cute, a little nerdy, and totally in her own world.

"Hey, Owen," she says with a warm smile. She's got the same long dark hair and thick bangs she's had since she was little, but the wire-framed glasses have been replaced with a cool pink retro pair that matches the color of her cheeks. "How's it going?"

"Good, Delilah," I say, crossing my leg over my knee and leaning back in my chair. My back is killing me. I try to keep up a semi-regular home yoga practice, but I've been sleeping like shit lately. Maybe I need a new mattress? Or a new pillow?

And then I remember that this is not the time to assess my sleep hygiene. I'm on a speed date with a beautiful woman, one of only two at this whole event who are in the same generation as me. And if the stubborn spitfire behind the bar is going to keep pretending I don't exist, then I should at least try. So I put a smile on my face and try to focus. "How are you doing?"

She grimaces. "Ugh, completely exhausted. My feet are killing me. This is my first night off after a week of doubles."

"And you're spending it here?" I ask, cocking an eyebrow at her. This speed dating event is for charity, and I'm here entirely against my will. Felix demanded we all show up, and I'm pretty sure he's only here to get Keeley Wentworth's number. I glance over at him and see him leaning across her table, a grin on his face as she tosses her head back and laughs. Every time a guy has tried to hustle him out of his chair, one stern look from Felix sends him on to the next open seat.

"Couldn't miss the good company," Delilah says. "I chatted with Mrs. Tingle earlier and got three new book recommendations! She's got me into bully romance."

I frown. "I don't know what that is."

"You don't want to," she replies with a laugh. Then she rests her hand delicately on my forearm, leaning in like she's got a secret. But before she can get it out, the sound of a glass shattering fills the air.

"Wyatt, are you drunk?" Ernie calls from the other end of the bar.

I turn and see Wyatt reaching for the broom and dustpan. "No, just tired," she grumbles. This is the second glass she's broken tonight. The first was when Libby sat down across from me.

Ernie rolls his eyes. "Well, wake up, or I'm gonna start taking those out of your tips."

I bring my focus back to Delilah, whose hand is still resting on my arm. She's gorgeous, no doubt about that, with her shiny, deep chocolate hair and milky white skin, a gentle dusting of freckles across her cheeks. And she's always been kind, ready to shut down mean girls who made fun of her friends for playing board games in the cafeteria. Speed dating is stupid, but I shouldn't waste this opportunity in front of me by pining over a woman who's made it very clear that nothing is going to happen between us.

"Sounds like your night's turned around, then," I say.

She smiles, then drops her voice to a whisper. "If I'm being honest, I actually just started seeing someone," she says with a sheepish smile. "This woman I met at my D&D night in Bloomington. She's great, and I think it's going to be something."

Well, there you go. Speed dating really is a total bust.

"Why did you come here, then?" I ask. "You don't need to get propositioned by Jasper Francis just for fun!"

"Because I signed up for this the day before I met Kirsten, and Mrs. Eberle scares the shit out of me. I was too afraid to back out. Luckily there aren't a whole lot of good candidates for me here. I mean, it's clear Felix has a hard-on for Keeley, Archer looks like he'd rather be chewing glass, and Carson is terminally straight. You would have been my only hope," she says. "But now I don't need you!"

I flinch. Yeah, get in line, Delilah.

She grimaces. "Sorry, that was meant to be self-deprecating, but I think I just sounded like an asshole."

I wave her off. "It's fine. I didn't have a whole lot of faith that Mrs. Eberle's speed dating would find me a girlfriend. I only came because Felix threatened to switch my toothpaste for Bengay if I didn't."

That, and because I was hoping Wyatt Hart would cut the shit, jump over the bar, and drag me out into the alley.

I look back over and lock eyes with the tiny bartender, her brow furrowed as she watches me with Delilah. Is it my imagination, or does she look almost…jealous?

"Oh, please, like you need help finding someone," Delilah says, rolling her eyes. "I mean, have you seen you? Women all over town would cut a bitch to get in line. That jawline alone!"

I laugh and feel my cheeks going red. My embarrassment is punctuated by the sound of another shattering glass.

"Dammit, Wyatt!" Ernie yells.

"Time!" Mrs. Eberle calls, her voice slicing through my awkwardness like a hot knife. "Everybody write down your picks on your index cards and bring them to me. I'll send out emails with your matches tonight!"

"I'm just writing down Mrs. Tingle," Delilah says to me.

"Same," I reply, and we laugh again. Behind the bar, Wyatt spins on her heel and pushes through the swinging door to the kitchen with a little more force than is necessary.

Maybe speed dating wasn't a total waste of time.

I pass my card to Mrs. Eberle, who narrows her eyes when she reads it. But I don't stick around to hear her admonishment. Instead I head straight for a stool in front of Wyatt. She's back behind the bar, drying freshly washed pint glasses with a white towel, her toned arms flexing.

"Pick up any chicks?" she asks, her tone spicy.

"We'll just have to wait and see what Mrs. Eberle has to say," I reply with a grin.

"Seems like you and Delilah hit it off," she says, then immediately presses her lips into a firm line, like she can't believe that slipped out.

Shit, she really *is* jealous.

I love it.

I think back to that night last month, how fun it was to play with her. It was the most fun I've had in a while. In longer than I'd like to admit, honestly. Women are lining up for me, according to Delilah, but until recently, I never noticed. Not until Wyatt sat down at my table in that dive bar. That night, it was like something came online in my brain. Something I hadn't felt in years. Even though I drove home frustrated and half hard, it was worth it just to wind her up. To feel her pressed between me and my truck.

I'm just about to remind her of that night when Wyatt's mother sidles up to the bar. She opens her mouth like she's got something to say, then pauses, her gaze ping-ponging between Wyatt and me.

"What?" Wyatt finally snaps.

Libby puts her hands up in surrender. "I didn't say anything. Just wanted to let you know that I'm going to walk home."

"Isn't it thirty degrees out?" Wyatt says.

Libby shrugs. "I spent eight and a half years letting other people tell me when I could go outside. I've got eight and a half years of fresh air to make up for. I'm going to take a walk whenever I damn well please."

Wyatt rolls her eyes, but Libby ignores it, shrugging on her coat. "I'll see you at home, honey bun," she says.

When she's gone, I turn to Wyatt. "Honey bun?"

"Don't you fucking *dare*," she replies with a glare.

"How's that going?" I ask, nodding toward the door that's shutting behind Libby's retreating form.

Wyatt shrugs, but there's nothing nonchalant about it. "Six months ago I lived alone, and now I'm crammed into a tiny house with my sister, a baby, and my mother the felon. It's going peachy," she grumbles, and I can tell she needs a change of subject.

So I give her one.

"So about that night," I begin, and just as I expected, a light glitters behind her eyes.

"The night you attempted to set my panties on fire during an impending ice storm?"

I laugh, nodding. "That's the one. I just wanted to apologize, in case I pressured you—"

She holds up a hand. "First of all, don't prostrate yourself like you took advantage of some fair maiden. I don't do *anything* I don't want to do. Not even your golden boy magic can sway me if I'm not into it."

I linger on the notion that she *wanted to*. It seemed pretty evident from the way she parted her lips for me, writhing against me, that she was interested, but it feels pretty fucking good to hear it confirmed.

Wyatt slings the towel over her shoulder and leans over the bar. "Second, it was Friday the thirteenth. I feel like that's Vegas rules or something. We don't have to count it."

I roll my eyes, then catch her gaze with mine. "I count it."

She arches an eyebrow. "Do you, now?"

Several times while alone in the shower.

"I'm just glad we were interrupted before we could do anything stupid," she says.

"Like what?"

"Something that might get in the way of your obvious connection with Delilah Perkins," she says, and I can see the question mark in her eyes. She doesn't want to ask, but she wants to know. She's using that smart mouth of hers to try and get it out of me.

I *could* tell her that Delilah is dating someone. That the only name I wrote on my card was that of an eighty-year-old widow with a penchant for smutty books who *also* doesn't want a relationship.

But I don't.

I like that Wyatt's jealous. I like the look on her face, the way she crosses her arms over her chest and pops a hip.

When I don't respond, Wyatt sighs. She leans back into the bar, chin in her hand, and shrugs. "It's probably for the best. Nothing could ever happen between us anyway."

"And why is that again?"

She points at my chest. "Relationship guy." Then she taps the exposed black ink of her tattoo at her collarbone. "Decidedly *not* a relationship girl."

Someone down the bar calls for a Coors, and Wyatt gracefully pulls the pint. But the whole time, she keeps her eyes on me.

"It's a real shame too. Because…" She slides the pint in front of the customer, then taps her tattoo again. My eyes follow her finger as it brushes her skin, then moves across the bar to tap my chest. "This thing between us would be really fun."

I shift on my barstool, trying not to visibly adjust my scrubs. "I'm not going to beg, but—"

"That's too bad, because I bet that would be hot." Her voice dips low and sultry, sending a chill up my spine.

"I think you're on the verge talking yourself into something," I say.

"I think you're dreaming."

"Only of you," I say.

She rolls her eyes, but she's biting her lip *hard* to keep from smiling.

"I'm so sorry to interrupt," Mrs. Tingle says as she and her cane thump up behind me. "Owen, I was going to call an Uber, but according to the app, Joe has been sitting at the bowling alley for the last half hour. I don't think I stand much of a chance. Can I trouble you for a lift?"

"Absolutely, Mrs. Tingle," I reply, sliding off my barstool and reaching for my keys. "I'm parked in back, so just let me pull around and I'll pick you up at the door."

"Boy Scout," Wyatt quips.

"Eagle Scout, actually," I reply. I hold up three fingers in a Scout salute and grin, enjoying the flush in her cheeks and the widening of her eyes as she takes in the size of those three fingers. Neither of us is thinking about salutes at the moment. "Until next time."

Five minutes later I've got Mrs. Tingle loaded into the front seat of my truck and we're making our way through downtown to her little white house. "So how'd you do tonight, Mrs. Tingle?"

"I met two nice young ladies who wanted book recommendations, and at my age, I'm just happy to make friends. Though Larry Andrews from the VFW asked if I'd like to go for a cup of coffee sometime," she says. "And you?"

I shake my head. "Tonight wasn't really for me."

"Oh, I think there was *someone* there for you tonight," Mrs. Tingle says. "You should work on that girl, you know."

I shrug. I could pretend I don't know who she's talking about, but I respect Mrs. T too much for that. "Unfortunately she's not interested in what I have to offer. We want different things."

I feel her eyes cut over to me. "Let me guess—she's only interested in sex, and you're a relationship guy?"

I throw my hands up. "Why does everyone keep saying 'relationship guy' like that?"

"Like what, dear?"

"Like it's a euphemism for 'serial killer.'"

Mrs. Tingle laughs. "See, I knew you had spunk."

I pull up to her driveway and leap out, racing around to open her door. The truck is high for a woman with a cane, so I offer her my arm to help her out. When she's got herself situated on the driveway, she turns to me.

"The way I see it, you have two options. You can apply some of that hustle I remember from your high school baseball days, work a little harder, change her mind," she says.

"Or?"

She gives me a knowing look. "*Or* you can change your own mind."

"Meaning?"

"Don't be a prude, young man. There's nothing wrong with a

little hit it and quit it," she says with a wink, and then she turns and heads up the stone path to her front porch.

I climb back into my truck but watch her until she's safely in the house. The whole time I'm clutching my phone, staring down at the glowing screen. At Wyatt's text messages from that night a month ago when I got so close. When we were both willing to ignore all the warning signs and take a risk.

Why are we both so adamant now? What has changed?

Nothing, as far as I can tell.

And that's the push I need.

OWEN

Turns out Delilah's dating a woman she met at her D&D club

It takes a minute for the response to come through, the little animated dots bouncing for entirely too long before I receive her entirely-too-short message.

WYATT

Were you trying to make me jealous?

OWEN

Did it work?

My phone lights up with a selfie of Wyatt, her eyes closed, her tongue out, and her middle finger raised. Her curly bob, dyed lavender now, skims her jawline. My fingers itch to tuck that one rogue curl behind her ear.

OWEN

I'm adding that photo to your contact. It's what'll appear when you call me

WYATT

Who CALLS?!

OWEN

Not into phone sex?

I type that last message without even thinking, and as it pops up in a little blue bubble, I'm simultaneously turned on and terrified.

But Wyatt fires right back.

WYATT

It's really too bad you don't do casual. I think we could have a lot of fun

There it is. Another invitation.

I'm thinking about what to say back when another text comes in.

WYATT

Maybe in another life, Doc

I think about Mrs. T's advice, my two choices. There's the hit it and quit it. And while thinking about that makes my pants tight, I know it's not what I want. I want more than one night. I want more of *her*.

But the hustle? The competitive spirit? That makes my blood run hot. So I type one more text.

OWEN

Us Eagle Scouts are persistent, Wyatt. Unless you tell me to give up, I'm not done.

I wait a solid five minutes, staring at the glowing screen of my phone, but there are no bouncing dots.

No messages.

And so I'm not done.

CHAPTER 9

WYATT

Hey Doc, is it true what they say about swallowing gum?

OWEN

No. And you don't have to wait thirty minutes after eating to swim, and your face won't freeze that way

WYATT

Snarky. Not the bedside manner I was expecting

OWEN

You're welcome to help me work on my bedside manner anytime

WYATT

Damn, Doc

FEBRUARY 29 AT 5:14 PM

OWEN

Today I met an emotional support pig named Petunia. I don't think it's violating HIPAA to tell you that J'Nisha Abbott now has an emotional support pig

WYATT

Well today I met my mother's parole officer

I win

OWEN

Was he nice?

WYATT

First of all, she's a woman, you casual misogynist. And second, what could that possibly matter? It's my mother's PAROLE OFFICER. As if our relationship isn't fucked up enough, now I can say I've met my mother's *parole officer*

OWEN

Rehabilitation should be the goal of the criminal justice system, right?

WYATT

AAAAHHHHHH

OWEN

If you're feeling the need to scream, I can definitely help with that

WYATT

Finally, a response I can work with

MARCH 10 AT 8:11 PM

OWEN

I just saw your truck in the parking lot of Don Diono's

WYATT

I'm on a date

OWEN

Seriously?

And you answered my text?

WYATT

Yes. That's how bad it is

He "forgot his wallet" after ordering an entire bottle of wine that he proceeded to drink before the appetizer even hit the table. His understanding of subject-verb agreement is questionable, and he's had a piece of spinach stuck in his teeth since the salad course. We are now at dessert and (his) third bottle of wine, and he looks like he's about to pass out

He's sitting across from me as I type this and seems to have no idea I'm on my phone. Or that I'm even here

I think I'm the DD on this date

OWEN

Call him an Uber and get the hell out of there

WYATT

You're a genius

MARCH 11 AT 8:29 PM

WYATT

A very weird thing just happened. I tried to pay
the bill for the worst meal in history and the
waitress told me it had already been taken
care of

OWEN

Lucky you

WYATT

Yeah…you wouldn't happen to know anything
about that, would you?

OWEN

Have a good night, Wyatt

CHAPTER 10
WYATT

March 17

"The party's here!" I call as soon as I wrestle the stroller through the front door of Dog-Eared Books, Grace's new bookstore.

"My favorite ladies!" Grace hustles out from behind the counter. She immediately drops to her knees in front of the stroller, chucking Eden on the nose and cheeks and eliciting the most delicious belly laugh.

"We're hitting the town so Mama can do her online botany class without that pterodactyl screech you've been working on, right?" I say to her gummy little smile, and in reply, she gives us a perfect demonstration of the ear-splitting scream she's become so fond of.

"Good lord, you're gonna be a loudmouth just like your auntie Wyatt, aren't you?" Grace says.

"The world should be so lucky," I reply.

The bell on the door of the shop tinkles, and in walks Carson, fresh from school dismissal. Or at least I hope she is and that the red tights, red bubble skirt, and red blouse aren't some new monochromatic fashion statement.

"It's color week at school," Carson says before I can even ask. "Today was red day, and that's why I look like a jar of marinara."

"That skirt is cute, though," I tell her. It emphasizes the way her round butt narrows to her nipped-in little waist. With her long, loose strawberry-blond curls and dangerous curves, she looks like she was painted by Botticelli.

"Thanks, my mother thinks it's too short," Carson replies.

"You're twenty-five, what could it possibly matter what your mother thinks of your clothes?" I ask. Lord knows I'd be tempted to throw hands if Libby uttered one word about the contents of my closet. Of course she's too buys stealing my clothes to get on me about them. I'm damn near ready to put a padlock on my closet door.

"It's hard to claim the high ground when I'm still living in her house," Carson grumbles, and then she groans. "I've *got* to get out of there. Ever since my dad retired it's like micromanaging my life is their new hobby. Don't they know they're supposed to be playing pickleball, not trying to set me up with every eligible man at their church?"

"If you can hang on until our house is done, you can move into my apartment," offers Grace. She and Decker bought a few acres out near the quarry and are in the process of building their dream house, complete with a half-size indoor rink out back. As soon as the season is over—and we're all hoping that doesn't happen until the Stanley Cup Finals—he'll be back in Cardinal Springs for good.

"How long do you think that'll take?" Carson asks, her eyes alight with hope.

Grace grimaces. "It's probably going to be about a year of construction."

Carson groans and drops her head onto the counter with a dull thud. "If I'm still living with my parents next year, please put me on a raft and push me out to sea. What about Decker's apartment?"

When Decker was in Cardinal Springs last summer for reputation reasons, he rented the place across the hall from Grace, and even though he moved back to Chicago for his final NHL season, it's still full of his furniture.

"I wish you had asked me earlier. I absolutely would have handed you the keys," Grace says. "But Dan needs a place to stay, and he's sick of Archer's guest room, so Decker offered the place to him a few days ago."

Carson's cheeks pink up.

"Dan's living here? Like, permanently? What about New York? And his job?"

"You're welcome to ask him when he comes to get the keys, which should be any minute now," Grace says, glancing at her watch. "If you're able to get any real answers out of my brother, you have my congratulations."

As far as I know, Grace's brother Dan is some kind of finance bro in New York. A trader? Frankly, the entire stock market is none of my business, and while I know Grace's other brothers pretty well, what with their penchant for drinking in my bar and pinning me against pickup trucks with their tongues (okay, just the one, but *my god*, Owen's tongue, it haunts me), I barely know Dan at all. Until recently, he never came back to Cardinal Springs. Then he showed up last summer, unannounced and with no explanation. He's been drifting in and out, crashing at his dad's or in Archer's guest room and then disappearing for a while. It's all very mysterious.

"Hey, do you have the new Janice Andrews?" Carson asks, and Grace hustles to the back to find the box with the new shipment. I pull Eden out of her stroller and settle her onto my lap, selecting a copy of the Mötley Crüe memoir from the nearest shelf and flipping it open.

"You know, I have a robust, beautifully curated children's

section right over there," Grace says when she reappears with Carson's book.

"Yeah, but I need to start teaching her the red flags early. Like, don't snort ants and don't date drummers," I reply, giving my niece a raspberry on her chubby little cheek.

"You don't date *at all*," Carson points out.

"If you expand your definition of *date*, I do that plenty," I say, then sigh. "*Did* that plenty, anyway. But then this little nugget showed up, and now all I want to do is figure out ways to make her giggle."

"So you seriously haven't seen *anybody* since Eden was born?" Grace asks. "That seems like a record for you."

I glance over at my best friend. I've been wanting to tell her for a while. I hate keeping a secret from her, and at this point I don't think there's a reason to. It's not like kissing Owen changed anything. We've just become better friends. Yeah, we flirt a little (a lot), but what's a little flirting between friends? It's been two months since I had Owen McBride's tongue in my mouth, and nothing else has happened. I think it's safe to tell her now.

"It's true. I've barely had time for any extracurriculars. I did go on one epically bad date the other night, but that's been it, uh…" I bury my face in Eden's roly-poly neck like a coward. "Other than that one time I made out with your brother."

Carson gasps, and Grace drops the roll of pennies she's holding.

"*What?* Which one?" Grace cries.

"Owen," Carson says.

I whip my gaze to her. "How did you know?"

"Please. I have eyes," Carson says, rolling them. "I saw the way you were staring holes into his chest at that speed dating thing."

"Where was I during all this?" Grace asks.

"Hockey," we reply in unison, because Grace spent that entire night muttering swear words at the officials while staring at her phone.

"Ugh. Sorry," Grace says. "I've become that girl who disappeared because she got a boyfriend."

"Don't be sorry! You're in love, and I love that for you," I tell her. "And anyway, it's not a big deal. It was the night before that big ice storm back in January. It was just a one-time thing. We agreed it was a mistake. We're just friends."

"January? It's March! That was two months ago!" Grace cries, Eden startling in my lap at the sound. "I can't believe you didn't tell me!"

I wince. "I'm sorry. Are you mad?"

Grace shakes her head. "Of course not. Mostly I'm just annoyed that I could have spent the last two months trying to shove you guys together. I've noticed the chemistry between you. I just figured you were both oblivious."

"Nothing's going to happen," I tell her.

"Why not? Owen's a good guy," she says.

"Exactly," I reply. "Owen's a good guy, and I'm *not* a good girl."

"That's bullshit," she says.

"Okay, fine. I'm a fucking *great* girl. But he wants a girlfriend, and I don't want to *be* a girlfriend. I just want to fuck around, and I'm not about to fuck around with your *brother*. So there's no sense in getting everything tangled and confused when we obviously want different things."

"Nobody knows what they want until they get it," Grace says. "I mean, look at me. I was sure Decker was the absolute last man on the planet I wanted to be with, and now we're moving in together. I can't imagine my life without that hot hockey disaster. Give things a try with Owen. See what happens."

"There's no zealot like a convert," I mutter. I glance at Carson for support, but she nods at Grace.

"I'm with her on this one. Owen is hot and sweet and he wants you," Carson says matter-of-factly. "It's really nice to be wanted. I don't know why you'd run away from that. Figure out the label stuff later."

"Yes, we'll just wait until I grind his heart into the dust and leave a trail of misery through my best friend's entire family," I say.

"Or maybe you're afraid he'll break *your* heart," Carson says, raising her eyebrows at me.

"Please. Owen McBride? Heartbreaker? Bullshit," I say. I look over at Grace. "Right?"

She shrugs. "Don't ask me. Everyone thinks Dan is the mysterious one, but Owen hides his shit behind all his good deeds. I have no idea what his deal is. I know he dated Francie during residency, and that was pretty serious, but one day he called and said it was over. I don't think there's been anyone since."

"None of that says perfect hookup for Wyatt," I say. "I mean, maybe the mysterious part, but the good deeds? The long-term girlfriend? No. No way."

Grace shrugs. "It's your life. I'm just saying, don't let *your* mysterious shit get in the way of something good."

My cheeks heat at that, because as close as I've grown with Carson and Grace over these last couple of years, I haven't shared very much with them about my past. They know my mom went to prison and that I came to Cardinal Springs to care for Hazel. They know I stuck around so Hazel had a home to come back to during college. But they don't know about my time in Nashville or that it ended in disaster even before I got the call that my mother had been arrested. That despite my best efforts, I once let a shitty man take advantage of me.

The bell on the door tinkles again, and in walks Dan McBride. His brow is furrowed, his blue eyes dark, and he strides into the brightly colored, sunshiny space in a dangerously well-fitting black suit, a black leather carry-on slung over his shoulder. Standing on the rainbow rug in the middle of the store, he looks like the squarest peg in the roundest hole. Like a certified Suit Daddy, which is wildly at odds with the corn-fed smiles you usually find in Cardinal Springs.

"Keys?" he asks, his voice low and rumbly from disuse.

"Lemme grab them. They're in my office," Grace says, not bothering with the usual pleasantries. She knows how to easily communicate with her brother.

But I've never liked easy.

"So, are you fresh off a flight?" I ask, nodding at his bag.

"Yeah," he says. His jaw flexes, his eyes dropping down to my niece, bouncing and squealing in my lap, then rising back to my face. He's got the kind of intimidating gaze that I'm guessing usually shuts people up. Not me, though.

"From New York?"

"Yup."

"Why were you in New York?"

The muscle in his jaw jumps. "Work."

Okay, this is fun. I can barely suppress a grin. "What do you do?"

"Finance." It's the first multisyllabic response I've pulled from him.

I pause, cocking an eyebrow at him. "Are you in the CIA? Or a spy of some kind? A hit man or a hired gun?"

"No," he replies, his gaze steely, his vocabulary back to one-syllable words deployed like gunshots.

Grace returns from her office jangling the keys.

"Here ya go. All Decker's stuff is still in there, but he said feel free to donate whatever you don't want to Habitat and move your own stuff in," Grace says. Then her eyes light up. "Oh, or you could give it to Carson! She's looking to get her own apartment, so she'll need furniture."

Carson stands stock-still, her eyes wide, unable to speak.

Dan's eyes cut to her, sweeping over her all-red outfit, her cheeks growing crimson to match. I'm pretty sure Carson has it *bad* for Dan. That or she's just terrified of him. Maybe a little of both? Danger can certainly be fun in the right context. And from the way his gaze lingers on her for a fraction of a second longer than necessary, I wonder if there's not a little spark of something on his end too. Though using the word *spark* to describe anything about stoic Dan McBride feels wrong. The man carries himself like a Secret Service Agent, only the things he's guarding are his own thoughts and feelings.

"Thanks," Dan says, taking the keys from Grace and shoving them into the pocket of his suit pants. He looks at me, then slides his gaze over to Carson before he nods and turns, striding out the door like he's heading into battle.

"Good talk, buddy!" I call as the door swings closed behind him.

Grace sighs. "Something is going on with him, but he's a total vault."

Carson lets out a little puff of breath, shifting from foot to foot like she's finally coming back online. "That man scares the shit out of me," she whispers.

"Yeah, but scary can be a little bit sexy, huh?" I wink, and her whole face goes pink.

"As much as I love encouraging my friends to date my brothers," Grace says, giving me a trademark *stop meddling* look, "Dan is not for Carson."

"Why not?" I ask.

"Because Dan is barely for *Dan*," she says. "You ladies both deserve to be with men who adore you and treat you like queens. Guys who have their shit figured out. That's why I think you and Owen would be a perfect match, Wyatt. He would worship you."

"And while I definitely *deserve* to be worshipped, it's not what I want," I say gently. "One and done—that's my motto."

That's how you avoid getting hurt.

Grace rolls her eyes, but the pressure releases when a customer walks into the store and she springs into action. Within moments she's walking the older woman to the romance section, peppering her with questions and pulling selections from the shelves. Carson settles into the overstuffed leather chair in the corner, scrolling through apartment listings on her phone, and I set Eden down on the carpet so she can practice her independent sitting. She still slumps forward, but her core strength is getting there. Soon she'll be out of the happy little potato phase and on her way to becoming a person.

I can't wait.

And then a voice coming from the store's stereo system jerks me into awareness.

I haven't heard her voice in years, but I know it well. I used to hear it coming out of our tiny bathroom as she washed her hair in the crappy apartment we shared in East Nashville. I heard it during closing at the dive bar where we worked, singing Dolly and Patsy and Reba and Shania as she placed chairs upside down on the tabletops. I heard it as she wrote her own songs, strumming her battered old Martin on that gaudy floral chair we found on the side of the road.

We always talked about what it would be like, hearing one of her songs on the radio for the first time. How we'd take a bottle of champagne to the Bluebird, toast, and pour out a glass on the stoop as an offering to the country gods.

And now there she is, clear as a bell, singing about all her worst mistakes.

I know those mistakes better than anyone.

I know that voice like it's my own.

And I haven't heard it since that day I left Nashville.

"Wyatt, are you okay?"

Grace is looking at me, brow furrowed, and I don't think it's because Eden is about to shove the corner of the Mötley Crüe memoir into her gummy mouth.

"What? Yeah, I'm fine," I say. "Just zoned out for a second."

Through the speakers, the satellite radio DJ announces Romy Maxwell's debut single, "All I Done Wrong."

Eden squirms in my lap, but I can't move a muscle. Because the DJ isn't done talking.

"Romy Maxwell's hitting the road this summer, opening for country superstar Griffin Stone on the Midwest leg of his US tour. You can hear that single and the rest of her debut album, *Bad Mistake*, which is rapidly climbing the charts, in Milwaukee,

Chicago, Detroit, Indianapolis, and Cincinnati. So head to Griffin Stone's website for tickets."

She's coming to Indianapolis. My former best friend has finally achieved country stardom and is touring with my ex-boyfriend, the man I caught her kissing right before he wrote a song about me and hit number one with it.

CHAPTER 11

MARCH 21 AT 9:21 PM

WYATT

Are you dating?

OWEN

Right this minute? Or ever?

WYATT

Dealer's choice

OWEN

I don't know why I felt the need to clarify. The answer is no on both counts

WYATT

Why?

OWEN

Why?

WYATT

Just curious

OWEN

You know that killed the cat

WYATT

Luckily I have a few of my nine lives left. I'm
happy to sacrifice one to my curiosity about you

OWEN

Are you thinking of changing your mind, Wyatt?

MARCH 21 AT 10:45 PM

WYATT

Are you on any apps?

OWEN

Dating apps?

WYATT

No the NYT crossword

Yes apps

OWEN

No, I'm not on any apps

Except the NYT crossword. I do it daily

WYATT

Nerd

How do you meet people?

OWEN

In person

WYATT

Okay grandpa

OWEN

That's how I met you

WYATT

Doesn't count. We knew each other before.
You're telling me you would have walked up to
me in a bar if I were a stranger?

OWEN

Absolutely. Have you seen you?

WYATT

In fact I have. What would your line have been?

OWEN

I don't have a line. I would have asked if I could
sit beside you, then offered to buy you a drink

WYATT

Boring

OWEN

You know, I'm not really into sunsets, but I'd love
to see you go down

WYATT

DOC!

OWEN

[sunglasses emoji]

MARCH 30 AT 2:39 PM

OWEN

I've joined a bowling league

Deliver to me my AARP card

WYATT

What? And why?

OWEN

Because Larry Andrews asked me twice and I
don't know how to say no

WYATT

I could have an awful lot of fun with that little
personality quirk

OWEN

My door's always open

CHAPTER 12
OWEN

April 1

It's six fifteen p.m. The office closed at five, but my last patient left only a few minutes ago.

That's the kind of day it's been.

April Fool's indeed.

We kicked off the morning with a fire alarm that had all our patients standing in the parking lot while the fire department fixed the loose wire that had tripped the sensor. That totally borked our schedule for the rest of the day, leaving our waiting room packed with fussy kids and their equally fussy parents. It was like someone had inserted a key into the space between my shoulder blades and begun turning it, drawing the muscles in my back and neck taut as guitar strings.

Just before lunch, a mother arrived for her child's vaccination appointment, to which she had brought all *five* of her kids. And because we weren't going to send her off with four unvaccinated children, we hustled to make it work. But her youngest was terrified of needles, so that took some finessing.

The tension key made another quarter turn.

By the time I actually got to eat, I was hanging on by a thread, which might explain why I took my tomato soup out of the microwave and promptly dropped it onto the floor.

I stared at the culinary murder scene that was our tiny office kitchenette and felt the tension key between my shoulder blades make another full turn.

The rest of the day involved working to meet everybody's needs while pretending I didn't want to run into the back parking lot and scream myself hoarse. Sitting here in my blessedly quiet office, I realize I'm clenching my fists so tightly that my nails are cutting into my palms. My traps feel like they've been replaced with a combination of sharp rocks and steel bars. I can't look to the left without a bolt of pain racing down my shoulder blade, and I have a headache that feels like my brain is trying to escape my skull.

I'm leaning back in my desk chair and trying to remember that breathing technique I saw on Instagram when my phone lights up.

And there it is, the only bright spot in this garbage day: a text from Wyatt.

WYATT

How much ibuprofen is too much ibuprofen?

OWEN

Literally? No more than four every four hours for twenty-four hours, but if you feel like you need that much, maybe check in with your doctor

Metaphorically? The limit does not exist

WYATT

Maybe I'll just stick with pinot noir

OWEN

You okay?

WYATT

Just a shitty day. Nothing a glass of wine and a
bath hot enough to cook a shrimp can't fix

I let out an involuntary groan, my eyes closing as I conjure up the image of Wyatt's tight little body in a bath, the water sluicing over her breasts. I think about sitting beside her tub, running a soapy washcloth over her perfect skin, dragging my fingers through her damp hair, gripping it to pull her lips to mine…

Fuck the ibuprofen, that's what *I* need.

Unfortunately, not even my prescription pad can help me with that kind of relief. No, I'll be stuck with my usual method of stress relief: a long, hot shower alone with my hand.

Alone.

I'm suddenly very tired of being alone.

When Francie and I broke up early in our last year of residency, I was in a bad place. I was overworked and underslept. I was eating whatever crap I could scrounge up from vending machines or fast food restaurants near the hospital. My blood was made up almost entirely of burnt break room coffee. I was a disaster waiting to happen.

And then there was no more waiting. Disaster found me.

When Dylan Anders, the smiling kid with the missing front teeth, showed up in the ER, telling me all about his new Minecraft builds while his mom explained that he'd taken a tumble at the playground, I wasn't too worried. She assured me he hadn't lost consciousness, hadn't thrown up. He'd barely even cried, she said. She just wanted to be sure.

And so did I. So I ordered the head CT, laughed at his knock-knock joke, and moved on to the next patient. It was a busy night at the start of flu season, and everyone was coming in with wheezing and fevers.

When I heard the code blue, it didn't even occur to me that it could be him.

Brain bleeds are like that.

I'd ordered the right scan, but I could have pushed, made sure he got it faster, not underestimated the danger. If I'd stayed with him, had a nurse stay with him, been clearer with his mom about the risks... Hell, if I'd wheeled him to CT myself and made the tech scan him right then and there, Dylan would still be alive.

Everything sort of fell apart after that. I kept freezing in the ER. I could barely sleep. I often forgot to feed myself, and when I remembered, everything sat in my stomach like hot coals. I was on the verge of quitting medicine entirely when I got the call from Dr. Putnam back home. She wanted to retire, and she offered her practice to me.

So I gritted my teeth through the last couple of months of my residency, and then I left Philadelphia.

Was it my plan to move back to my hometown?

No.

But it seemed like the right thing to do. Walking into the ER day after day was excruciating. I saw Dylan's face on every child. Private practice would be better. It would be slower. I could get myself back on even ground.

Needless to say, dating fell completely by the wayside. I had a few hospital hookups, but they always left me feeling empty, like I'd just woken up from a hangover.

So I focused on the practice. Those first two years I worked myself to the bone, making sure every one of my patients got the care and attention they deserved.

By last fall, that same wrung-out feeling of desperation was starting to creep back in. My sleep grew sporadic, my headaches more frequent.

That was when I hired Fatima.

And things have been better since then. I trust her, and that means I can step back a little. Suddenly there's space for me to feel alive again.

Unfortunately, there's also space to want.

To want something I can't have. *Someone* I can't have.

"Look alive," Fatima says as she steps into my office, tossing the on call phone at me. I jerk to attention and catch it just before it smacks into my chest.

Fuck, I forgot I was on call tonight.

When Fatima came on board, she brought a few new processes with her. Gone are the days of the after-hours line forwarding calls to my personal cell phone. Gone are the days of the after-hours line entirely. Now we have an app that allows patients to message us directly, including photos. It helps keep a lot of smaller-scale things from escalating, like they often can when you have a frantic parent on the phone.

There are still plenty of calls, though. And tonight I was really counting on attempting to unwind.

"You okay, Owen?" Fatima asks, cocking her head and studying me.

I give my shoulders a quick, painful roll and smile. It's not her job to tend to me.

"I'm good. Just one of those days," I reply.

"Lord, that was a wild one. I pulled *four* beans out of a kid's nose this afternoon, and *then* he tested positive for strep." She sighs. "I know your day sucked too, but I'm so glad to hand off that phone. I need a margarita the size of my head tonight."

"No worries, I've got it," I say. I stand and wince at the cracking sound my right knee makes.

"You sure?" Fatima asks.

I wave her off. "I'm good. Go enjoy your tequila."

She grins. "See you tomorrow."

On the way home, I remember that there's no food in my house other than mustard and beer, so I swing my truck around and stop at the grocery store. The bright fluorescent lights set my teeth on edge, and the jangly nineties alternative rock on the store stereo has my shoulders creeping toward my ears.

"In and out," I mutter to myself as I grab a basket, working to breathe slowly, and head for the produce section.

CHAPTER 13

WYATT

It took two weeks for my past to fully muscle its way into my present. The irony that it arrived on April Fool's Day was not lost on me. No one has ever made me feel more foolish than Romy Maxwell and Griffin Stone.

It's been a week since the text from Romy arrived—the first since I left Nashville, when she sent me a string of apologies and explanations and desperate pleas.

I told her never to speak to me again, and at least she gave me that.

Until now.

The text is heavy with all the things she left unsaid. That she'll be in Indianapolis for a show. Her first big tour. Opening for my ex-boyfriend. The one who wrote a hit single about me breaking *his* heart. The one she kissed on the couch that she and I had carried two and a half miles home from Goodwill because the battery on my truck had died and they wouldn't hold it for us.

In another life, the three of us would be thick as thieves, celebrating their success. In a life where they didn't cheat, where my mom didn't go to prison. Where I didn't leave Nashville behind, the city full of every broken, battered hope and happy memory.

Nashville was my first and last chance to live my own life the way I wanted, without the bad influence of my mother and all her mistakes.

Turns out I didn't learn shit from her mistakes.

And yet every time I pick up my phone to tell Romy no, that I don't want to see her, not now and maybe not ever, something stops me. But I need to solve it soon, because that text is like an open wound that's starting to fester.

Until then, I'm treating it with a smorgasbord of my favorite snacks.

I'm just leaving the candy aisle, my basket half full of high-fructose corn syrup and good old-fashioned sugar, my internal compass pointing toward the chip aisle, when I see him.

He must have come straight from the office, because he's in those khaki pants that are sexier than khaki has a right to be, fitted around his ass and his muscular thighs. He's wearing a blue button-up shirt, the sleeves rolled to show off his corded forearms.

But I don't ogle his forearms for long, because right away I can see that something is off with him. He's facing a cooler, glaring at rows of packaged chicken breasts. His shoulders are pulled in and up, one fist clenched at his side. He's got his feet planted on the scuffed white linoleum like he's prepared to take a tackle from an NFL linebacker.

But it's the expression on his face that stops me in my tracks beside an endcap of Capri Suns.

He's *glowering*.

The golden boy's easy smile is nowhere to be seen, his brows drawn in, his lips drawn down. I don't know what's going on, but whatever it is, it's not good.

I approach slowly, but he doesn't seem to notice anything besides the illuminated shelves of meat.

"You're staring at the chicken like it wronged your family," I say when I'm beside him.

His head whips around, and when he realizes it's me, there's just the tiniest bit of softening in his face.

"You okay?" I ask, and he tenses again.

"Rough day," he says, his voice gravelly.

I glance down into his basket, which contains a package of basmati rice, a head of broccoli, and a bottle of soy sauce. I glance from that to the chicken and back.

"You had a rough day, and you're not soothing it with cake and wine? Or ice cream and beer? Or sixteen different flavors of ruffled potato chips?"

The corner of his lips twitches, and then he studies my basket.

"Are you throwing a birthday party for a nine-year-old?"

"This is dinner," I reply. "I too had a crappy day."

His brow furrows. "There's no protein in there. You're going to feel like shit tomorrow."

"Tomorrow is not the point. We care only for tonight, Owen, and tonight we dine on the finest snacks Food Town has to offer."

He reaches in and plucks out a cellophane bag of Circus Peanuts. "You're seriously going to eat these?"

"Orange marshmallows shaped like peanuts that taste like bananas? You bet your high and tight ass I'm going to eat these," I tell him, then watch the blush climb into his cheeks. Damn, I love a man who blushes. "The question is, why aren't you?"

"Because unlike you, I actually *am* thinking about tomorrow and the inevitable headache and stomachache and self-loathing."

"See, just one more reason we wouldn't work. I'm impulsive and you're a planner."

"Except when I'm not," he says, and the look in his eye says he's thinking about pressing me against his truck. That smoldering look is enough to ignite a fire inside me, and it's only the blinding overhead light of the grocery store that keeps me from dropping my basket and leaping into his arms right here in the meat section.

We've been flirty texting for weeks, and I'm practically Pavlov's dog, salivating every time I hear the ping of my phone. But our schedules are completely opposite and equally full, so we haven't talked in real life.

Standing here in front of him, listening to the voice I've been imagining as I read all those teasing texts, each one walking the line of appropriateness, is like lighting a fire beneath our attraction.

At some point during this conversation, we must have stepped closer together. Suddenly I'm craning my neck to stare up at him, my chin even with his pecs. I watch his chest rise and fall, long to press my face into it, to feel the warmth of him, to listen to the sound of his heartbeat. To figure out if it's as fast as mine is right now.

I reach up, take the candy from his hand, and drop it back into my basket. "Such a good boy," I practically purr. I let my eyes rake over him. "Milk really does do a body good."

His left eyebrow rises. "Wyatt, if you want me to show you what does a body good, you just have to ask."

I arch a brow in return, heat flooding my body. "Damn, Doc."

And then it's his turn to drag his eyes over my body, and fuck, do I feel every inch of their path. He pauses at my hips, sweeping across to the flash of belly button just above the waistband of my jeans. His tongue darts out, moving over his bottom lip, and I wonder if he's imagining sucking the gold ring there into his mouth, tugging on it with his teeth.

Because that's what *I'm* thinking about.

And he doesn't even know about my other piercings yet.

His eyes narrow when he reaches the deep V of my shirt, the red lace of my bra peeking out, the scrollwork of my tattoos rising even higher.

For the last three months, ever since that night back in January at Sorry Charlie's, I've wanted him. I've always been willing to admit that to myself, like letting the thought in would keep things from going any further. But dammit, I don't just want him in the abstract. I want to *do* something about it. Something that will help me forget my crappy day and my pain-in-the-ass mom and the unanswered text from my past. Suddenly all those roadblocks and warnings, all the danger signs, are fading from view.

Owen seems like a very good bad idea.

And knowing that I've helped unwind him right here under the fluorescent lights of the grocery store feels so good.

It makes me want to unwind him completely.

Or maybe to wind him up again.

But then his phone buzzes, and the spell breaks.

Owen steps back, pulls out the phone, and studies the screen with a furrowed brow.

"Everything okay?" I ask.

He sighs. "Yeah, I'm on call tonight. And it looks like I'm heading back to the office to stitch up a forehead."

And I'm…*disappointed*. This interruption wasn't welcome. It wasn't serendipity. It didn't save me from making a bad mistake.

Because now I know for sure that letting myself go with Owen McBride would be the best kind of mistake.

He slides the phone back into his pocket and reaches for a package of chicken. After all that staring and glaring and studying, he plucks one off the top without even looking and tosses it into his basket.

His eyes? Those are still on me.

"We're not done," he says. His voice is a delicious warning.

"So go home, eat your trash food, enjoy a hot bath, and think of me. Because eventually, we won't be interrupted."

All I can do is nod, my voice snatched from my throat as I watch him turn and stalk toward the front of the store, his shoulders no longer tense, a smirk playing at the corners of his mouth.

CHAPTER 14

APRIL 2 AT 8:15 AM

WYATT

You feeling better?

OWEN

I really am

WYATT

It was the stitches, wasn't it?

OWEN

It was you, actually

WYATT

…back atcha

APRIL 14 AT 8:37 PM

WYATT

What kind of women are you looking for?

OWEN

Tiny bartenders who are mean to me

WYATT

I'm not mean to you!

OWEN

Yes you are and I like it

WYATT

...noted

APRIL 15 AT 10:15 PM

OWEN

No questions about my dating habits today?

WYATT

Nothing today. Eden is teething. And when Eden doesn't sleep, nobody sleeps

OWEN

I'm sorry

Freeze a bagel, it's a great teething ring for her

WYATT

Why does it turn me on that you know that?

OWEN

Don't look at it too closely. Try to focus on the being turned on part

WYATT

This is not a problem I have when it comes
to you

I'm off Friday night

OWEN

Fuck. I'm going to a conference in Cleveland

Wanna come with? I've got a room in the finest
Holiday Inn the Forest City has to offer

WYATT

I'd follow you to Cleveland for a Motel 6, Owen.
Unfortunately we've got a meeting with my
mom's parole officer Saturday morning

I can't believe that's the thing keeping me from a
sex weekend in Cleveland

OWEN

I'm just glad we're on the same page

Like I said...one of these days we won't be
interrupted

APRIL 20 AT 11:36 AM

OWEN

Are you going to this dance marathon thing?

WYATT

Grace told me I had to or she wouldn't be my
friend anymore

Are you going?

OWEN

Yeah. The practice is one of the sponsors. Save
me a dance?

WYATT

Is that a euphemism?

OWEN

Wyatt, you know I'm down to dance with you wherever, whenever, in whatever state of undress you choose

WYATT

See you at the dance Doc [winking emoji]

CHAPTER 15

OWEN

April 28

This gel is only barely strong enough to tame my thick hair, and despite my attempts, a rogue curl keeps popping free and draping itself over my forehead. It detracts from the polished Navy pilot image I'm going for, but I like imagining Wyatt brushing it off my forehead tonight.

My dad's girlfriend—and yes, it's still weird to say that about my father, a bachelor widower for the last twenty-five years—is on the board of a nonprofit that supports women leaving violent relationships. They offer housing, legal and financial support, and counseling. For this year's gala, Corianne decided to "put the *fun* in fundraiser" and switch from the usual boring plated rubber chicken dinner to an all-night eighties-themed dance marathon.

Which means that not only do I have to stay up all night, I have to do it in costume.

But it's for a good cause, and my dad has bent over backward for the five us his whole life. Corianne makes him happy, so I'll do what I can to make *her* happy. That's what family does.

Which is why I'm wearing an army-green flight suit and black boots, a pair of aviators perched on top of my head.

I reach for the faucet to wash the pomade off my hands, but when I turn the knob it just sputters and dies.

"Felix!" I shout, already halfway down the hall to hunt him down.

I find Felix on his back on the kitchen floor, his head in the cabinet beneath the sink. The kitchen is a disaster, wet towels surrounding him, half the cabinet doors leaned up against the wall, waiting to be painted.

They've been waiting since President's Day.

My brother has been a tinkerer all his life, from Lego sets as a kid to gathering up the wood scraps Dad had lying around his workshop to make avant-garde birdhouses. He went to school for engineering, finishing his BA and master's in five years, but after only a month at his first job with a big Chicago firm, he realized a desk job wasn't for him. So he moved home and became Cardinal Springs's most sought-after handyman while he worked toward his contractor's license.

Unfortunately, he spends an ungodly amount of time honing his craft in the little house we share. There's a newly built deck off the back that still needs staining, our hall bath is partially tiled, and the basement has an in-progress wet bar in the far corner. And that's to say nothing of our living room, which sports six different paint samples splotched on the wall and an uncaulked chair rail.

My brother is as reliable as they come if you hire him to work on your house, but when it comes to *his* house, his ADHD gets the better of him.

But I can't complain. The rent is cheap, and when he *does* manage to finish a project, it always turns out spectacularly. Like the outdoor kitchen with a gas grill, flat top, brick oven, and weatherproof sixty-five-inch television with surround sound. The first time he grilled steaks while we watched the Cubs opening day, I forgave him for all the early mornings he woke me up hammering on the wall outside my bedroom.

But when he does things like turning the water off without telling me, I get testy.

"Where's the water, dude?" I ask, kicking the sole of his dirty work boot. "And also your costume? We're supposed to leave in ten."

Felix gives whatever tool he's holding a final twist, then slides across the partially stripped wood floor of our kitchen.

"Needed to fix this leak, so I shut off the water. But it's fine now, so I can turn it back on." He wipes his hands on a rag and looks up at me. "Good look, Goose."

"I'm Maverick," I scoff. "Goose dies. What the hell are you?"

My twin brother is wearing a pair of jeans, a plaid pearl-snap shirt, and dusty, beat-up old work boots.

Which is what he wears every day to the jobsite.

"I'm the guy from *Footloose.* Kevin Bacon?"

I roll my eyes. "Kevin Bacon is the actor. And that's a weak costume, bro. Those are your regular clothes."

Felix shrugs. "You're just jealous you didn't think of it. Going to be kind of hard to drag Wyatt Hart to the janitor's closet when you're wearing a onesie."

"It's a flight suit," I say, glancing down at my costume. "And don't talk about Wyatt like that."

Felix's eyes shoot up at the heat in my tone.

"'Sup, Goose," Dan says as he strolls into the kitchen.

"I'm Maverick!" I tap the patch on my chest where I wrote it out in Sharpie. "Where's your costume?"

Dan is wearing his usual crisp black suit, tailored within an inch of its life. The only variation on his usual workwear is the blue-and-white-striped dress shirt, paisley tie, and matching suspenders.

"This is my costume," he grunts. "I'm Gordon Gecko. From *Wall Street.*"

"You guys have no sense of fun," I grumble.

"What the hell are you two supposed to be?" Archer, our oldest brother, booms as he walks in, studying Dan and Felix. He's dressed as a ghostbuster in a light beige jumpsuit, complete with a homemade laser gun on his back.

"Sweet proton pack," Felix says.

Archer spins to show off the blue and red lights that actually glow.

"Betsy made it," he says, his grin wide, as it is whenever the twelve-year-old daughter of his beautiful next door neighbor comes up. She's become the joy of my brother's life these last few months. "That kid is so fucking creative, unlike you jokers. *Footloose* and Gordon Gecko? Snooze."

And then, without breaking eye contact, he holds up a hand and silently high-fives me.

"Where are Betsy and Madeline, anyway?" Felix asks.

"They're meeting us there. Betsy wanted her costume to be a surprise."

"You guys are hanging out again?" I ask. The last time I drove by, I noticed that the BMW that's been in Madeline's driveway the last few weeks has disappeared.

Archer shifts in his work boots. "Same as always," he replies, and before I can pepper him with more questions, he raises his eyebrow. "You hanging out with Wyatt Hart?"

Archer and I glare at each other. *I'll show you mine if you show me yours*, he's saying silently.

Not a chance in hell, I reply with my eyes.

"Good talk," I finally say.

"Back atcha," he replies.

Dan silently rocks on his heels.

"The three of you need to loosen the fuck up," Felix says as the slams the lid of his toolbox. "Now let's go dance."

———

I've barely seen Wyatt in the two weeks since I ran into her at the grocery store. That night had all the makings of a disaster. I remember the panic coursing through my body, coiling tight in my muscles. My temples felt like they were being squeezed in a vise, and all I wanted was a dark, quiet room.

Not that sleep would have come for me. I knew I was well on the road to lying in my bed, staring at my dark ceiling, and willing my brain to slow down, to cut me some slack, to get a fucking grip. Those kinds of nights used to plague me often back in medical school, and I'd lie awake combing through all my mistakes, noting my near-misses, and cataloguing my catastrophes.

Now that I'm out of the pressure cooker of med school and residency and life in the emergency room, sleepless nights come less frequently, but they still come. Usually after a day when everything's gone to shit, but sometimes for no reason at all.

When they come, I try my best to do the calming breathing techniques the therapist gave me back in residency. But usually I wind up just waiting it out. By the time the sun rises, I can take the fresh start and move on. Well, after some ibuprofen and coffee to deal with the insomnia-related migraines.

Anxiety hangovers, if you will.

But that night in the grocery store, everything went a different way. Wyatt showed up out of nowhere, interrupting my thought spirals, catching the herd of squirrels racing around my brain and soothing them to sleep.

If I hadn't had to put seven stitches in Erica Montour's forehead, I would have taken Wyatt home and used all that energy to show her my appreciation. Because after months of reticence, whatever hang-ups have kept her from me seem to have dissipated. She wanted me that night. She's ready to let go, and I am too.

And tonight, I'm finally going to be alone with her.

Well, her, my entire family, and damn near everyone else in this town.

Still, I don't plan on letting *anything* interrupt us tonight. Even if I have to get creative.

As soon as I step through the doors with my brothers, I begin scanning the crowd for her. Last I saw her, the streaks in her dark curls were a gentle lavender, and that's what I look for in the sea of dancers in brightly colored costumes clustered around the half court line of the Cardinal Springs High School gym. The smell of bleach layered over old basketballs and body odor brings me right back to my teenage years. In fact, with the balloon arch, the refreshment table, and the DJ set up underneath the scoreboard, it looks almost identical to our senior prom.

I spot three different Cyndi Laupers bopping around the floor and a number of hair metal wigs, but I don't see her.

Beside me, Archer busts out laughing so hard he nearly falls over on me.

"What the hell?" I mutter, rubbing my arm, but then I see the little girl weaving through the crowd wearing a denim shirt and bell-bottoms, a paint palette and brush in her hand and a brown permed wig on her head.

And then I'm laughing too.

"Betsy, that costume is incredible," Felix says, giving her a high five, and even Dan is grinning.

"What did I tell you about this kid?" Archer says as he pulls her in for a noogie on her Bob Ross wig. "Creative as hell."

"Don't light a match near her—I filled that wig with enough hairspray to burn a hole in the ozone layer," Madeline says, pushing through the crowd behind her daughter. She's dressed in a white lace corset and skirt, and she's got a drawn-on beauty mark and a bandana in her hair, looking just like a brunette Madonna.

Archer's laughter dies in his throat, his mouth hanging agape as he takes in his neighbor in costume.

"Be cool," I mutter beneath a cough.

Archer's mouth snaps shut, but it takes him a couple of slow blinks to finds words again. "You look great, Madeline," he says, his voice cracking only a little bit on her name. Felix stifles a laugh beside me.

"Thanks," Madeline replies, and I can't tell if it's the lights, her makeup, or the way Archer can't stop staring at her that's causing the pink in her cheeks.

"Can we *dance*?" Betsy pleads. She starts dragging Archer toward the dance floor with one hand, the other reaching for her mother's hand.

"Yeah, of course, kid," Archer says, and the three of them disappear into the crowd as the DJ cranks up a Whitney Houston tune.

As much as I want to stand around watching Archer try to dance to "I Wanna Dance With Somebody" while attempting not to drool all over Madeline, I have to find Wyatt.

I leave Felix and Dan and take a lap around the dance floor, but I don't spot her. I do spot Mrs. Tingle, dressed as Prince in a purple suit, shimmying with her cane.

"Looking good, Mrs. T. You in it for the long haul tonight?"

"I'm only staying until ten," she says, fanning herself with a sequin-gloved hand. "After that I turn into a pumpkin. But I couldn't resist the chance to rock this costume. Betsy says I have 'rizz,' which from context clues seems like it's pretty good!"

"You have mad rizz, Mrs. Tingle," I assure her—I learned the word from the kids at the practice. They keep me young, even if they look at me like I'm a hundred and five.

"Well, don't waste your time standing here with an old lady. Tonight is a perfect night to make your move on your favorite bartender." Mrs. Tingle gives me her sauciest grin.

"Way ahead of you on that one," I assure her. "I just need to find her."

"Good luck, my dear!" she replies, and then "When Doves Cry" echoes through the gym. "They're playing my song!" And then she's gone into the crowd.

I take another lap, but I still don't find Wyatt. I do find Decker and Grace, though. It's hard to miss them in their green spandex, giant cardboard turtle shells strapped to their backs.

"Nice costume, man," Decker says. "Wish I'd thought of it. These tights are really riding up."

"Hey, I wanted to be Barbie and Ken, but you nixed that," Grace says.

"Too obvious," Decker says, and Grace opens her mouth to object—it's obvious they've already had this little fight a few times—but Decker charges on. "If we weren't Ninja Turtles, you wouldn't have gotten to show off your mad crafting skills. You know, she made these costumes from scratch."

I realize he's talking to me a beat too late because I'm busy scanning the crowd for Wyatt.

"She's running late," Grace says. "She got stuck at the bar."

"Who?" I ask, as if it's not obvious. Even I can hear how pathetic I sound.

Grace rolls her eyes. "Don't even try it, Owen. She told me you kissed her."

I smirk, calling up the memory of her fingers digging into my back as her tongue tangled with mine. "I think she did some of the kissing too."

Grace squeals, loud enough that I hear it over the crowd shouting along to "Don't Stop Believin'."

I shake my finger in her face, which I know she hates, but I also know it will get her attention. "Nope. Nuh-uh. None of that. Wyatt doesn't want it, and I'm not going to push her."

"She told me that too," Grace says with a smug smile. "I'm on *your* side."

"No meddling, Cherry," Decker warns. I don't know what that nickname means, and given the way my sister blushes, I won't be asking.

"I need a drink," I mutter. I underestimated how loud and social this event would be without Wyatt to distract me, and while I'm very good at extroverting, there comes a point at which it exhausts me. And I'm starting to hit my limit with the loud eighties playlist ringing in my ears.

"It's a dry gym, unfortunately," Decker says, and my heart sinks, but then he reaches beneath his cardboard turtle shell and pulls out a flask. He passes it to me with a wink. "Just like old times."

"Back in high school, I'm pretty sure you and Archer filled your flask with flat ginger ale and jalapeños and tried to convince Felix and me it was moonshine," I remind him.

Decker laughs. "You guys acted like you were wasted for a good hour before you figured it out."

"Yeah, and Felix still barfed because that shit was disgusting." I shake my head, laughing. I'm definitely going to have to remind Felix of that memory later.

I head off through the crowd, the flask tucked in the pocket of my flight suit. I drop my aviators over my eyes like I'm on a covert mission, and when I get to the refreshment table, I quickly fill a cup with pink punch from the enormous crystal bowl at the end. Then I tuck myself into a corner, glancing around like Principal Paterno is going to appear and give me detention at thirty-one years old, and top off the punch with what I think is gin.

The cup smells like every one of my high school indiscretions, and it nearly goes tumbling right out of my hand when I see her.

Because Wyatt steps through the doors of the gym, backlit by the lobby lights, wearing only a black leotard, a soft gray sweatshirt hanging off one shoulder, and a pair of short black leg warmers.

I've never seen *Flashdance*, but that doesn't mean the movie poster didn't imprint itself on my teenage brain.

She looks delicious.

As if she can feel my eyes on her, her gaze finds mine right away. She raises her hand in a little wave, the other tugging at the hem of her sweatshirt in a way that is demure and sexy and scandalous all at once.

I toss the cup into the nearest trash can and feel myself moving before I even realize I'm doing it. I think I hear Mrs. Tingle say, "Go get 'er, tiger," but I can't be sure. All I know is that I need that woman in my arms. *Now.*

But Ernie, the owner of the Half Pint, beats me to her. He holds out his hand, and with a quick look my way that says *what are ya gonna do about it*, she steps into his arms for a slow dance.

What am I gonna do? I'm gonna wait until this song is over like a goddamn gentleman and then claim her as my own. That's what I'm gonna do.

But the eighties synth slow jam barely ends before Archer steps up. Some yacht rock song fills the gym, and they sway together to the gentle beat. I grit my teeth, stepping a little closer so I'll have a better shot next time, but still, I wait. As soon as the song starts to fade, I'm striding over.

Only Decker, the motherfucker, slides up, pulling Wyatt into his arms and dipping her to the Phil Collins song that's just starting. Beside them, Grace covers her mouth and giggles. I thought she was on *my* side.

"Traitor," I mouth in Decker's direction, but he just gives me a devious grin.

And on it goes, Felix jumping in, followed by Dan, who I didn't even realize knew how to dance. Mrs. Tingle is next, and luckily for me, she tires before the end of Toto's "Africa." Unluckily for me, Archer is back and ready to take her spot before I can even come close to gathering Wyatt to my chest.

I'm about to hip check Archer directly into the bleachers when Felix appears at my side, distracting me so Dad can take his turn with Wyatt on the dance floor.

"What the fuck are you doing?" I say to my twin brother, exasperated.

"Good things come to those who wait," Felix explains, shoving his hands deep into the pockets of his jeans in a classic Felix McBride *aw, shucks* little brother move even though he's literally four minutes younger than me.

"You're fucking with me."

"You bet your ass I am. After Dad comes his whole bowling league."

I glare at my twin. "Why are you doing this to me?"

He shrugs. "Because it's fun. And because I can't remember the last time you had a crush."

"I don't have a crush!" I throw my arms up. "This isn't high school!"

Felix grins. "Look around, brother. It's *literally* high school."

I grind my molars. "Fuck off."

"Hey, Wyatt doesn't do anything she doesn't want to do," he says.

And that's when I catch her eye.

She looks at me for a long beat.

And then she winks.

Goddammit. She's playing with me too. Again.

CHAPTER 16
WYATT

I have to laugh when the DJ starts playing "Take My Breath Away" and my Maverick is glaring at me from the refreshment table while I dance with his dad.

"I think my son's about to have a little come apart," Mr. McBride says with a chuckle. He's got one hand resting lightly on my waist, the other clasping mine as if we're about to do a very respectable nineteenth-century waltz.

I lock eyes with Owen and watch his jaw flex, the only betrayal of his annoyance. Felix is laughing beside him.

"Probably the most polite come apart the world has ever seen," I say. "You raised a real gentleman, Mr. McB."

"Please, call me Jack," he says, then glances over at his son, who's starting to make his way across the dance floor toward us. "And keep an eye on that one for me. He thinks being a good guy means hiding the cracks."

I'm left to contemplate that as Owen strides up to us, hands clasped at his lower back, stance strong like the military man he's dressed up as.

"Excuse me, Dad. Mind if I cut in?"

"Well, that's up to the lady," his dad says.

Owen doesn't even roll his eyes at the use of *lady* to describe me. Man, these McBride men are built different.

Owen locks eyes with me, those brilliant baby blues piercing. He gives me a gentle grin and holds out one of his big hands. "May I?"

"Well, I guess it can't hurt," I say, smiling at Mr. McBride, who releases me and takes a step back. Owen quickly takes his place, his hands snaking around my hips. I drape my arms over his broad shoulders and let him pull me close enough that I can rest my cheek on his firm chest.

"What took you so long, soldier?"

"You made me wait, tiny bartender," he growls.

"That a problem?"

"I've been waiting an awfully long time," he says.

"So what's a little longer?"

"You know, at first I thought it was our schedules that were keeping us apart—me at the clinic during the day, you at the bar at night. Then it looked like my brother was trying put one over on me. But all this time it was you, playing your little games." He laughs, giving my hips a squeeze with those large hands. "Now I see that if we're going to get anywhere, I'm going to have to take the reins."

"You think you've changed my mind?"

"I think *you've* changed your mind," he says. He gives me a little shove, spinning me away from him and back in again. I crash into his chest with a little *oof*, liking far too much the way he takes charge of me. He grins down as if to say, *See what I can do to you?*

I sigh, an ache deep in my chest. "I do want to be with you, Owen. But that's not the point."

He scoffs. "It's entirely the point."

"What I want is irrelevant. I *want* to quit my job and run off to Southern California to live on the beach. I want to eat a diet consisting only of fountain Cokes and Cool Ranch Doritos. But I don't do those things because they're bad for me. Relationships are bad for me. I end up losing things. People. Myself."

Owen pauses, staring down at me with a little crease in his brow. He looks like he's just finished a puzzle only to discover that the last piece doesn't fit.

"Who hurt you, Wyatt?"

I don't like the serious look on his face, the concern written there. I want banter. Low-stakes fun and games. I don't want him looking at me like he's trying to excavate my pain. It scares the hell out of me.

So I give a dramatic eye roll and force out a laugh. "Why, you wanna hurt them back?"

His eyes go thunderous. "I want to *ruin* them."

It's not what I expected, not from this sweet man who cradled my niece so gently on her very first day on this planet. And I believe him. Not just that he wants to, but that he actually could —*would*—lay waste to Griffin Stone and his manicured stubble and his stupid cowboy hats, and he'd *enjoy* it.

I pull Owen closer, winding my arms tighter around his neck. I have to rise up on my tiptoes to reach his ear, but I get there and whisper, "Why did you have to go and say something like that when we're standing in the middle of a dance floor surrounded by everyone we know?"

I drop back down onto my heels, relishing the foot of difference in our heights. His grip tightens around my waist as he grins down at me.

"What is it that you want to do and can't, Wyatt?"

I give a saucy little shrug. "I'm open to feedback, but my plan involves far fewer clothes."

The man looks downright cocky. "I might have a solution."

Without explanation, he takes my hand and starts walking. To anyone else, it probably looks like he's gently leading me through the crowd. But his firm grip on my much smaller hand is anything but gentle. It's demanding and possessive. It reminds me of his confidence that night at Sorry Charlie's when he invited me outside, shoved me against his truck, and gave me a panty-melting kiss.

I've done a lot of thinking about how Owen McBride might fuck, but this? This possessive, almost bossy thing he's got going on? I did not see this coming.

It's always the nice ones.

We push through the doors of the gym and into the hall, but he keeps going. With his long legs and determined gait, I have to trot to keep up.

"Where are we going?" I ask as we fly past banks of red lockers.

"Somewhere we can be alone."

At the end of the hall, we duck into a stairwell, and Owen immediately backs me into the corner, his hands on my cheeks as he pulls me toward him. He claims my mouth, a true *claiming*, and all I can do is surrender to him. I moan into his mouth and press against the hard ridge inside his flight suit.

"Hardly private, Doc," I whisper against his lips.

"This isn't our final destination," he replies with a curl of his lips. Then he traces his tongue along the edge of my jaw. "I just couldn't wait."

And then he's taking my hand again, pulling me after him down two flights of stairs, through a set of double doors, and past more lockers. At the end of the hall, he turns and shoulders into a classroom, the heavy wooden door smacking hard against the wall before he closes it behind us. There are tall tables and metal stools, shelves against the back wall full of glass beakers and jars. And in the corner, a little nook with a sink and a counter.

Owen drags me back there, turns, and in one swift motion, grasps my hips and lifts me, depositing me on the countertop. Tucked back in this nook, we wouldn't even be seen if someone opened the door and poked their head in.

"How do you know about this spot?" I ask, breathless.

"This is my high school," he reminds me, then grins. "And I

may have brought Suzie Parrish here during the homecoming dance."

I roll my eyes as if I'm not completely charmed by the idea that the golden boy has a few dirty little secrets. "Way to make a girl feel special, Doc."

"We just made out a little," he says, peppering my collarbone with soft kisses. "That is not at all what I have planned for you."

Owen places his hands on my bare knees, sending a sizzle of heat through my body.

"Open," he says. It's a command, issued in a low, stern voice. It's an Owen I haven't seen before, and I like it way too much.

Still, I take pleasure in smirking at him. His lips twitch, trying to suppress his own smile, as I press my knees together.

"You're being a brat, Wyatt," he says with a warning in his tone.

I grin. "Do you like it?"

His eyes grow dark, and this time he lets his lips curl into a smile. "Yes."

Everything around me fades to black as this man in front of me becomes the center of my universe. His smug smile, the way his fingers flex into the skin of my thighs. As much as I want to keep playing with him, pushing him, something about the commanding look in his eyes causes my knees to drift apart.

And when he realizes that he's won, that I'm opening for him, he parts my legs the rest of the way with a firm press of his palms, dropping to his knees before me.

He looks up and meets my eyes.

"That's a good girl," he says, then gives my inner thigh a slap.

I gasp.

A guy called me a good girl during sex once. It sounded porny and demeaning, and—entirely instinctively—I kneed him in the balls. (Okay, it was a little bit on purpose.)

But when Owen says it, it's like my body comes online, erogenous zones lighting up like a slot machine, the little air traffic controller in my brain setting every nerve ending ablaze.

My lips part and a moan escapes.

"Tell me yes, Wyatt," Owen says, and this time it's part demand, part desperate plea. When I don't respond immediately, when I press my lips together, a brow arched, he bends down and sinks his teeth into my inner thigh.

"*Yessss*," I hiss, holding my thighs open for him, wanton and free.

It's the affirmation he needs to send his lips ghosting over the thin strip of fabric covering me. This leotard was an even better costume choice than I imagined.

Because while I certainly planned to have fun with him tonight, getting eaten out in a high school chemistry lab is miles better than any of my dirtiest fantasies.

I lean against the wall, arching my back and pressing myself into his lips, desperate for contact. But Owen pulls back, exhaling a soft puff of air that drags a desperate whine out of me. It feels so good, and yet it's not anywhere close to what I want from him.

"Needy, are we?" Owen chuckles, running a finger along the damp spot blooming on the fabric. "You know, when I think about that night in the parking lot and all the things I regret not doing, tasting you is at the very top of the list."

And then that same long, strong finger hooks into the elastic at the apex of my thighs and drags it to the side. When his tongue dips between my folds, I nearly levitate off the counter.

"Fuck please yes oh my *god*," I babble as his tongue makes gentle circles around my clit.

Owen's hands slide beneath my thighs and lift them onto his shoulders. Then they slip beneath my ass to tilt me until I'm at the perfect angle for him. I let him manipulate my body as he pleases. I'm so far gone for him and for this that he could stand me on my head or suspend me from the ceiling and I'd simply beg for more.

Which is what I do when he sucks my clit hard between his lips.

"Please don't stop," I whine, followed by a string of expletives and pleas and prayers. My fingers thread into the thick waves of his hair, pulling him closer as my hips began to buck against his tongue.

Through the flood of pleasure, the absolute electric current of his attention, I think I hear sounds that could be distant footsteps, but it's not enough to pull me away from this, from him. I feel like I've gone over the first hill of a roller coaster, and I'm not stopping until I've come screaming into the station.

And maybe I say something like this out loud, some garbled plea for more and harder and *now*, because Owen pulls back just long enough to run two of his fingers through my slick heat before sliding them inside me. I feel the delicious stretch, the glorious fullness all the way in my throat, or maybe that's just the scream I'm suppressing as his tongue laves my clit.

"Fuck fuck *fuck* I'm coming!" I cry, my head dropping back against the wall as Owen coaxes me to the most explosive orgasm of my entire life. My ears are ringing, and every nerve in my body is alight as I ride the wave of pleasure back down like a feather floating gently from the sky.

"You are delicious," Owen says, his lips ghosting across the tender skin of my inner thigh.

I'm still heaving in breaths, my heart thundering in my chest, when I hear the creak of the door.

"Occupied!" Owen shouts in his most authoritative voice, the sound of which nearly makes me come again.

"Got it," a man's voice replies. The door shuts, and it takes me two full breaths to realize I recognize it. And the giggle that comes after it.

It's Decker and Grace.

I huff out a laugh as I finally lock eyes with Owen, still on his knees between my thighs, wiping the glistening evidence of my orgasm from his lips.

"A popular hookup spot, I take it?"

Owen grins. "I got it from Dan, who got it from Archer, who I'm guessing got it from Decker."

I shake my head. "You McBride boys are bad news." I reach

down for his elbows, trying to haul him to his feet, though of course he stands on his own. There's not a thing I could do to move this wall of muscle against his will. He leans in to kiss me, and I lose myself in his lips and tongue once again. But as I reach for the zipper at the top of his flight suit, he pulls back.

"We're done for tonight," he says.

"Excuse me?" I try to sound indignant, but I think I just sound like a petulant teen.

Owen shakes his head. "I'm not fucking you for the first time in Mr. Dillon's chemistry lab," he says, and though I immediately begin to pout and start to formulate ways to change his mind (my hand on the shockingly large, hard ridge of his erection is my first gambit), he remains resolute. "When I finally get to be inside you, I want to take my time. I want you laid out beneath me. I want you to scream as loud as you want."

"What makes you think there's going to be another time?" I ask, cocking an eyebrow at him, but he levels me with that furrowed brow and those piercing blue eyes.

"Cut the shit, Wyatt. I want you, and once was not enough," he says, reaching for a paper towel from the dispenser beside my head. He gently cleans me up and settles my leotard back into place. "I'm done dancing around this, debating semantics. If you don't want to call this a relationship, that's fine with me. I'll call it whatever you want. A hookup. A situationship. Fuck buddies." He throws his hands up, a smile on his face. "Hell, call it a pineapple. I just know that I'm not done making you scream my name. Not even close."

I laugh hard enough that I hiccup. I don't think I've ever laughed like this with a man, and certainly not after he's made me come so hard I can barely spell my own name.

"Okay, then," I say, swallowing the fizzy feeling in my chest. Because if Owen can take a detour from being a relationship guy, then maybe I can meet him halfway. "Let's call it a pineapple. A pineapple sounds good. I want to…pineapple? Be a pineapple? Have a pineapple?"

He presses his finger to the crease between my brows. "Stop overthinking," he says, then kisses the spot. Then he focuses his blue eyes on me like I imagine he used to focus on chemistry experiments at that table right over there. "Tonight we dance. Tomorrow we sleep. And tomorrow night? You're mine."

My stomach does at least four full cartwheels, landing somewhere high in my chest. I'm filled with an absolute blizzard of emotions, from desire to nervousness to a wicked case of church giggles and back again. I try to center myself, to return to this cold, empty classroom, to listen to what this man is saying to me.

I appreciate that he doesn't invite me to sleep over, even if there is a very loud part of my brain that is screaming that being Owen's little spoon would be the fucking best. But a) we both desperately need sleep, and if we get into a bed together, spooning will not happen—only forking. And b) that's too much too soon. It's too close to what scares me the most. I need to walk away from this man while I'm still able.

So I just nod, letting him be in charge. He's so very good at it, after all.

Satisfied, Owen grasps my hips and lifts, gently lowering me to the floor. Taking my hand in his, he leads me back through the blessedly empty halls, up the stairs, and past the lockers.

But I pause just outside the doors to the gym.

"We walked out of here together with an awful lot of purpose, Dr. Boy Scout. If we go back in together—"

"With you all flushed like that," he says, running a finger along the apple of my cheek.

"Yeah. If we go in there together, it's going to look like—"

"A pineapple?"

I snort. "The metaphor might be breaking down."

Owen drops my hand and shoves his into the pocket of his thrifted flight suit. He looks bashful, and it's sexy as fuck. "Whatever makes you comfortable," he says, with not a trace of judgment. "You go ahead. I'll sneak in the back door by the locker rooms."

"Shit, you know all the secret spots in this place."

He grins. "I'm not *always* a good boy, Wyatt."

My body lights up. "Don't I know it."

He winks, and then he's gone, striding down the hall with all the confidence of a man who just brought a woman swiftly to orgasm in a chemistry classroom.

CHAPTER 17

WYATT

I'm trying to pour myself a cup of punch and adopt the look of a woman who didn't just come in a high school chem lab when Grace comes skidding up beside me so fast she nearly takes out the entire refreshments table.

"You were in the hookup nook!" Her voice is pushing the limits of a whisper.

I raise my eyebrows. "It has an official name?"

"I went there with Tyler Jessup during junior homecoming," she says, working to catch her breath. "So, you and my brother? It's happening?"

"It's just sex," I say.

Her nose wrinkles. "Okay, ew, I don't need the details."

I roll my eyes. "No, I need you to hear me. Owen and I talked about it. I'm not his girlfriend. We're just having fun," I say, like I'm laying out a business plan. "I don't want to sneak around or hide things from you, but I also don't want this to become..."

"A relationship?" she says, her voice hopeful.

"A thing," I say, because the *r*-word sticks in my throat. "It's categorically *not* a thing. Please hear me on that."

She nods solemnly. "Okay. Absolutely. Just..." She wrinkles

her nose, clearly uninterested in labeling her brother my fuck buddy.

So I help her out. "We're calling it a pineapple," I say.

Now she looks really confused. "A what now?"

"I swear it sounded a lot less insane a few minutes ago." I shrug. "Just go with it."

"Well, okay, then. I support you in your…pineapple."

Carson slides through the crowd and sidles up beside me.

"I heard about you and Owen!" she squeals, and at my wide eyes, she points directly at Grace. "From her. I heard it from her, and I told no one else."

"Nor did I," Grace chimes in. "I mean, Decker was there, so he knows, but—"

"We can keep it quiet," Carson assures me.

"They're calling it a pineapple," Grace says.

"Excuse me?" Carson looks from me to Grace and back. "Isn't that, like, the symbol for swingers?"

"Oh my *god!*" Grace cries.

"No! Good Lord, the two of you are ridiculous. We're not swingers, nor are we in a relationship. We're just—"

"If you say fuck buddies, I'm barfing in that punch bowl," Grace warns.

"—not labeling things," I say firmly. "And I definitely don't want this circulating around all of Ye Olde Cardinal Springs, so we're going to play it cool for the rest of the night."

"And you want us to help with that?" Carson asks.

"I mean…" It hadn't occurred to me that I'd need help, but as my gaze drifts across the dance floor to where Owen is twisting the lid off a beer bottle with a quick flex of his forearm, rocking back on his heels like the cat that ate the canary, I realize this is going to be a *very* long night. What am I doing here? Charity? Dancing? What's my name, even? "Yes. Please keep me occupied so…"

"So the entire town doesn't pick up on your seismic sexual attraction," Carson finishes.

"Consider us your wingwomen," Grace says.

Across the gym floor, Owen catches my eye and winks. It's the wink of a man who knows what I taste like, and while I'm no virgin bride, I find the look on that man's face downright scandalous.

Fingers snap in front of my face. "Are you sure you want us to do this?" Grace asks. "Because we can step aside and you can go, uh, do it like they do on the Discovery Channel or whatever."

"Seriously, I have never seen a woman look so horned up in my life," Carson says, laughing.

Oh god, I'm in so much trouble.

"Help me, Obi-Wan, and all that," I mutter.

"Okay, then eyes on me, Hart." Grace is using the voice she reserves for rowdy toddlers at the library. And you know what? It works. I snap my eyes to hers, and she's looking at me like a general about to lead me into battle. "We're going to dance our asses off. *Away* from Owen. Capisce?"

I nod, resolute. "Capisce."

For the rest of the night, we dance and snack and hype each other up to make it to seven a.m. Grace and Carson are true to their word, keeping me from drifting toward Owen whenever he's on the dance floor, even though my body feels magnetically drawn to him. I find myself turning toward him like a flower finding the sun.

The only time he slips past their defenses is just before Corianne declares the dance marathon complete. We're all gathered on the floor, a sudden surge of adrenaline battling with the yawns as we collectively realize how close our beds are.

I feel him behind me immediately, his warm, strong presence there just before I feel his breath on the shell of my ear.

"You good to drive home?" he whispers, his big hand drifting gently over the curve of my hip. The crowd is tight as we all gather near the stage, and I let myself lean my weight into him just for a brief, delicious stolen moment.

"I'm good," I say, because the jolt of electricity I feel at the contact gives me enough energy to *sprint* home.

"Good. Sleep well," he says, then takes a gentlemanly step backward. I glance over my shoulder just in time to see his smile. "Tonight," is all he says before disappearing into the crowd.

———

Exhaustion catches up to me as soon as I pull my truck into the driveway. I'm seconds away from having to hold my eyelids open with my thumbs. With my bed as my only target, I trip through the front door and begin shuffling down the hall.

"Pancakes?"

My mother's voice slices through my fatigue, as does the smell of butter and vanilla and…something burning?

Against my better judgment, I veer into the kitchen to find my mother standing over the griddle, a spatula in one hand and a dish towel in the other. She's attempting to wipe up the drips of batter rolling down the front of the oven and pooling on the floor. There are also spatters on the counter, a puff of flour on the cabinet door, and dripping eggshells lying near the sink.

And a burner spattered with pancake banner glowing, nothing cooking on top.

Suddenly I'm wide awake.

I huff out an exasperated sigh and march over to the stove, hustling her aside with my hip so I can turn off the extra burner. Then I snatch the dish towel out of her hand and set about cleaning up the mess.

"Honey, I was gonna get to all that as soon as I finished with the pancakes," Libby says in that leathery, syrupy Southern drawl that I know started out fake but by now is probably her true voice.

"Right," I mutter, because in the four months I've been roomies with my mother, I've become all too familiar with her brand of cleaning. It usually consists of sweeping everything into an overfull trash can, stacking the dishes in the sink to "soak" (until someone else comes along to rinse them and load them into the dishwasher—spoiler alert, it's never her), and fucking off to vape in the backyard.

"I was!" She flips the pancakes, rogue batter flying.

"Good morning!" Hazel says, padding into the kitchen with Eden on her hip. Her eyes go from Libby and her culinary disaster to me. Ever the peacemaker, Hazel plasters on a smile. "Oooh, pancakes! We love pancakes, don't we, Eden?"

"That's right, Little Edie!" Libby says in that sickly baby voice she uses.

"You know Little Edie was a tragic figure, right? Emotionally stunted by her abusive mother? Quite the legacy to bestow on your granddaughter," I say.

Libby rolls her eyes like a snotty teenager. "Give it a rest, Wyatt."

Noticing the way my jaw is clenching as I try to bite back my words, Hazel passes me the baby while she starts making Eden's morning bottle.

"How was the dance marathon?" she asks.

Like she's cast a spell, my tension melts away. Owen McBride is a gift that keeps on giving, apparently, because simply calling up the memory of last night floods my body with heat.

"That good, huh?" Hazel grins.

"Be careful, that kind of starry-eyed glow is how you wind up saddled with one of these," Libby says, taking Eden out of my arms.

And just like that, my body cools. "Wow, you've managed to insult both your daughters *and* your granddaughter in one sentence. Impressive."

Libby waves me off with the spatula, hoisting Eden higher on her hip. "Oh, that's not what I meant."

I drag the trash can over and swipe the eggshells into it with a little too much force. One pings off the edge of the lid and skitters across the linoleum floor. Watching the gooey bits settle beneath the fridge makes something snap inside me. Twelve years of resentment bubbles up all at once, everything I've been holding back since Libby showed up on the curb back in January. Suddenly my exhaustion is secondary to the rage adrenaline boiling inside of me.

"Really? Because that's the message you gave me when you sent me packing at eighteen."

Libby's eyes go wide, like I've slapped her, and I take a sliver of satisfaction in the notion that I've caught her off guard. I've been playing nice for Hazel and Eden and the Indiana State Board of Corrections, but a girl can only bite her tongue for so long.

"That's not what—" Libby protests, and then Hazel steps between us.

"Come on, guys, it's early, we're all tired," she says.

"Oh, I'm tired, all right. Tired of her pretending she has any authority to hand out motherly advice," I snap. "She gave up that right more than once. Like the time you went to that casino after work and left me waiting at school for *three hours*. Or the time you forgot to pay the water bill and they shut it off for a *week*. Oh wait, that happened twice! And of course, let's not forget the time you went to *prison* because you cared more about some lowlife dead-beat boyfriend than your own daughter."

Now Libby's mad, and she passes Eden back to Hazel so she can wave her spatula in my face. "Don't talk to me like that," she says, the venom overtaking the Southern drawl.

"Or what, you're gonna kick me out of this house too?" I say, toe-to-toe with her.

"Stop it!" Hazel shouts, and at the unusual rise in her voice, Eden begins to cry.

"Fine," I grind out, spinning on my heel and stomping out of the kitchen.

In my room, I pace, hands on my hips as I mutter all the angry words I want to say to Libby. It would be such a relief to tell her once and for all that she fucked up my childhood, that she fucked up Hazel's childhood, and that I won't let her do the same thing to Eden. The notion that she should *ever* feel entitled to offer me advice or correct me like a naughty toddler is *laughable*. It's downright offensive.

A gentle knock at my door freezes me along the track I'm wearing into the carpet. "What?" I call, because I am not letting Libby into this room. Not now, not ever.

"It's me," Hazel replies, then cracks the door.

I let out a breath. "Come in."

Hazel steps in, closing the door gently behind her, then settles onto the end of my bed.

"I can't, Hazel. I can't deal with the fake mother shit," I say, feeling the anger boil up inside me anew.

"I know. And we need to deal with it. With…well, everything. But that's not going to happen right now. Not after you've been up all night doing unspeakable things with Owen McBride," she says, her lips curving into a Cheshire Cat grin.

"That obvious?" I ask, huffing out a rueful laugh.

"You blushed head to toe when I asked about the dance marathon," my sister says. "Nobody has that much fun doing the Electric Slide."

I bite my lip and fall back onto the bed beside her, my eyes on the water-spotted ceiling. "I like him."

"I can tell," Hazel says. "I think the whole town can tell."

I groan.

"Hey, it's your business, and I support whatever boundaries you want to put up. Lord knows we're in need of some around here," she says, then flops back to lie beside me.

I sigh. "I'll try not to…" I trail off, trying to figure out what I can reasonably promise.

"Just don't go all Khaleesi on her," Hazel pleads. "At least not until we can get ourselves to a therapist."

"Oh god, anything but that," I beg.

Hazel sits up. "Steel yourself, because it's happening. It's the only way Eden is going to grow up in a happy home. I'll do anything to protect that kid, and that includes busting through your walls and making you confront all your shit."

"How do *you* not have shit? She abandoned you too."

Hazel rolls her eyes. "I have shit. And I handle it in my own very unproductive ways. The difference is, I want to change that. And I'm going to make you change with me, okay?"

I sigh. "Fine."

"Good girl," she says, patting my head like I'm the little sister. "Now get some sleep. I've seen what a nightmare you become when you don't get a solid eight hours. You after an all-nighter might just be lethal."

I let out a leonine yawn that I feel all the way down to my toes. "Okay," I say, my eyes already fluttering shut. I roll onto my side and hug my pillow.

Hazel lets herself out, the door clicking quietly behind her—she's developed ninja-level stealth skills since having a baby—and I'm seconds away from sleep when my phone vibrates in my back pocket.

The pull of Owen is the only thing that keeps me from dreamland. I slide the phone out and read the text that I knew would be from him.

OWEN

I hope you're in bed, maybe even asleep already.
I need you well rested for later.

The grin starts at the corners of my mouth, and soon I feel the thrill of his message radiating out through my body. I start to tap at the screen, but another message appears.

OWEN

I see you typing

Stop

Go to sleep

> Text me when you wake up. 8 hours minimum please

The please is a nice touch, considering the orders he's dishing out. And while my reflex is to send him a smart-ass little message, to push against the control just for fun, I find myself happy to let him boss me around.

That doesn't mean I won't have a little lip for him after eight hours of sleep, though.

Good thing he likes it.

CHAPTER 18

APRIL 29 AT 6:01 PM

WYATT

I'm rested. Revived. Ready

OWEN

Exactly eight hours since I sent you to bed. Good girl.

Now come over for dinner

WYATT

At your place?

Like a date?

OWEN

It's a pineapple, Wyatt

WYATT

I heard that's the international symbol for swingers

OWEN

I don't share

But you can relax, it's not a date

Let me feed you, Wyatt

WYATT

Promise me it's not going to be a tofu kale salad
or some shit

OWEN

I have actually met you

WYATT

Intimately

CHAPTER 19

OWEN

My immediate instinct is to say yes. I want nothing more than to introduce Wyatt to Francie. I have no doubt they'd get along famously; they'd probably instantly team up against me in a festival of playful taunts the likes of which the world has never seen.

There's also the fact that now that I've convinced her to be with me—even if it's in some messy, inscrutable way—I want her by my side as much as possible.

But I also know that what Wyatt and I have is tenuous at best.

I've had to coax her to me like a stray cat, and any sudden movement could scare her off. That's precisely why I sent her home by herself this morning. The prospect of curling up around her in my bed, listening to her gentle breaths and feeling her relax, *really* relax, into me was like a siren's call. But I knew it would be too much. Wyatt needs to establish distance, even if every part of me wants to obliterate it.

So extending an invite to my ex-girlfriend-turned-best-friend's engagement party five weeks from now is probably not the move with Wyatt Hart.

And yet …

OWEN

Yes

FRANCIE

Seriously?

Don't bring a rando app date or a call girl to my engagement party

OWEN

I'm offended, Frank

FRANCIE

You will tell me everything about this girl, Owen McBride

But later. We're doing dinner with my parents and Josh's parents, and I have to steel myself for nonstop hint-dropping about grandkids

OWEN

You can't fault them for loving you so much they want you to make copies

FRANCIE

Save the charm for your mystery girl

OWEN

I've got plenty of charm to go around

FRANCIE

LORD

Half an hour later I've confirmed that Felix is spending the evening in Bloomington with Margo, his latest short-term girl-friend. I'm putting the finishing touches on a charcuterie board and uncorking a nice-but-not-too-nice bottle of red.

A spring storm has blown in, the rain pounding the roof in sheets so loudly that I barely hear the knock at the door. I mentally curse Felix for once again ignoring my pleas to fix the doorbell.

Wyatt is standing on my doorstep in her usual uniform of jeans and combat boots and a deconstructed T-shirt. This one is baby blue and advertises the Deluxe Town Diner in red, a little cartoon coffee cup below it with a speech bubble reading, "LIFE IS BREW-TIFUL." It's been cut up the sides and crosswise into strips, which are tied together to make the shirt fit her narrow torso like a second skin. The sleeves have been cut off and the neckline cut into a dangerous deep V that displays the top of her tattoos.

Tattoos I'm still dying to see.

There's so much of Wyatt Hart that I'm dying to see.

And so much I worry she'll never show me.

The whole tableau is only made more delicious by the fact that she braved the pouring rain to get to my doorstep. Her thick dripping curls are pasted to her cheeks and forehead, her shirt clings to her body, and her jeans are blooming with dark wet spots down her thighs.

A bolt of lightening flashes behind her.

"Wow, that really came out of nowhere, huh?" I peer at the dark clouds over her shoulder.

"I've been thinking that since last night, Doc," she replies with a wink.

"Get in here, you." I grab her wrist and tug, pulling her into my arms. I rest my chin on her head and enjoy the feeling of her arms wrapping around my waist.

She doesn't squeeze, though, doesn't pull me close to her. I'm starting to recognize the distance Wyatt always leaves herself. She's careful.

So am I.

"I'm glad you're here," I tell her, and when she doesn't say anything, I add, "Are you glad you're here?"

She glances up at me, that wicked gleam in her eye I'm starting to know so well.

"That remains to be seen. You mentioned food?"

I release her and lead her through the house by the hand, pointing out all Felix's unfinished projects as we make our way to the kitchen. Now that she's here, I don't want to let her go. Having her hand in mine feels like snapping the last piece into a puzzle I've been working on for months.

"I promised to feed you, and I always deliver," I say when we get to the kitchen island. The large cutting board Felix made in high school shop is covered in a swirling selection of salami and prosciutto, Gruyère and Brie, raspberries and dried apricots, wasabi peas, almonds, dark chocolate–covered golden raisins, and a selection of crackers. A warm, crusty baguette sits atop a dish towel, ready to be torn to yeasty bits.

"Where did you get this?" she asks as she circles the board like a lion circling her prey.

"I made it. I know your penchant for snacks, so this is, you know, grown-up snacks. Well, mostly."

And then she dives straight for the center of the board.

"Circus Peanuts!" she cries, holding up a candy.

"They were out at the grocery store. I can only assume you bought all of them, because I refuse to believe anyone else eats those things. I had to drive to four different gas stations before I found these, and I can't promise they're not twenty to thirty years old."

She plucks one off the board. "That's okay. They're good when they're a little stale."

She holds it up between her thumb and forefinger, then sinks her teeth into the neon-orange marshmallow, and shit, she makes it look delicious. *She* looks delicious, even eating an unholy lump of sugar, food dye, and artificial flavoring.

I watch her in wonder as she chews and swallows, still not believing that she's here. The taste of her is still so vivid on my lips from last night.

"Oh, I forgot. I brought something," she says, then digs into the worn leather tote bag still hanging over her shoulder. She drags out a heavy can and thunks it onto the bar. It takes me a few seconds to get it.

Pineapple.

"I figured it was on theme," she says with a grin.

I roll my eyes and reach for the wine bottle, pouring two glasses and passing one to her. Then I raise mine. "To pineapple," I say, and instead of clinking my glass, she clinks the can.

"To pineapple."

And then the words just fall right out of my mouth, all thoughts of taking it slow and not scaring her gone. "Do you want to go with me to my friend Francie's engagement party?"

I immediately cringe. I couldn't have let her have a glass of wine first? Some food? Maybe coaxed her through four or five orgasms? I couldn't have waited *a day*?

But the truth is, this woman makes me lose all self-restraint and discipline. Any notion of being thoughtful or delicate? Just *gone*.

I'm gone.

For her.

Shit.

Wyatt swallows hard. "Francie your ex-girlfriend who's now your best friend?"

"Yeah."

Her eyes narrow. "When?"

Well, I opened the can—might as well shake out the worms. "First weekend in June."

She sets her wineglass down on the counter to another rumble of thunder.

"Owen, we need to talk about what this is."

My heart starts to thud like I've got my own thunderstorm in the center of my chest.

"What is it?" I ask.

"Not that. Not me being your date to your ex-girlfriend's engagement party five weeks from now."

The thunderstorm blows from my chest into my brain, my thoughts flashing like lightning as I work to save this moment.

"Which part bothers you? The fact that Francie and I used to date? That I asked you to go? Or that it's five weeks from now?"

"I…well…" Her nose scrunches, her eyebrows furrowing as she fumbles for an answer. "Yes?"

The hesitation, the questioning lift of her voice, shows me that I haven't scared her off. Not yet. Because Wyatt Hart is nothing if not stubborn. If she didn't want to do this with me, she wouldn't still be standing here. She wouldn't have come in the first place. We just need to get on the same page.

"First of all, I didn't ask you to be my date. I asked you to go with me. It's going to be fun, I don't want to go alone, and I think you'd like Francie. I want to take you even if I never manage to get you into bed," I tell her, and the tension in her brow begins to ease. "I meant it when I said I don't need this to be a relationship. I want to be around you. I want to receive your weird non sequitur texts. I want to flirt with you shamelessly even if it never comes to anything.

"I don't want to trick you, Wyatt, or make you guess. We can decide what we want this to be. Right now. You can tell me the rules. Tell me what you want to call it. All I want is you."

She nibbles at her lip, but the tension in her brow doesn't return. "What if I can't…"

"Whatever you have to give me, Wyatt, I'll take it."

She inhales, holds the breath for a moment before she blows it out with a little nod.

"Okay," she says, then again, more sure. "Okay. Then we need an agreement."

I nod. "Okay, let's talk terms."

"No labels," she says.

"Agree."

"No commitments," she says.

"Okay."

She pauses, then adds, "No flowers."

I scoff. "Seriously?"

She gives me a stern look. "That's boyfriend shit. I was serious, Owen—flowers make me sneeze. I'm allergic to boyfriends."

I shake my head and let out a little chuckle, but I agree. "No flowers," I say, and she appears satisfied. She reaches for another Circus Peanut, but I'm not done. "I have one condition too."

She glances up, waiting.

"Nobody else."

She frowns. "That sounds an awful lot like a commitment."

I shrug. "I told you, Wyatt. I don't share. If you're with me, I don't want you to be with anybody else."

"Okay, but—"

"You need an escape hatch. I get that. You're not tied to me. If you want to be done, or you want a break, or you want to change the terms, you just talk to me. I won't fight you. If you want out, I'll let you go. We'll both walk away. I promise." I place my hands firmly on the counter, leaning across the island. "But I'm serious. I. Don't. Share."

She breathes out a little *hmmm* that makes my cock stir.

"Okay, then let's make it official." She reaches for the cup on the counter that's filled with pencils and pens. She finds a black Sharpie and uncaps it with her teeth, then reaches for the can of pineapple. She scribbles on the top, then pushes it across the island to me. In her crooked handwriting, it says:

No labels
No commitments
No flowers
Nobody else

And beneath it, her messy signature.

"Sign it," she says, and I do. Then she takes the pen back and adds a note at the bottom. When she spins it back toward me, I see the title of our little contract.

Owen + Wyatt 4Now

I grin. "We good?" I ask.

She nods. "We're good. Which means I can properly devote my attention to this pile of meat and cheese."

"There's veggies and fruit on there too," I tease.

"Oh, I thought those were just for decoration," she says, leaning over the board. A raindrop breaks free of her curls and rolls down her cheek, landing on the counter with a splash.

"We really should get you out of these wet clothes first," I say.

She grins. "My, my, quite the smooth operator, Dr. McBride."

I roll my eyes. "I'm serious. I did laundry earlier. There's a stack of dry clothes on my bed. Go grab something. I'll throw your clothes in the dryer. Then we can feast."

"Awfully bossy," she says, but she's already moving in the direction I'm pointing. I've noticed she likes to be told what to do, but she can't do it without a little lip.

I like it.

"My house, my rules," I tell her.

She tosses a devious grin over her shoulder. "We'll see about that."

CHAPTER 20

OWEN

From that twinkle in her eye, I'm prepared for Wyatt to play with me.

But I am not prepared for the moment she walks back into the kitchen wearing my high school varsity letterman jacket.

And nothing else.

The jacket is entirely too big for her, which is a real shame, because it means the red-and-black hem rests just below the curve of her ass. The black leather sleeves fall well past her hands, and the only exposed skin is the thin, milky-white column from her neck down to the band of her lace panties.

I set the wine bottle down with a dull thud, because I don't trust myself to pour with this woman standing in front of me. I can practically hear the blood rushing through my body, all heading in one direction.

"I figured you'd go for the sweatpants," I say, my tongue feeling thick in my mouth.

She smirks. "I had a moment alone in your bedroom. You think I wasn't going to do a little snooping?"

"Seems like you found something interesting." Last year my dad turned the room in his house where Felix and I once slept into a home gym to help with rehab from his accident. He delivered boxes of our high school memorabilia early one Saturday morning, and I remember thinking, *What the hell am I supposed to do with all this shit?*

I've never been so thankful for the pang of nostalgia that made me put it all away in my closet.

"I did." Wyatt pokes her delicate hand out one of the sleeves and runs her finger along the red felted letter on the breast and the little black, red, and white emblems sewn onto it. "Baseball and soccer, huh? I didn't know you played soccer. And is this one cross-country?"

I nod, my breath already ragged. I work to get control of myself, even though my teenage fantasy is standing in front of me.

"And this one?" Her finger lands on a little circle with a torch embroidered on it, just over where I imagine her nipple must be, pebbled and pink beneath the jacket.

"National Honor Society," I tell her, my voice gravelly as I struggle to control my breathing. I grip the counter, partially to keep me upright, partially to keep me from hurdling this kitchen island and pressing her against the wall.

The corner of her full red lip quirks, her eyebrow arching sharply. "You were the valedictorian, weren't you?"

All I can do is nod, my eyes following that finger, which is now running up the stretch of bare skin between the buttons. Well, bare save for the black scrollwork that spreads beneath the jacket and dips down to her sternum. I can see now that it's a network of curling stems and leaves, dotted with little flowers that look like stars. I want nothing more than to peel that jacket off her body and appreciate the whole canvas.

"Such a good boy," she purrs. "I was busy smoking under the bleachers while you hit home runs and did logarithms or whatever."

I can't help but laugh.

"Math was never my best subject," I confess.

"Poor baby, what did you get, a B?"

I laugh, but I shake my head. Wyatt laughs.

"Oh my god, Owen. Straight A's? Of course," she teases. "I sure would have liked trying to corrupt you."

"I don't think you would have had to try very hard," I say.

Her eyes leave mine only to follow the trail of her finger as it hooks into the opening of the jacket, just next to the varsity letter. She slowly—*so* slowly—drags it open until I finally see that pretty pink nipple…and the silver ring through it.

"Would you have let me wear your letter jacket?"

I swallow hard, using every bit of control I have to keep myself still. I know I have to let her come to me, but fuck, I want to rush her, take that nipple between my lips, the ring between my teeth. I want to throw her over my shoulder and march her to my bedroom.

But I stay stone still.

"Only so I could take it off of you," I say.

She hums, dragging her finger in a lazy circle around her nipple, then pausing to give the ring a gentle tug. My cock throbs, practically reaching for her.

"You sure this is what you want?" she asks, raising her hooded eyes back to mine. She slips the jacket down over her other shoulder to reveal the matching ring in her other nipple, the constellation of stars tattooed just over her breast. I watch her, the most beautiful thing I've ever seen, a study in contrasts between the milky-white skin and the bold swirls of ink, the soft swell of her breasts and belly and the glint of the metal rings in her nipples and navel.

She looks tough and…delicate.

And I want her.

Wyatt sinks her teeth into her full bottom lip, just barely suppressing a smile. But the smile doesn't quite reach her eyes. I can almost feel her slight intake of breath, how she holds it, before her voice comes out husky and low. "I can't be your girlfriend, Owen."

I nod.

"Then I won't be your boyfriend, Wyatt," I tell her evenly. I sense we're standing before the last hurdle. She wants to be sure. "I'm just here to figure out what you want and then give it to you."

She releases her lip from her teeth, her smile spreading wide, her eyes crinkling wickedly.

She crooks one finger.

"Then get over here," she says.

I need no other invitation. I haven't moved so fast since I stole home to win the state championship senior year. In no time, I'm around the island and have her in my arms, her back pressed against the wall, my lips covering hers, swallowing the delicate *oof* and then the moan that escapes her.

Wyatt tastes like sugar and sass, and I'm ravenous for her. I push the jacket farther down her arms, settling it in the crook of her elbows so I can finally explore those tattoos that have been taunting me for months.

"Beautiful," I say as I trace one swirling vine with my tongue, deviating only to journey down to her nipple. I flick one of the delicate silver rings before taking it between my teeth and tugging. "These are a good surprise."

She moans in response.

"You'll tell me if I hurt you?" I say into her skin, my fingers toying with the other ring.

"Well, that's a little bit the point," she says.

I groan and pull her nipple back into my mouth, sucking her, flipping the ring with my tongue. I'm rewarded with a full, deep-throated moan.

"You're sure Felix isn't coming home?" she pants as I lavish her art with my mouth.

I pause. He said he wasn't, but with Felix you can never be sure. And I'm not about to be interrupted. Which means I can't spread her across the kitchen island and feast on her how I want.

In answer, I bend my knees, wrapping my arms low around her ass, and lift. She lands over my shoulder in a fluid movement.

"I can walk," she says with a laugh as I march down the hall toward my bedroom.

"Not fast enough," I reply.

I pause only long enough to slam the bedroom door and turn the lock. Then I heave her onto the bed, where she lands with a bounce and a giggle.

"I'm really torn, because as much as I'd like to climb onto this bed and edge you until you've forgotten your name, I've also been dreaming about being inside of you since January," I tell her as I shed my T-shirt. I revel in the way her eyes travel down the expanse of my chest, glad I've managed to hit the weight bench in the garage lately. She looks like she wants to lick the ridges on my chest, and I want to let her. "So if you don't object, I'd really like to fuck you right now."

"No objections from me."

She props herself up on her elbows, the jacket falling open so once again I can take in the full expanse of her.

Well, almost.

I hook my thumbs into the lace waistband of her panties and drag them down over the black illustrations on her thighs and calves, brushing my lips over each one as I go.

"So fucking beautiful," I whisper, moving back up to the apex of her thighs. And when I can't help but dip my tongue between her folds to taste her, I'm rewarded with more sweetness. "And so wet."

Wyatt moves to shed the jacket, but I press my hand into her sternum, lowering her down onto the bed.

"Leave it on," I say, then remove my jeans and boxer briefs. My erection springs free as I tower over her, and I'm reminded that in all these months of sexual tension and teasing and frustration, Wyatt has only felt me through my pants. I pause, fisting the hard length, and watch her tongue dart out to sweep across her bottom lip.

"If I'd known that's what you were working with, I don't think I'd have let you out of that chemistry classroom last night," she says.

I laugh as I move to the nightstand and take a condom out of the drawer. I love that she can make me laugh like this even when I'm hard and aching for her.

"This will be a whole hell of a lot more comfortable than an aluminum countertop," I tell her. I grab a pillow and then a handful of her ass, lifting her hips so I can slide it beneath her. Then I press my hands to her knees, opening her to me completely. I run the pad of my thumb up the glistening length of her opening, circling her clit and then back to her entrance. She moans and arches into my hand.

"I thought you were saving the teasing for later," she pleads.

"I'm going to fuck you, Wyatt," I say, dipping my thumb just inside her. "But I'm not about to neglect you."

I hover above her, one hand pressed into the mattress just beside her cheek. Then I lower to capture her mouth, parting her lips. She tangles her tongue with mine, like a more intimate version of the rapid-fire banter we've been trading all these months. I'm so lost in the kiss that when the swollen head of my cock brushes against her warm, wet entrance, I gasp.

"Fuck, Wyatt, I've wanted you for so long." I'm practically trembling. She lifts her hips, tilting into me so I slide across her clit. "I just want to give you *everything*."

Wyatt stills. She reaches up and grabs my chin between her thumb and forefinger, angling my face sharply to meet her gaze.

"Owen," she says. Her voice is stern, but there's the tiniest quiver there. Just the smallest hitch. I hold my breath, waiting to hear what she wants from me. Her brow is knitted, but a smile unfurls across her face. "Fuck me like I'm not your girlfriend."

Her tone, her eyes, the way her thighs grip my hips as I hover over her—it snaps every last bit of my control. When she reaches down and wraps her hand around my cock, guiding me, I lock on to her eyes and press my hips forward, sinking into her in one smooth, tight glide.

Wyatt cries out, head thrown back as she wraps her legs around my waist and pulls me closer, deeper. Her lips are parted and ruby red, and a flush climbs her chest, painting her tattoos like watercolor.

I want to kiss her so bad I can taste it. Can taste *her*. The flavor of Wyatt Hart will probably never leave my mouth.

But that's not what she wants.

And I'm in the giving-Wyatt-Hart-what-she-wants business.

So I pull back and snap my hips, rolling at the base of her so her clit hums along my pelvis.

"Oh my god," she moans, urging me on with her ankles locked at my lower back. "Please, just like that."

I thrust and roll, thrust and roll, my eyes roaming her body. Part of me is terrified that despite our agreement, she's never going to let me see her like this again. That this will be my only chance to watch the column of her neck as she tips her chin up in ecstasy. That I won't get another opportunity to see how her nipple rings glint in the lamplight, shimmering each time I push into her. That I'll never again get see the lavender streaks in her curls splayed out on my bedsheets. She is the most erotic sight I've ever seen, and it's taking every fiber of control in my body to keep from spilling inside her before she comes.

I lower down to one elbow so I can tug on her nipple rings with my lips, the other hand drifting down the curve of her petite breast, the dip of her belly, and the contour of her hip, before playing across her body to find her clit. I fuck her hard, just like she wants, but I stroke the delicate bundle of nerves softly, delicately, as if I can tell her how I feel about her with my touch.

I won't fuck her like she's my girlfriend, but she'll come like she is.

Her breath is growing ragged, her body writhing as these incredible little moans pour out of her.

Her orgasm is close. I can feel it from the way her nails dig into my skin and the fluttering of her inner muscles around my cock. And just as I can feel that she's on the brink of coming apart, her lips drop open and her eyes drift shut.

I raise myself onto my palm so I can watch the way her body reacts, my other hand still working her clit. I'm desperate to see her, for her to let me watch. But even though I want to beg her to open her eyes, to look at me, I let her have this small bit of distance. As much as I want her to open herself to me, I know she needs this one wall.

I told her I'd take her however she was willing to give herself to me, and I meant it.

So I watch her come apart, her eyes closed, as I guide her through the explosive peak of her orgasm. She lets out a soft scream, her lips forming my name as she shudders through her release.

And when she's finally undone, her hands clenched around my forearms, chest heaving, *then* her eyes flutter open. Her gaze meets mine, her emerald eyes alight.

She holds me with those eyes.

And that's the moment I follow her over the edge.

CHAPTER 21

SUNDAY, APRIL 30 AT 7:07 AM

OWEN

Wyatt?

WYATT

Yes?

OWEN

Did you sneak out of my bed in the dead of night?

WYATT

It was more like 5 am, but…

Yes

To be fair, there was very little sneaking. I tripped over your boots trying to find my underwear and nearly took out your bookshelf. You sleep like the dead

I didn't want to run into Felix in the kitchen. Or my mother at my house

OWEN

Don't do that again.

If you leave when it's still dark, I want to know that you made it home safe. If you want to keep this from other people, that's fine. I'll help you do that

But no hiding from me, okay?

WYATT

Okay

OWEN

Do you want to keep this a secret from everyone else?

WYATT

I don't know

I don't think so

I mean, I told Grace

And Carson

And Hazel

And it's fine if your brothers know

OWEN

Okay. Around town we'll be circumspect

WYATT

SAT word

OWEN

I got an 800 on the verbal section

WYATT

You are VERY good with your mouth

MONDAY, MAY 1 AT 5:45 PM

WYATT

You free tonight?

OWEN

Booty calling me already?

WYATT

You have a problem with that?

OWEN

I absolutely do not

Unfortunately I'm volunteering at the after-hours clinic in Elletsville. I'll be there until 2 am

TUESDAY, MAY 2 AT 4:35 PM

OWEN

You free tonight?

WYATT

I'm closing the bar. I could be there around midnight?

OWEN

I've got rounds at the hospital at 8 am, and then I have to drive to Bloomington to speak at a med school alumni event

WYATT

Sleep is for the weak

OWEN

And for people who are no longer in their twenties

WYATT

Fair

WEDNESDAY, MAY 3 AT 3:23 PM

WYATT

You free tonight?

OWEN

I caught a stomach bug from a patient

WYATT

Oh god. See you in a few days

OWEN

You don't want to come take care of me?

WYATT

I…no?

OWEN

Good. I don't think I could summon the energy to bar the door

You're the last person on the planet I want to see me like this

WYATT

Thanks for looking out for me, Doc

FRIDAY, MAY 5 AT 2:17 PM

OWEN

You free tonight?

WYATT

FUCK YES I AM!

I get off at 8

OWEN

Can I feed you and fuck you?

WYATT

In whatever order you desire

And if you really want to have fun, at the
same time

OWEN

I hope your mouth is otherwise engaged, Wyatt

WYATT

[fire emoji]

CHAPTER 22

WYATT

Friday, May 5

ROMY

Hey. I haven't heard back from you, and that's totally cool. I understand. But I miss you and I have to keep trying. So I'm putting your name on the VIP list for the concert. Saturday May 12. I go on at 6. Go to security gate C and give them your name. You can bring someone. I just really miss you, and it would mean the world to me if you came

None of this feels right without you

The only thing keeping me from coming completely undone is the knowledge that later I get a repeat performance of my night with Owen McBride.

Well, that and the fact that Carson and Grace are sitting across from me at the bar. As soon as I got the text from Romy, I called in reinforcements.

"I hate that we have to do this here," Grace grumbles as she stirs her Arnold Palmer. "As soon as the playoffs are over, my schedule is going to blow wide open."

It's been hard to get together with my friends lately. Grace has been jetting off to every playoff game she can to watch Decker try to win another Stanley Cup before he retires. She flies to Winnipeg tomorrow for Games 3 and 4 of the second round.

"It's not all your fault. I've been going through the end-of-year death march of Field Day and parties and art shows. Kindergarten graduation is next Friday, and then I'm finally free!" Carson says, raising her arms over her head like she's approaching the finish line of an ultramarathon. Then she points at me. "And this one here is so busy sneaking around with your brother it's a wonder we see her at all."

Grace squeals. "Yes! First order of business, how goes the…pineapple?"

I keep my eyes on the limes I'm quartering for later, when the rush hits. The muscles in my jaw practically cramp as I try to suppress a grin.

"It's good." From the way they lean across the bar, wide, nose-crinkling grins on their faces, I have a feeling I didn't do a very good job keeping my voice even.

"Tell us everything," Carson says. "Tell me all the dirty details. I want to hear about every orgasm."

"Ew!" Grace grimaces as she leans back on her barstool.

"What? He's not *my* brother, and I'm so hard up a stiff breeze could make me come," Carson says. "Do you know how miserable it is on the apps? I must have been a war criminal in a past life to be subjected to so many hoisted fish and dick pics!"

Grace shoots me a warning look. "Just, could you save the details for tomorrow, when there's no chance I might overhear a single life-altering, brain-scarring detail about my brother's sex life?"

"We have the spring carnival tomorrow," Carson whines. "I have to bake four cakes for the raffle and bully three other teachers into volunteering for the dunk tank. Otherwise it's going to be *me*, and I'd rather walk into traffic."

Grace sighs. "Okay, how about this? I'll go to the bathroom and set my timer for five minutes. You can spill as much as you want in that time, and then we can turn to purer topics, like how I'm already planning your wedding! I'm thinking backyard boho?"

Now it's my turn to look miserable. "Come on, Grace. We talked about this," I warn.

"I know, I know. I'm teasing," Grace says, hands held up in surrender. "But I do want to hear about how things are going with you guys. You've both seemed so happy since the dance marathon. Owen came to family dinner this week and didn't check his phone *once*. You can deny it all you want, but you two mean something to each other."

I can't suppress my smile.

"I *am* happy," I say, savoring the idea that I make *him* happy like it's a good piece of chocolate.

"Oh, *blast*," Carson says, staring at the glowing screen of her phone.

"Everything okay?" I ask.

She sighs. "Yes, I was just desperately hoping my parents' flight would be delayed, but it looks like they're taking off now, which means I need to head up to Indianapolis to pick them up. They've been visiting my aunt and uncle in Boca for the last two weeks, and having the house to myself has been a *dream*."

"Still no luck with the apartment hunt?" Grace asks.

"I saw a listing last week that looked promising, but it turned out to be an unfinished basement with a mini fridge and a hot plate." Carson drags her purse off the bar and hops down from her stool. "I want those details, though. Next week? Thursday is the last day of school, so I'm free Friday."

"If the Grinders don't sweep Winnipeg, I'll be in Chicago for Game Five," Grace says. "So send prayers to the hockey gods."

"I'll be here, so whoever's free and wants to hear about my

orga—" I stop myself before the word—*plural*—escapes, but Grace squeals nonetheless. Then she mimes zipping her lips.

"I'll pretend I didn't hear that because you're my best friend," Grace swears, and because she's my best friend, I know better than to believe her.

Carson heads out to pick up her parents, and I brace for an interrogation from Grace. But then an unholy crash comes from the back, followed by a loud, low groan.

"Ernie?" I cry, dropping the knife and racing through the door to the back. I find him on his ass on the floor next to a keg, clutching his bad arm. "What happened?"

"I was just grabbing another keg of Blue Moon and the damn thing shifted," he says, and that's when I notice that his arm is hanging at a weird angle, the sharp point of his shoulder visible through his T-shirt.

"Oh my god, it looks dislocated!" I say, rushing to his side.

"Yep," he says through gritted teeth.

"Ernie, I *told* you. *I* heave the kegs," I say.

"You can chastise me later. Right now you can help me off the fucking floor."

I squat beside him and throw his good arm over my shoulders, gingerly dragging him to his feet. It takes every ounce of my strength, and he cries out when he stumbles, jostling his arm.

"Everything okay back here?" Grace peeks her head through the door.

"This ding-dong fucked around and is now deep in the finding out stage," I say as Ernie shoves me aside to grip his bad arm.

"Either of you know how to pop a shoulder back in?" Ernie asks, but Grace and I both shake our heads. "Your boyfriend here?"

It takes me way too long to realize he's talking to me. "He's not my boyfriend!" I cry.

"Ask me if I give a shit about your relationship status right now," Ernie grumbles. "I just need a doctor."

"He's at the practice until six," Grace says.

"You cannot sit around this bar and wait two and a half hours for a pediatrician to show up and pop your shoulder back in," I say.

"Well, my truck is a stick, so I don't have any other choice," he fires back, then winces—even talking is enough to hurt his shoulder.

"I can take you in my truck," I tell him.

"Someone's gotta watch the bar," he replies.

"I can drive you," Grace says. She comes over and tries to get Ernie's good arm over her shoulders, but he shakes her off.

"I can walk just fine," he says, and when I shoot him a warning glare, he adds, "Sorry. And thank you. For the ride."

"It's not a problem. The urgent care by the highway opens at four, so we'll go there," Grace says, then shoots me a smile. "Let's just pray for a sweet of Winnipeg so I can finally catch up with my friends."

"Thank you," I tell her, and follow them out into the bar.

It's not until Ernie is gone and I'm back to prep that I remember that with Ernie gone, I'm going to have to stay until closing.

Which means I can't meet Owen.

I tip my head back and stare at the dim neon lights on the ceiling. "Fuuuuuuuuck," I groan, because that's what I *won't* be doing tonight. Or at least not until very late. I was hoping for sex *and* a good night's sleep.

I pull out my phone and fire off a text to Owen.

WYATT

> Ernie's out tonight with a dislocated shoulder, which means I have to close the bar at midnight and then clean up. You down for a booty call in the wee hours?

He replies in seconds.

OWEN

I volunteered to be medical support at the soccer
fields tomorrow. Archer bullied me into it. I have
to be there at 6:30 in the morning.

I let out another groan that sounds dangerously close to a
growl. I know I should be mysterious and flirty, but it's been six
days since I was in Owen's bed, and that is five days too long. I've
never done hard drugs, but I imagine Owen's lips on my bare skin
produce the same kind of high. I'm addicted and want more.

WYATT

Goddammit. I need you.

The three dots dance and disappear, dance and disappear,
before a message finally arrives.

OWEN

You get a break at any point tonight?

I'm suddenly *very* very aware of the ache between my thighs,
the heat and the slip of my skin. I press my legs together, but that
only makes the throbbing worse.

I glance down the bar, where our new hire, a raggedy hipster
called Jacob or Jonah or Jimothy—he's only been here a day, so I
haven't bothered to learn his name—is staring at the cash register
like it's one of those puzzle boxes in an escape room. He'll be very
little help tonight, since he knows how to make barely any drinks
that don't come directly from a tap. Still, we usually have a slight
lull around eight before the late-night crowd shows up.

WYATT

I can get off for a few around 8

OWEN

Yeah ya will

WYATT

Doc!

———

I expect time to crawl by until Owen's arrival, but it's Friday night and we're down a man. I spend the hours pulling drinks and closing tabs, hauling kegs and wiping up spills. Jonah proves just useful enough that I learn his name.

And when I have a spare moment to catch my breath, it's Romy's text that invades my brain, not Owen's.

I was already in a bad place when I walked in on her and Griffin all those years ago. I'd just gotten the call about Libby's arrest, and my mind was whirring with plans. I'd have to quit my job, probably find a subletter for the apartment I'd moved into with Griffin. And my bank account was empty enough that I couldn't survive long without a job. I'd visited Cardinal Springs a few times for holidays so I could see Hazel, but I had no idea what the job landscape there was like. Or how to care for a thirteen-year-old by myself. Or if the state of Indiana would even let me.

And there he was, pressing Romy into the couch, her guitar on the floor, his slung around his back like a cowboy.

I took in the scene just long enough for him to look up and see me.

He smirked.

I remember Romy yelling my name. I remember that Griffin didn't.

I walked out.

I spent that night sleeping in my truck at a campground

outside of Nashville. I ignored all her texts.

He sent only one:

C'mon, Wyatt. Things haven't been good between us for a while

 No apology. Barely an explanation. More like an excuse.

I waited until I knew he was at the studio where he was trying to crank out his debut EP before going back to the apartment, throwing things in suitcases and trash bags like I was on a fucked-up episode of *Supermarket Sweep*. I was so wracked with rage and heartbreak and fear about what awaited me in Indiana that I could barely think about the scene I'd walked in on.

But now, eight years later, I try to call up the image.

I can see it. Surprisingly clearly. Romy's hands were on his chest, and her guitar was on the floor.

In all the years I'd known her, Romy had never *once* put her guitar on the floor. It was a Martin acoustic that had been passed down from her grandfather. It was her most prized possession, not only because she hoped it would make all her dreams come true, but because it was the only thing she had left of her grand-dad. He had died only six months prior but had been lost to her for much longer thanks to Alzheimer's. When she put that guitar down, it was always on a stand. She kept one in her room and one in the living room. She had a fold-up one she brought to gigs.

That guitar was *never* on the floor.

And her hands were on his chest.

Like she was trying to push him away.

The first year I was in Cardinal Springs, I could barely hold myself and my sister together. Hazel fell to pieces when Libby went to prison, and she had nothing—*nothing*—but me and my half-assed attempts to provide a stable home. By the time I got my feet under me, it felt too late to reach out to Romy. I was living a different life by then. There was no way I was getting down to Nashville, and I figured her life had moved on too.

But now I have another chance. My friend, my homegirl, my ride or die—I can have her back in my life.

All I have to do is go to a Griffin Stone concert.

I'm cashing out a group of construction workers when Owen shows up, dragging my mind away from the churn of memories and regrets.

I see his blue scrubs first, hanging loosely over his muscular shoulders in the most delicious way. I notice his blue eyes next when they lock on mine. His brow furrows with the kind of determination that screams 4.0 GPA.

He stomps through the crowd and stops right in front of me, pressing his hands into the bar like he personally has to secure it to the floor.

Without taking his eyes off me, he barks at Jonah, "You're covering."

Jonah looks up with what might be alarm, but I hardly spare him a glance. I'm too busy taking Owen's hand, letting him lead me around the bar.

CHAPTER 23

OWEN

I know I'm practically dragging Wyatt through the bar. I know people are looking.

I don't care.

I need her.

I'm not entirely sure where I'm going, but Wyatt quickly takes charge and pulls me past the bathrooms and through a door at the end of the small hallway. Inside are shelves of cardboard boxes, stacks of napkins wrapped in plastic, extra pint glasses and dishware. There's a wonky table in the middle with two torn chairs beside it.

"Storage closet meets break room," Wyatt says, already breathless. She pulls the door shut and clicks the lock. "We've probably got about fifteen minutes before Jonah forgets how to use the register and comes knocking."

I don't hesitate. In two long steps I'm pressing her against the door, my mouth covering hers.

Immediately I feel the knots of tension in my neck and shoulders begin to loosen.

My day hasn't been particularly difficult. It was good, even.

Just a day of well-child visits where I got to assure a parade of nervous parents that their kids were perfect.

It's usually my favorite kind of day. But I still couldn't manage to stave off the tension headache that's been plaguing me since lunch.

But with one swipe of my tongue across Wyatt's, something releases. When I thread my fingers through the hair at the nape of her neck, my thumbs stroking her jaw as I kiss her, there's immediate relief.

I coast along her jawline to her ear, pressing my tongue to the spot just behind it that makes her sigh, then nip at her earlobe.

"The scrubs are a good look," she says between gasps.

"Yeah?" I keep my mouth on her neck, licking and sucking and pulling all kinds of delicious little gasps from her. I forgot I was even wearing them. I keep extras in my office for when disaster strikes. Today it was a four-year-old who threw up—I caught it with the trash can, but her mother went green at the sight, and I wasn't quick enough to transfer the trash can to her.

Not a story I intend to tell Wyatt, especially when her palm is exploring the shape of my cock, which is growing harder by the second.

"I never thought I was into the whole 'playing doctor' thing, but you're changing my mind."

I bite down on her neck and she yelps, then laughs.

"You want an exam, Wyatt?" I growl into her ear. "I'd be happy to check you out."

I tilt my head and catch the delicious flare in her eyes. So I coast one hand up her torso, letting my thumb linger for just a second on the hard peak of her nipple under her tank top, then travel higher. I drag my fingers along the column of her neck, resting them just below her jaw.

I press, and her pulse jumps beneath my touch. I watch the dusty old plastic clock on the wall over her shoulder, the second hand ticking.

"What are you—" she gasps, but I kiss her again.

"Hush," I scold her. "I'm counting."

She stills, her chest barely moving.

"Breathe, Wyatt," I whisper, enjoying the view of her chest heaving as she tries to breathe normally. When she settles into a rhythm, I count. "Ninety-two beats per minute. Good. Steady. Perhaps a touch elevated. Are you experiencing any…excitement, Ms. Hart?"

Wyatt huffs out a tiny laugh. "Well, a tall, dark, and handsome doctor dragged me to a storeroom to have his way with me, so I'd say yes."

"Mmmmm." I can practically feel her pulse in my cock. I release her neck and drop my hand immediately to her thigh, enjoying the goose bumps that rise on her skin as I move my hand beneath her skirt. "You know, there's another spot you can take a pulse."

"Oh?" she says, playing along, then moaning when I nudge the hem of her panties and press my fingers into the crease at the top of her thigh.

"The femoral pulse," I say, finding the flutter of her heart. And then I take my other hand and dip into her panties, taking a swipe at the warm, wet, delicate bundle of nerves. Wyatt's body reacts immediately, her pulse skittering beneath my touch.

I force myself to pause.

To count.

"One hundred and sixteen beats per minute," I whisper, still circling her clit and pressing kisses along her jaw. "How high do you think we can get it?"

Wyatt lets out a sound that is somehow both a laugh and a moan, then reaches for the drawstring of my scrub pants. "Enough playing," she says, dipping into my boxer briefs to wrap her hand around my cock. She squeezes, giving me a rough stroke that pulls a growl from deep in my chest. "Fuck me, Doctor."

The words nearly have me tearing her panties from her body, but I manage to remember that she's going to have to finish her shift in this skirt. The thought of her walking around the Half Pint bare is the sexiest fucking thing; it practically drives me to madness.

I quickly drag her panties down her thighs, pausing to lick the mess I've already made of her pussy with just my hand. The taste of her coats my tongue, and as long as I live, I know my mouth will always water at the thought of Wyatt Hart.

Wyatt seems equally frantic, stepping out of her black lace panties and kicking them into the corner as she yanks on the waistband of my scrub pants.

"Easy, trigger," I tease, slowing her down so I can retrieve the condom I stashed in my back pocket.

"You can't drag a girl into a storeroom and bring her seconds from orgasm and then fault her for getting a little frisky," she says with a dramatic pout.

"You'll hear no complaints from me," I tell her as I roll the condom on. Then I grab her hips and lift, her legs wrapping around my waist as I press her into the door and bury myself inside her in one frenzied thrust.

I have to pause for a moment so I don't come immediately. The feeling of being inside her, her ankles pressing into my back to pull me in deeper, her breasts heaving—it's all too much. I can't believe this feisty, funny, dazzling woman is letting me fuck her. Is letting me *have* her, even when I know she hates to give any part of herself away.

I don't take it for granted. Not for a second.

"You counting heartbeats again, Doc?" Wyatt gasps as she squirms on my cock, urging me to move.

"Give me a second, woman." I give her ass a squeeze. She responds by squeezing her inner walls until I groan. I lock eyes with her, brows furrowed, trying to hide my grin behind a stern look. "You brat. For that I'm going to fuck you until you scream."

Wyatt just arches an eyebrow as if to say, *Don't threaten me with a good time.*

And so I spare her no mercy as I fuck her against the door of the storeroom at the Half Pint. I fuck her until the glasses rattle on the shelf beside us, fuck her until her lips part, her moans mingling with the muffled sounds from the jukebox, fuck her until a flush climbs her chest and settles into her cheeks. I thrust and roll my hips so I catch her clit with every movement, and when I feel her getting close, I reach down and swipe across it with my thumb.

And just as she comes, I watch her eyes flutter shut, watch her disappear inside herself as she falls apart in my arms.

I want to beg, to plead, to will her to open her eyes. I want to see her—really *see* her—as she comes, want to connect with her as I make her shatter.

Instead, I press my lips to hers, caressing her tongue with mine, tasting her satisfaction, as my own orgasm roars through me.

When my atoms feel like they've arranged themselves into human form again, I put her down and watch her eyes flutter open. They're wide and sparkling, her pupils dilated, and when she's finally able to focus on me, she bites her lip and smiles.

"Want to go to a concert?"

CHAPTER 24

OWEN

May 12

The knock at my door is loud and out of rhythm, like Wyatt's mind is elsewhere. When I open the door, I find my tiny bartender on my stoop in the smallest pair of denim cutoffs, cowboy boots, and an oversize Dolly Parton T-shirt that's somehow sexier than a string bikini top. Her eyes are smokey, the dark liner thick like a warning, with only a hint of iridescent shimmer on her lids.

And she's frowning.

"You look like you're taking your nine-year-old daughter to a Taylor Swift concert," she says, eyeing my dark jeans and army-green linen short-sleeved button up. My pants are cuffed, and I'm wearing leather loafers with no socks.

"Thanks?" I say, reassessing my outfit, which I thought looked pretty good until six seconds ago.

She huffs out a sigh and pushes past me into the house. "You look fucking hot and you know it. It's just not the right vibe for where we're going."

She's in my living room now, pacing back and forth in front of the couch. I have to grab her by her forearms, bend my knees, and make her face me to get her attention. "To be clear, you didn't tell me where we were going. You just said 'a concert.'"

She bites her lip, her eyes on the ceiling as she sorts through her thoughts. Then she sets her jaw and looks me dead in the eye like a challenge.

"We're going to see Griffin Stone."

It takes me a minute to place the name, and when I finally do, I can't control my expression. "The guy who sings the song about truck nuts?"

She groans. "Yes. It's a long story."

And from the look on her face and the way she's bouncing in her cowboy boots, practically vibrating with tension, it seems like it's a complicated story too.

And I want to hear it. But more than that, I want her to be comfortable.

"Do you want me to change?"

She eyes me, a slow appreciation of my body that makes my pants go slightly tight in the crotch. Her gaze lingers on my biceps, where the sleeve of my shirt is tight in a way I'm frankly pretty fucking proud of.

"No," she finally says, a saucy look on her face. "Like I said, you look fucking hot."

The urge to drag her into my bedroom and keep her there until tomorrow is strong, but she pivots on her heel, and I can't not follow her heart-shaped ass in those tiny little shorts.

"I'm driving," she calls over her shoulder as she strides through the door.

"You sure? I'm happy to drive." I glance at my truck, just a year old and much bigger than her ancient little Toyota pickup.

She levels me with a look that has me shoving my keys into my pocket as I pull open the squeaky passenger door of her truck. Wyatt slides into the driver's side like it's home, then reaches across the console to grab a shoebox full of cassette tapes and sets them on the dusty floor.

"Feel free to pick one," she says as the truck starts with a surprisingly robust roar. Grace has mentioned that Wyatt knows how to work on cars, and I try not to linger too long on the image of her, cheeks marked with grease, wearing a tool belt...and nothing else. We've got an hour-long drive and a Griffin Stone concert to get through before I can get my hands on her, so I need to get hold of myself.

I reach for the box. Inside is a pile of tapes in plastic cases, bands my dad loves: Heart, Fleetwood Mac, Foreigner, Journey. There are also several that don't have cases, just words scrawled on their labels.

"Old-school," I say, holding up a mixtape with a tie-dye design done in marker. "Where did you even get these?"

"Yeah, the old girl has an old sound system," Wyatt says, patting the dashboard. "Record stores sell used tapes for cheap. I can usually get them for less than a dollar a pop. But my favorite is finding mixtapes at garage sales and estate sales. I can sometimes get a whole box for a couple of bucks."

"You mean you didn't make these?"

"Nope. These are all vintage specimens. I love them. My favorite is when they don't have track listings on the liner. It's a fun surprise to hear what's on them, imagine the types of people who made them, what they were going through. Some of them were even taped off the radio, so I get old commercials and DJ bits."

We hit the highway, and Wyatt drapes her wrist over the top of the steering wheel, her sunglasses perched on her nose as she leans across and digs into the box. She pulls out a tape in a black case with a handwritten track list.

"I went to this estate sale in Columbus a couple of years ago and found a box of mixtapes. Turns out this guy had made them for his girlfriend, a woman named Debbie, and together they told the entire story of their relationship. It was amazing, like this epic musical about the two of them falling in love." She holds up the tape for me to take. "This one is my favorite. Check it out."

I lean closer to read the tiny, blocky text.

> Jeff Buckley - Lover, You Should've Come Over
> The Cranberries - Linger
> Bryan Adams - Please Forgive Me
> Cake - I Will Survive
> Foreigner - I Want to Know What Love Is
> Journey - Who's Crying Now

I gape. "Is this their breakup?"

She grins.

"This guy scored his breakup? And sent it to her?"

"Yup. It's an amazing listen. I'm guessing it's got to be from 1996 or '97. The Cake cover is from '96, so it's after that."

"I don't know what's more heartbreaking—that he made this, or that she sold it at a garage sale almost thirty years later," I say.

Wyatt plucks the tape from my hand, flips open the case and slides out the tape one-handed, popping it into the tape deck. I have to shout over the opening strains of Jeff Buckley. "All these love letters, and this one is your favorite?"

She casts a glance at me sideways, a half grin on her face. "I've never lied about who I am."

"Then why are we going to a Griffin Stone concert?"

She freezes, frowning, then sighs, her chest sinking in on itself. "He's my ex," she says.

Thank god I'm not driving, because I think I would have swerved off the road at that little piece of information.

"Your ex? I'm sorry, you had a *boyfriend*?"

She lets out a rueful laugh. "I love that you're more shocked that I had a boyfriend than that it was that poser douche-canoe."

She tips her head back against her seat and presses harder on the gas. "Remember how you said you were gonna hurt him? Don't do that."

I'm putting it all together now: the way she charged into my living room like a lit sparkler, the way she holds back, the walls she's built.

That fucking guy? *Really?*

"I think you're going to do that just fine on your own in that outfit."

I watch the tension melt off of her as she laughs, deep and throaty. But she doesn't say anything else, just keeps her eye on the horizon, the two-lane highway rushing at us as we head toward Indianapolis.

"You don't have to tell me anything, but we've got about an hour on the road, so…"

I can practically feel her eye roll, but she starts talking anyway.

"First, I should tell you that we're not actually going to see Griffin Stone. I don't plan to hear that asshole sing a note," she says. "We're going to see Romy Maxwell, who's opening for him. She was my best friend and roommate back in Nashville…and I haven't spoken to her since I walked in on her kissing my boyfriend. Griffin. Well, *he* was kissing *her*. But I don't really know what all happened, because I walked out and moved here the next day."

It's then that I realize just how little I know about Wyatt Hart. And it's not because I'm not curious. She plays her cards so close to the vest that I'm not even sure *she* can see them.

I let the information roll around in my brain. She poured that story out like it was bullet-pointed, like she was testifying in court. Just the facts, no emotion.

But when I glance over at her, I see that despite the way she's holding her face still, impassive, focusing on the road, there's a watery sheen to her eyes that betrays the heft of this situation. When she finally looks over at me, there's a touch of fear in her expression.

Like I'm going to ask more questions.

Or bolt.

Or both.

Instead, I turn back to the road, settling back into the surprisingly comfortable passenger seat of the ancient truck.

"So what do you need from me?"

CHAPTER 25

WYATT

My whole sordid story, and that's all he's got to say?

"From *you*?" I ask.

"Yeah. Are we beating him up? Yelling at her? Do you need backup? Or just a getaway driver?"

I have to force my gaze back to the road, because otherwise I will just stare open-mouthed at this beautiful man. I poured my mess all over him, and he didn't even blink. Didn't push me for details or explanations. Didn't look at me like I was something he'd stepped in. Just asked me how he could help.

He's *such* a good guy.

And I never should have dragged him into my disaster.

But he's here, and the truth is I'm really fucking glad to have him on my side.

"To be honest, I'm not totally sure," I confess, partly to him and partly to myself. Because since I texted Romy and told her I'd be at the show, I've refused to think about what that meant. What would happen when I got there. I just…said yes. Because I knew I'd have Owen by my side.

But now, staring at this seemingly endless stretch of rural

highway, cornfields whipping by on either side as the sun glows orange and pink in the clouds, I actually consider it.

"I think I'm ready to listen to her," I say, working out my thoughts as they come. "Not him. He can get fucked. But…I miss her. And I think I might have made a mistake back then, cutting her off."

"Linger" by the Cranberries begins. The tape's a little scratchy and tinny, but it works for the guitar, for Dolores O'Riordan's haunting voice.

But Owen's voice, deep and strong, cuts right over the vocals.

"I'll follow your lead," he says.

———

Just like Romy said in her text, when I pull up to security and give my name to the very beefy guard at the gate, we're waved into a small parking area and escorted into the bowels of Lucas Oil Stadium, where a tall, broad-shouldered woman with platinum-blond hair, several dainty face tattoos, and a pink Nudie suit is waiting for us.

"The mysterious and elusive Wyatt Hart," the woman says in a Southern-accented voice that is somehow both fizzy and syrupy. She holds out a tattooed hand. "I'm Sienna Walker, Romy's manager."

I like her firm handshake and the arrow tattooed just above her lethally arched right brow.

I don't particularly like the way she eyes Owen like she wants a taste.

"Nice to meet you," I say. "I'm not sure I'm particularly mysterious or elusive."

Owen stifles a snort beside me, and I elbow him in the ribs hard enough that he gasps.

Sienna watches us, appraising, then lets out a deep, throaty laugh.

"I knew I was gonna like you," she says, turning and gesturing for us to follow. "Romy's in her dressing room. She goes on in fifteen, and she'll play a thirty-minute set before that walking Mountain Dew bottle full of snuff spit goes on."

Suddenly Sienna is my favorite person in the world.

The backstage area is cavernous and bustling like a train station, full of crew members wearing black clothes and earpieces like Secret Service agents and rushing around in a hurry. But that makes it easy to follow Sienna's 1940s bouffant and sparkling pink figure through the crowd until we arrive at a closed door.

And just when I feel my heart start to pick up the pace like a marching band is making its way from my chest cavity into my throat, Owen slips his hand into mine. The warmth, the weight, the feeling of him puts me immediately at ease.

What do you need from me?

He just knows.

As soon as Sienna opens the door, my eyes go to Romy. How could they not? My ex–best friend lights up the tiny room.

Her fiery-red hair is somehow deeper, the curls cascading over her shoulder. She's wearing a denim halter-top jumpsuit covered in rhinestones and a pair of silver-toed, bright red cowboy boots. And even though she's bigger and brighter and just...*more* than I remember, she's also exactly the same. The big green eyes that betray her every thought. The sliver of a gap between her front teeth that makes her smile slightly rascally. And her old Martin on a stand beside an old green velvet couch in the corner of the room. I know it's the same guitar from forever ago because it bears a scratch down the body from the night a drunk hurled a pint glass at her during a set and I summoned pull-a-car-off-a-child energy and hauled him out of the bar with my bare hands.

"Hi," she says, her eyes watering. "You came."

Ever since her first text—hell, ever since I drove away from Nashville—I've imagined what I'd say if I saw her again. I tried to formulate something that felt true. Honest. As if I even knew what I felt. When everything went down with my mom, my laser focus turned to Hazel. There was no space for reconciliation.

I can't believe I almost missed this.

And as soon as I see her and that guitar, the words come easy.

"I wouldn't miss it," I tell her, and it takes only a beat, one long, conspiring look between us, before we're rushing to each other, crashing into a big hug almost nine years in the making.

"I'm so sorry," she rasps into my hair.

"Forgiven and forgotten," I tell her, and I mean it.

"I was so drunk, and he was—"

"A bastard," I finish for her.

She pulls back and dabs at her eyes before her thick mascara stars trailing down her rouged cheeks. "I slapped him as soon as you left."

"I hope you left a mark," I say, swiping at my cheeks, though it's too late for my mascara.

Romy grins, grabbing my hands and squeezing them. "A good one. I was wearing that big old Masonic ring that belonged to my granddaddy."

I return her squeeze. "That thing's like brass knuckles."

"I heard it took four stitches to close the cut on his cheek. They had to airbrush the scar on his album cover."

"Good girl," I say.

I lose myself in a momentary spiral of shame that I waited so long to have this moment, but I come out of it when I realize Romy is staring over my shoulder, eyes wide.

I forgot he was even here, but when I turn, there's Owen standing behind me, hands in his pockets, relaxed and grinning.

Waiting.

Following my lead.

"This is Owen. He's my…" And now, after the words of absolution came so easily, my brain just…short circuits. I have no words. Pineapple? Can I say pineapple?

But Owen just steps forward and shakes Romy's hand. "I'm Owen. Pleasure to meet you, Romy," he says, his voice warm and deep like a hot toddy on a cold night. "Excited to hear your set tonight."

Fuck, he's so *good*. Not pushing me. Not making me explain. My own personal safety net.

"Speaking of, we're just here to see you," I add. And like we haven't missed a day, Romy fills in everything I don't say.

"You don't have to worry," she says, giving my shoulders a squeeze. "He never leaves his green room before he goes on. There's always a preshow tailgate full of whiskey and women. Sienna'll show you where you can watch from the wings, and I'll meet you offstage after."

Then she pulls me in for another hug. "I missed you," she says.

"I missed you too."

———

Romy is incredible.

As good as I remember, maybe even better. She's confident and sassy, her fingers flying over the strings of her guitar. She has an incredible rapport with her band, and she soon has the audience—who didn't even come to see her and trickle in throughout her set—in the palm of her hand. She somehow manages to get them singing along to songs they've never heard before.

I watch the whole set from stage left, tucked into the wings beneath lights and rigging and next to the smoke machines I imagine will later obscure the fact that Griffin Stone can't play guitar for shit.

And Owen stands with me, first beside me, then behind me so I can lean back into him, his arms wrapped around my waist. I like the feeling of being cocooned by him, the smell of his soap or detergent or cologne or whatever it is putting me at ease. Throughout the show he ducks his head every so often to whisper in my ear, just little comments like, "I've heard this one" or "She's really good." But it has the same effect as if he were whispering utter filth, his warm breath sending shivers up my spine. I just keep sinking further and further into him as the show goes on.

Romy finishes the song that I know is her biggest hit, the one I heard on the radio in Grace's shop and that I've been covertly streaming on my phone here and there. Then she motions for the roaring crowd to quiet.

"When I was just starting out, I used to always close my sets with this last song," she says, leaning into the mic and smiling like she's got a secret. My heart leaps into my throat. When she glances to the left with a smile, tears spring to my eyes. "It's been a long while, but I think it's time to bring it back." She unclips the capo from the head of her guitar and moves it to the neck. "A lot of you might know it, so feel free to sign along."

When she strums the opening chords to "Can the Circle Be Unbroken," I want to laugh and sob at the same time. Listening to the first verse is like time traveling out of the cavernous arena and directly back to the open mic nights in tiny bars, the gigs where she went on at two a.m., all the backyard bonfire singalongs. My lips move without me even thinking, and if the crowd weren't singing along so loudly, they might hear me chiming in on the low harmonies, just like I used to back in Nashville. The song feels like a hymn, a prayer, one filled with gratitude for the return of my friend, for the fact that I've finally let myself hear her apology, accept the truth. It feels good to put down the grudge I've stubbornly carried for so long.

And having Owen here for this moment when the before and after of my life meet feels like opening a door inside myself and inviting him inside. It feels precious.

It feels right.

When the song ends, Romy slings her guitar around to her back and blows kisses to the crowd, then trots offstage and directly into my arms.

"Soon you'll be on your *own* headlining tour," I tell her. And I mean it. She was absolutely incredible.

"God, I hope so," she says, fanning herself. "I know you want to get out of here before he goes on, but I have something for you. Wait here, I'll be right back, 'kay?"

I nod and watch her move through the backstage area like it's her home.

She's only been gone for a moment when I feel his arrival like a summer storm.

When I turn, there he is.

Griffin Stone.

Exactly the same, but somehow smaller.

He looks like someone typed "country music asshole" into an AI generator. He's wearing skintight jeans and a black Johnny Cash T-shirt with a pack of cigarettes rolled into the sleeve, even though he's never smoked a day in his life. Hell, he used to call the cops on the hipsters who smoked Spirits on the sidewalk outside our apartment.

My stomach curdles when he smiles.

Which is not what I want. I *want* to be a badass. To deliver a devastating line and leave him grasping. If I have to run into him, I want to win.

Instead I'm frozen.

"I knew as soon as I heard that old Carter Family song on the monitors that you had to be here," he says, his eyes roaming up my bare legs. "Looking good, Wyatt."

I can't make my mouth move. I just let him stand there looking satisfied while he ogles me. The longer it lasts, the more paralyzed I become until I'm worried I won't even be able to walk away from him. I'll have to live here, rooted to this stage, for the rest of my life.

And then Owen leans in.

"I don't believe we've met," he says, holding out his hand. "I'm Dr. Owen McBride. And you are?"

I suck in a breath, watching as Griffin grits his teeth, barely hanging on to his smile.

"Griffin Stone," he says with a bro nod, ignoring Owen's outstretched hand.

"Sloane?" Owen asks, and I nearly snort out a laugh. It's only by the grace of God that I manage not to grin.

Owen takes his hand back, wrapping it around my waist and bending to nuzzle me just behind my ear, knowing full well that it's a spot that always makes me moan a little. I can practically feel his smile against my neck when the sound escapes.

In front of us, Griffin's eyes cloud.

"Stone," he replies through clenched teeth, his shit-eating grin now gone.

"Ah, right, the man of the hour," Owen says. "Sounds like Romy got the crowd good and warmed up for you."

Griffin's eyes flash, but it's less a warning than a malfunction. He looks like he's desperately trying to come up with a comment that'll put him back on top, but he can't find anything.

"She's great," he finally manages to say.

"And how do you know my Wyatt?" Owen asks him, flexing his forearm around my midsection to pull me closer. Griffin's eyes drop down to watch the way I settle my ass against him.

"We were together for three years," Griffin says, and finally that cocky smirk is back on his face. He thinks he's got me. That maybe Owen doesn't know, maybe he's exposed a lie.

But Owen just smiles, then drops his lips to my neck, brushing me with a gentle kiss. Then he looks back at Griffin, a smile on his face that I haven't seen before. It's…smug.

"And you let her get away?"

I don't bother to hide my gasp, and I know Owen feels it in my belly when his hand flexes against it. He bends down again to sink his teeth into my earlobe, letting out a light chuckle.

"Lucky me," he says, and it's meant for *me*, not for Griffin.

Country music's biggest douchebag clears his throat, looking anywhere but at us. "I gotta go get ready for my set," he grumbles, then walks away, his brand-new thousand-dollar poser cowboy boots clomping across the floor.

"Break a leg," I call after him, my voice finally returning.

"Or I could break your face," Owen mutters as Griffin disappears into the darkness of backstage.

I spin and practically leap into his arms, laughing.

"Oh my god, that was the meanest thing you could possibly have done to him," I say before planting a big sloppy kiss full on his mouth. "I loved every second."

Owen gives me a hearty *you're welcome* by slipping his tongue between my lips, a preview of later, and everything around us disappears in a haze of lust as I surrender my mouth to his.

When Romy returns, she has to clear her throat to interrupt our kiss.

"Thank you so much for coming," she says, enveloping me in another hug. "I'd ask you to stay, but I have to do my stupid cameo during his big party song. But I've got a day off before Cincinnati. I could rent a car and drive down."

"I'd love that," I tell her. "I'm working tomorrow, but I'll text you details."

"Great. This is for you." She hands me a little plastic case containing a mixtape, her familiar loopy script on the liner. "You know what they say—love is a mixtape. Hopefully you still have a way to listen to it?"

"Girl, I still drive my same truck," I tell her, and she laughs.

"Well, that's the soundtrack for your drive back," Romy says, then smiles at Owen. "It was nice to meet you, Owen."

"Same to you," he says with that dazzling smile. "You were absolutely incredible."

"Thank you," she says, then turns to me and mouths *I like this guy!*

"Me too, Rome," I say, as I lean into the firmness of his shoulder, letting him hold me up.

CHAPTER 26

WYATT

The next morning, I'm alone in the bar, swapping kegs and prepping glassware in anticipation of the Sunday sports crowd.

But my mind is back in the wings of that cavernous arena, Owen at my side.

My Wyatt.

The words ping around in my brain like a pinball, lighting up parts of my body I didn't even know were erogenous zones.

My Wyatt.

I want to have those words tattooed on me, just above my hip, where Owen rested his large, warm hand. I want to turn them into a song and listen to it for the rest of my life.

We said no commitments, no labels, but *my Wyatt* feels like something else entirely.

And it scares the shit out of me.

My spiral is interrupted by a grumble coming from the back.

"You talking to me, Ernie?" I call, dumping my bucket of soapy water down the sink and going to check on him.

"I *said* I need some help," Ernie barks, rubbing the shoulder supported by a sling. He managed to take twenty-four hours off before he got bored out of his fucking mind (his words) and came back. But he's under strict orders to lift *nothing*.

He's thrilled, clearly.

"Which one?"

"The summer shandy."

"On it."

I leave Ernie to wipe down the bar, but when I get back with the keg wagon, he's doing something absolutely bizarre.

He's smiling.

And that's because he's got the rag tossed over his shoulder, his good elbow leaning into the bar, as he makes conversation with Romy Maxwell.

"Watch out for that one—he's trouble," I say when my best friend turns on her stool and spots me.

And instead of snapping at me, Ernie just blushes.

My mouth hangs open. "Ernie, are you *starstruck*?"

He shakes his head, but then he turns to Romy and says, "I love that one you do about the blue dress."

Romy lights up like a disco ball. " 'Tears in Chiffon!' That's a B-side. You're a real fan!"

He shrugs, but he warms to the praise like a preschooler presenting an art project. "I like country. The classic stuff, not that pickup truck shit," he says. "You remind me of Linda Ronstadt."

Romy's mouth drops open. "Holy shit, that is the biggest compliment anyone has ever paid me."

"Ernie, you old flirt." I've literally never heard my boss talk to a stranger this much. But I'm proud of Romy and thrilled to watch her get her flowers.

"Let an old man have some peace," Ernie grumbles with a wave of his hand. He snaps the towel off his shoulder and goes back to wiping the bar.

The same spot he was cleaning when I left.

I pull Romy into a hug and then heave the keg into place. "I'm so glad you came," I tell her has I tap it.

She glances around the quiet bar. We don't open for another

hour, so it's clean and doesn't smell like stale beer and body odor yet.

"Wyatt, I love this place," she says. "Yours?"

"No, I just work here. Chatty Cathy here owns the place," I say, snapping a bar towel at my boss. I brace for a snappy retort, but instead he just shrugs his good shoulder.

"Couldn't run it without you," he says, his voice gruff. He eyes me. "I'm heading out to do my stretches with Corianne. You good here alone?"

"I'm not alone," I say, nodding at Romy.

"I'm happy to jump in. Wyatt and I tended bar together *a lot* back in the old days. I can pull a pint like you wouldn't believe."

Ernie looks like he might fall over at the thought of Romy Maxwell tending his bar, but he manages to school his face back into the lined grimace I know so well. "Jonah should be here in about half an hour. Call me if his ass is late, okay?"

I give Ernie a two-fingered salute and get back to my side work, the memory of what it felt like to do this alongside Romy rushing back.

"I'm glad to see you behind a bar still," Romy says. "You're so good at it. You always seemed so at home there."

It's true. When I moved to Cardinal Springs, the little brick ranch house was supposed to be home, but I didn't really feel at peace until Ernie hired me. Bartending's hard work, but I love it. It's physical, never dull, and I'm a people person, so I love the customers. Well, not *all* of them, but my regulars are like my second family.

"Speaking of home, you looked pretty dang comfortable on that stage," I say as I refill the toothpick dispenser.

Romy sucks in a breath, her eyes going wide with news. "Sienna's negotiating with the label to get me my own tour."

I drop the box of toothpicks, sending them skittering across the bar. "Seriously? Romy, that's huge!"

"Not stadiums, obviously. More like large clubs and small

theaters. Jingle Ball and music festivals and that sort of thing. But people would be coming to see *me*."

"Well, after seeing you last night, I'm not a bit surprised."

"I gotta get off Griffin's tour. It's such a redneck frat party." She takes a toothpick from the pile and starts strumming it across the bar like it's a lap steel. "I nearly cried when Sienna told me about his offer. Partially because I couldn't believe I was finally going to get to do it—travel around the country playing my songs. And partially because it's *him*. It felt so icky to join up after what he did to you. To us. He was the reason I lost my best friend, and now I had to choose between my career and *that*?"

"Well, I'm glad you chose your career, because now you get to show his audiences what a true artist sounds like. I'm glad you're using that dull mirror to reflect your own shine."

"You'll be happy to know he fumbled the bridge to his biggest hit last night."

The song about me: "Burning Heart." It was his first big radio hit, topping out at number two on the country charts and even crossing over onto the Billboard Hot 100. He wrote his own narrative of that night and everything that came before it, recasting me as an evil temptress out to destroy him or any other poor man who fell for my seduction. It's full of the most obvious kindergarten rhymes—no shit, the second verse pairs *love* and *dove*. It has a mind-numbingly boring melody and sounds like it was written in crayon on the back of a Longhorn menu. The title sounds like a symptom of a venereal disease. The worst people you know love to blast it from their lifted trucks.

Just the thought of it makes me want to shatter every glass in the bar.

Another perk of listening to most of my music on cassette in the truck? I never have to worry about accidentally hearing "Burning Heart" by Griffin Stone.

And I don't want to spend one single, solitary second of my time with Romy thinking about that asshole. Which she can obviously tell, because she changes the subject.

"So tell me about this Dr. Owen," she says in a syrupy, singsong voice like we're fourth graders on the playground. "He's a strapping fellow."

"He's …"

But I don't have words to describe him. Pineapple started out as a joke, but now it stands in for all the things I can't say, all the things I won't let myself feel. He's so good, and I'm such a disaster. I can't cast him in the role of one-man cleanup crew. I've always made sure my mess is mine to handle, but it's getting harder and harder to keep it from him.

Still, something shifted last night at the concert. Something feels bigger. That "4Now" doesn't quite cover it all anymore.

"Wyatt, you're blushing."

I duck my head, as if keeping her from seeing it will make it not real. "Well, he's a very good lay," I tell her.

Romy tosses the toothpick at me, and it lodges itself in my curls. "Don't do that," she says.

"Do what?" I ask, swatting at my hair to shake the toothpick loose.

"Diminish the things in your life that are good."

"I'm not!"

"You used to do it all the time back in Nashville, and it seems like you haven't changed. You neg yourself like you're ready for the floor to drop out. I think that's why you were with Griffin to begin with. You knew he was going to be a disappointment, so you didn't have to be surprised when he showed his true colors. You've always gotta be big tough Wyatt Hart, ready to muscle through disaster."

"That's a load of shit."

"Yeah. It is," she says, leveling me with a look. "Nobody's ready for disaster, for heartbreak. But when you try to prepare yourself like that, you just experience the misery twice. You can't enjoy the good parts."

I sigh. "But how can you call them good parts when they end in misery?"

Romy's eyes go soft as she studies me. "Oh, honey. That's just life. You take the good with the bad. You lean on the good to deal with the bad." She reaches across the bar, taking my hand in hers. "But you've got to let yourself be happy."

Then she swipes her thumb across my cheek, wiping away the tear I didn't even realize was falling.

I grab for a bar napkin, sniffling and trying to smile. "I don't *want* to be like this," I say. "I just don't know how to be any other way."

She smiles. "Maybe start with that very handsome doctor who looks at you like you invented orgasms?"

CHAPTER 27

MAY 15 AT 2:30 PM

WYATT

Eden is crawling!

OWEN

Way to go, kid!

WYATT

Holy shit, she's going straight for the outlets

OWEN

The hardware store has covers, want me to pick some up and bring them by?

WYATT

Please. This kid is barely 7 months old and she's scaring the shit out of me

MAY 19 AT 11:17 AM

WYATT

I just ran into Felix at the hardware store. He says you're getting an outdoor shower?

OWEN

We're probably just getting the plumbing for an outdoor shower. It'll be another six months before he finishes the job

WYATT

Ouch. Twin troubles?

OWEN

He started some rewiring and didn't finish, a thing I discovered when I grabbed a metal pull chain to turn on a ceiling fan and way too many volts coursed through my body

So forgive me if my faith in my brother's house projects is shaky

WYATT

Too bad. We could had some fun in that shower

JUNE 1 AT 4:47 PM

WYATT

Your brother is scary

OWEN

Which one?

WYATT

The big one

OWEN

What he he do? Do you need me to talk to him?

WYATT

Only if you think you can get me out of this
soccer game. 8 am on a Saturday is cruel and
unusual punishment

OWEN

Wish I could, but Archer's taking his job as
Betsy's soccer coach VERY seriously

WYATT

No kidding. He texted me a dress code

OWEN

Just be glad he didn't have time to make the T-
shirts he wanted us all to wear

WYATT

Oh, you didn't get yours? Mine was in my
mailbox this morning

CHAPTER 28

WYATT

June 3

"What are you doing up so early?"

The morning sun is just starting to filter through the kitchen window, casting Hazel and Eden in a warm glow at our kitchen table. Hazel has her laptop in front of her, a legal pad beside it, as she finishes up her final paper for the semester while Eden makes messy work of the peanut butter toast soldiers on her high chair tray.

As soon as she sees me, Eden starts shrieking and babbling. At almost eight months, she doesn't have any words yet, but that doesn't stop her from talking a blue streak. And nothing has ever sounded better to me than the nonsense spilling from her gummy little mouth.

"Morning, Princess Peanut Butter," I say, planting a kiss on top of her fuzzy red head, then stealing a bit of toast off Hazel's plate. "Betsy's soccer final is this morning. Archer has gathered the world's largest cheering section."

"That explains the outfit." Hazel snorts, eyeing the red Cardinal Springs Cardinals jersey tucked into a white skort and the red Converse on my feet. But before I can fire back, she sucks in a breath and sits up straight. "Oh, hey, can I come?"

I raise an eyebrow at her. "You want to come to a youth soccer game at eight a.m. on a Saturday?"

"Thanks to my Facebook stalking, I'm pretty sure the Parks Department director's daughter plays on Betsy's team," Hazel says, closing her laptop and retrieving the bottle Eden just chucked on the floor. "I'm trying to get them to hire me as a landscape intern. My advisor told me I could get practicum credit for it, and that would get me closer to an on-time graduation."

Hazel's been working her butt off doing online classes. It remains to be seen if she can finish her entire degree remotely. Her advisor at Cornell is being incredibly helpful and accommodating, but there's only so much you can fight the administration at an Ivy League institution. I'm trying not to imagine Hazel packing Eden and all her baby gear into the Subaru and driving away. The thought breaks my heart.

More than once I've considered following them to Ithaca, spending a semester or two in a tiny apartment watching Eden while Hazel goes to class.

But that was before Owen. I would do anything for Hazel, but that doesn't mean it wouldn't hurt like a motherfucker to leave.

And then there's a whole other stew of emotions that I try not to look at too closely. The last time I loaded up my truck and drove away from a man, I was in pieces. Owen isn't Griffin. The hurt would be different, but it would hurt all the same.

"What's up, buttercup?" Libby pads into the kitchen in leggings and an oversize sweatshirt, rubbing the sleep out of her eyes. She's been working days at the diner lately, which means I don't cross paths with her all that much, what with me working nights at the bar.

I'm not mad about it.

Before I can send Hazel some sister telepathy, she pipes up. "We're going to Betsy's soccer game."

Libby pours coffee and lets out a catlike yawn. "Who's Betsy again?"

I scoff, but Hazel ignores it and smiles at our mother. "Archer's neighbor's daughter."

"And Archer is?"

"The older brother of Owen, who is Wyatt's—"

"*Nothing,*" I say through gritted teeth. This time Hazel shuts her mouth.

"Oh, right, the good doctor," Libby says in a playground singsong. She waggles her eyebrows over her coffee mug. "How are things with the two of you?"

I ignore her and focus on Hazel and my promise that I would try to keep the peace. "Grace is arranging a whole pregame brunch thing on the sidelines, so I have to be there at seven thirty. You want to ride with me?"

"I want to go," Libby says.

"No," I reply.

She pouts. "Come on. I haven't had a morning off in forever."

"And you want to spend it watching children you don't know play soccer?"

"No, I want to spend it with my girls," she says with a theatrical touch of pain in her voice.

Hazel gives me a look. "It's fine," she tells me, as if saying it will make it so. Then she turns back to Libby. "You can ride with Eden and me. I need to scrub the peanut butter off this one, so you go ahead, Wyatt. We'll meet you there."

"Peachy," I mutter, suddenly dreading this soccer game a whole hell of a lot more.

———

I arrive at the field to find the whole McBride clan gathered by the soccer field at Whitlow Park. Grace told me she was putting together "a little pregame brunch," but this is another level.

"Jeez, you went full Ole Miss tailgate," I say as I peruse the folding table she brought, topped with a red linen tablecloth. Grace is a bomb-ass cook, and she's really outdone herself this morning. The table is practically creaking under the weight of platters filled with flaky biscuits, French toast sticks, bacon-wrapped sausages, egg bites, and a colorful fruit salad. A large pitcher of orange juice sits beside a stack of red Solo cups.

"There's champagne under the table," she whispers, lifting a corner of the tablecloth. "Be discreet. I'm pretty sure it's illegal, and Archer will kill me if I embarrass him at this game."

Across the field, Archer has his feet planted shoulder width apart, arms crossed over his chest, a whistle in his mouth. He's blowing it at regular intervals while his team of nine-year-old soccer players moves through warm-up drills like a squad of Navy SEALs.

"I don't think it's illegal, but getting tipsy at a children's soccer game is certainly frowned upon," Felix says, reaching for one of the cups.

Grace snatches it from his hand. "Then no mimosas for you," she retorts.

"Hey, no judgment!" Felix says, then looks around. Mr. McBride is standing hip to hip with Corianne, his girlfriend, as they share a heap of goodies from a red paper plate. "Where's Dan?"

"Archer said he was coming, but then Dad said he left last night to go back to New York. So as usual, I have no idea what his deal is," she says with a sigh, sipping her mimosa.

"Well, a guy in a suit stopped by *my* house this morning looking for him. Said he was with the SEC and left his card," Felix says. "Apparently Dan gave them my address when he was crashing with us? But that was months ago."

"SEC? Like the football conference?" I ask.

"The Securities and Exchange Commission," Felix says.

"What the *hell*?" Grace asks.

Felix shrugs. "I'll try to call him. I'm all for giving him space or whatever, but this shit's fucked up. Guy had a bad suit and a shiny badge and looked like he resented setting foot in the state of Indiana. Whatever's going on is straight-up not good."

Grace sighs again as Felix trudges away, phone to his ear.

"Hey, I'm sure everything is fine," I say, even though it sounds very much *not* fine. Dan has been slinking in and out of town for months, taking furtive phone calls and saying absolutely nothing to anyone. If the feds are looking for him in Cardinal Springs, Felix is right—shit's fucked up.

Grace shakes her head. "I highly doubt it, but there's nothing I can do about that right now. I'm just trying to focus on this food to distract me from my brother's troubles *and* the fact that the final round starts tomorrow."

Decker's hockey team just finished a brutal battle in the semis that lasted all the way to the final seconds of Game Seven, when a buzzer beater guaranteed them a trip to the final. Since Decker is retiring at the end of the season, this is his last chance to win a Stanley Cup, and Grace is as nervous as if she were donning skates and playing herself.

I reach beneath the table and find the bottle of champagne, which is wrapped in a red towel. "Girl, skip the OJ. Go straight for the bubbly," I say, tipping the bottle into her cup.

She smiles. "Bless you."

And then Grace is pulled away by some of the soccer parents coming by to fill their plates. Now that no one is paying any attention to me, I decide to take a nice stroll down the sideline to where a very handsome medic is setting up at the center line.

Owen is wearing a pair of black joggers that make my mouth water and a neon-yellow T-shirt that says MEDICAL VOLUNTEER in large black letters.

"Excuse me, Doctor, I've got an itch I just can't scratch," I say in a faux-breathy voice.

Owen looks up from the cooler he's filling with ice and grins.

"Hey, gorgeous," he says, his blue eyes slowly sweeping over me. "You look like a naughty cheerleader in that skirt."

I pop a hip and grin. "Wanna meet me under the bleachers after the game?"

Owen glances over at the small set of metal risers positioned across the field, only four rows high.

"I think I'm a little tall," he says with a laugh. "How about instead I take you back to my bed and fuck you until you scream?"

My mouth nearly drops open in surprise. I've been getting hot and heavy with Owen since January, and it still shocks me that the mild-mannered pediatrician has a mouth like that.

"Yoo-hoo!"

And just like that, my vagina dries right on up—my mother is walking toward us from the parking lot. She's wearing a pair of white cutoffs and a red V-neck baby tee, kitten-heeled sandals on her feet. Which is why she's wobbling on the grass like a drunk toddler, the heels sinking into the damp soil with each step.

When she finally arrives, she grins. "Wyatt, hon, introduce me to your man friend!"

"You've met," I deadpan.

"Yes, well, that was before he was your man friend," she trills.

I huff out a sigh. "Owen, this is Libby," I say, gesturing to my mother. "Libby, Owen."

"Nice to see you again, Libby," he says, reaching out to shake her hand.

"Oh, the pleasure is all mine," she says with a wink, and I want to *die*. I can't even be bothered to hide my eye roll. "Now, Owen, you're a doctor, so let me ask you—"

"Oh my god, *please* do not hit this nice man up for free medical advice," I plead.

"Fine, fine," she says, waving me off like *I'm* the one being unreasonable. She smiles at Owen. "Wants you all to herself, I see."

I groan. "Go get food. There's mimosas."

"Honey, you know I don't drink anymore."

Did I know that? My mother keeps up a near-constant stream of chatter, and I've gotten very good at tuning her out when I'm forced to be in a room with her. I guess I've missed a few things. Then again, I can barely picture Libby Hart without a beer in her hand, so I guess I'll believe it when I see it.

"I'll let you two have your alone time, though," she says. "I'll just go make conversation with your other friends."

I must have a panicked look on my face, because Owen takes a furtive glance around, then drops a quick, soft kiss on my forehead and nudges me toward her.

"I'll see you after the game," he says, then gives me quick a swat on the ass as I turn to walk away.

CHAPTER 29

OWEN

The game is a good one, if you're rooting for the Cardinals. The girls have three goals to the Blue Jays' zero. Betsy even drew first blood with her goal in the first three minutes.

And then she drew *actual* first blood when she slid in for a kick and took a girl out at the shins. It didn't seem like a legal move for a nine-year-old athlete, but the ref didn't blow his whistle, and Archer applauded like she'd just won an Olympic medal.

My job has been mostly slapping on Band-Aids and handing out ice packs, which the girls have needed more and more in the last third of the game. They're getting hot and tired and sloppy, and the Blue Jays are desperate to avoid a shutout.

I'm reaching for a bottle of water when I hear a dull thud followed by a scream. Out of the corner of my eye I see Betsy go down. Hard.

I react instinctively. I bolt from the bleachers, my brain making sense of what I saw as I run. A Blue Jay going in for a goal. Betsy trying to head the ball away.

Betsy taking a cleat to the forehead.

I sense Archer and Madeline behind me, but I get there first, dropping to my knees beside her in the grass.

Betsy's eyes are open, and she squints into the sun as she groans and reaches for her forehead. There's already a goose egg blooming there, red now, but it'll surely be a festival of colors later.

"Betsy, are you okay?" I say, my training warring with the increasing panic in my chest. I force myself to focus on the fact that she's conscious.

"Yeah," she says, and she starts to sit up, but I place my hand on her chest to keep her on the ground.

"One sec, I need to check you out first." I think my voice sounds steady, the pleasant *don't worry* tone I use with kids every day. But in my head it's too loud. Too forceful. I hold up fingers and ask her how many, which she answers with ease. I ask her what day it is and her mom's name and watch her eyes as they follow my finger.

She passes every test.

"Betsy, baby, are you okay?" Madeline grabs her daughter's hand and squeezes.

"Yeah," she says. "But that really fucking hurt."

Madeline gasps. "Elizabeth Jane!"

Archer, who's squatting beside Madeline, chuckles. "She got kicked in the head, Mads. I think she's allowed an F-bomb."

"Can I sit up now? This grass is tickling my ears," Betsy asks, and I help her sit slowly, watching for any dizziness or unsteadiness.

She seems fine.

"Okay, well, you may have a concussion, so you'll need to be observed," I tell her, the words transporting me back in time to another exam. Another kid. Another mother.

"Does that mean I can't go back in?" Betsy asks.

Archer puts his arm around her and helps her up. "There's only nine minutes left and we're up by three, killer. I think you can sit the rest out."

"Nooooo," Betsy whines, and tears finally gather in her eyes.

"Kicked in the head? Fine. Benched? Tears," Madeline says

with a nervous laugh as she slings her arm around Betsy's shoulders. The child is sandwiched between Archer and her mother, rolling her eyes and staring forlornly at the scoreboard.

"She's got the heart of champion," Archer says. "And the forehead of a heavyweight boxer."

Everyone is laughing and joking as they lead Betsy off the field, but I'm rooted to the grass. My heart rate is climbing, my chest tightening. My feet and hands begin to tingle. As my breath starts coming in faster gasps, I try to ground myself, trying desperately to remember the techniques my therapist gave me back in residency, but they're all just out of reach.

I scan the field, my gaze jumping from Betsy to Archer to Madeline to the scoreboard to the parents on the sideline to Wyatt, who is smiling at me, though her brows are knitted together.

But I can't even manage to focus on Wyatt's face. Everything feels a little fuzzy at the edges.

"Owen, are you okay?" Archer asks when he realizes I'm not following them.

I lock eyes with him, then look at Madeline. "You should take her to the ER," I say.

"What?" Archer asks, eyebrows raised.

The smile slips from Madeline's face. "You think so?"

I nod with enough force that it makes my head hurt. "Yeah. You need to get her a CT scan. To be sure."

"She seems okay," Archer says slowly, like he's trying not to frighten an angry bear. "Just a bump. We can watch her."

"No. You need to go," I insist. I feel sweat rolling down my back and gathering at my temples.

"I know concussion protocol, Owen," Archer says, his voice taking on that superior-big-brother tone.

"You're not a doctor, Archer," I say through gritted teeth.

"Are you really sure?" Madeline asks, looking from Betsy to me and back again. "The ER is—"

"*Yes.*" I hear my voice getting tight. I squeeze my fists at my sides like I can hold back the rush of anxiety with brute force. "You never know. Okay? You just…you never know."

There's a beat of silence, and I'm not totally sure what's happening around me. Everyone is just standing there. There's not listening. They should be going to the emergency room. They're not *going*.

"Please," I say, or maybe the word gets caught in my throat. I can't tell, because there's a ringing in my ears that's overpowering everything else.

"Okay," Madeline says with a short nod, her voice shaking slightly. She pulls Betsy closer to her. "Okay. I'll take her."

It should make me feel better, but I take one look at the fear on her face—fear *I* put there—and all I can see is the terror of another mother three years ago.

She's going, I tell myself. I repeat it like a mantra. *She's going*. If there's a problem, they'll catch it. Betsy will be fine.

She'll be *fine*.

"Owen?"

A hand falls on my arm, and I feel Wyatt at my side. Archer says something, but I don't hear it. I'm focusing on my breathing, chasing the panic away with all my might.

"Owen, let's go sit down, okay?"

Wyatt hooks her arm through mine and steers me over to the sideline. As we walk, I hear a whistle blow, and red and blue jerseys streak past me.

"That was really scary," she says.

"Yeah," I say, the word grinding past the lump in my throat. I try to breathe out, but it feels like all my air is trapped in my chest.

"Can I get you anything?"

I watch Madeline gather her bag and walk with Betsy toward the parking lot. *She's going*, I repeat again, and watch to make sure.

"Owen? How about a drink of water? You're sweating," Wyatt says.

"Yeah, it's really hot," I say, turning my focus to her. She's smiling at me like she's trying to comfort a kid who just woke from a nightmare, but she's also chewing on her bottom lip. I can feel myself coming apart, but I summon everything I have and try to smile back at her. "Water would be good."

Wyatt pulls a dripping bottle from the cooler. I take it from her, but I know as soon as it's in my hand that this isn't going to help me. It's not going to give me enough air or slow down my heart or make my thoughts stop racing, and it's not going to take the worry off Wyatt's face. I need to relax. I need to calm the fuck down.

I glance around and see people trying to avoid looking at me. I'm freaking everyone out.

Fuck, I need to get hold of myself.

I need to get *hold* of my myself.

About fifty yards off the field, I spot the little brick park bathroom. "I'll be right back," I tell Wyatt, and uncap the water bottle. I take a long pull and swallow hard to get it past the boulder in my throat. "I just need to wash my hands."

Her brows knit together. "Do you want me to come—"

"I'll be right back," I tell her again, already striding away. Everything is whirling around inside me, screwing up tight. I'm scared that if I let go, I'll spin out like a top.

And I can't let her see that.

I stride toward the bathrooms as fast as I can without actually breaking into a run. I bypass the door and head around to the back of the building where no one can see me but the trees. I lean forward, pressing my palms to the warm brick. I drop my head.

And I breathe.

In for four.

Hold for four.

Out for four.

Hold for four.

It takes a few rounds before I'm actually able to hold any breath at all. Another couple of rounds before I feel like my heart isn't trying to take flight. A few rounds after that before my vision clears and my ears stop ringing.

I keep breathing in the box pattern and feel the tension begin to recede a little. I breathe and count until it no longer feels like my heart is trying to Hulk out of my chest, until the world stops vibrating, until I'm sure I'm not going to throw up.

I breathe until the face of Dylan Anders and his mother's screams recede back into the dark corners of my memory.

I haven't had a panic attack like this in years. Not since I worked in the emergency room. I haven't even felt the tight grip of extreme stress since Wyatt came storming into my life.

I thought everything was good.

But seeing Betsy get kicked, seeing her go down like that—it triggered all those memories.

But I breathed, I remind myself before the knot of tension can tighten again.

And I fixed it.

When I stand back up, I am exhausted, like I could take a ten-year nap. My body feels like it's filled with wet sand, and it takes a herculean effort to walk. Every part of me wants to get into my truck, drive straight home, crawl into bed, and stay there until tomorrow.

Instead, I pick up the water bottle and chug. I run my hands through my hair. I roll out my shoulders. I practice smiling.

And then I head back to the field.

CHAPTER 30

WYATT

Owen is doing a really good impression of someone who isn't freaking out.

I mean, I get it. Just the memory of the sound of a foot connecting with Betsy's head makes me shudder. It sounded like the kind of injury that should have required an ambulance and lots of stitches.

But Betsy got right to her feet, walking easily off the field. Even though she was crying, I heard her begging to go back in the game.

When Owen came back from the bathroom, he had a smile plastered on his face. He chatted amiably with people as he made his way back to his spot. Everyone seems to have forgotten that minutes ago, his nerves got the best of him.

But not me.

And from the look of him, not him, either.

He spends the rest of the game scanning the field like a lifeguard searching for a drowning child. As the seconds tick by, I see his shoulders creeping upward, the flex of his jaw.

He may be fooling everyone else, but something is clearly off with him.

"Is Owen okay?" I ask Grace.

"Yeah, why?" She doesn't even look up from snapping lids on Tupperware as she packs up the remains of her brunch, now mostly decimated by spectators.

"He seems upset."

Grace finally looks up, squinting into the sun to inspect Owen. He's standing ramrod straight, his muscles bunched.

"I mean, he's always pretty intense about his job," she says with a shrug. "He's one of those guys who's really focused, but he doesn't let that get in the way of being a person, you know? He's probably got his shit figured out more than the rest of us."

Grace would know better than me, having grown up with him. But Owen doesn't look focused to me.

He looks terrified.

When the whistle blows and the Cardinals win 3–0, the players dogpile their goalie while Archer shakes hands with the opposing coach.

Hazel comes skidding across the grass, a sleeping Eden in the carrier on her back.

"I got it!" she says in a hushed squeal, which is ridiculous, because the kid hasn't been awoken by any of the whistles or raucous cheers. When Eden goes out, she really goes out. "Twenty hours a week, some in the office and some out in the field, working on the landscaping for parks around the entire county! And if the budget comes through in time, she said I can help design the new butterfly garden at Henry Park!"

Despite her attempts to be calm and quiet for Eden, my sister is practically vibrating with excitement. And I'm so happy for her that she's managed to have Eden and still pursue her dream. When Libby left, Hazel started taking care of the haphazard array of plants in the yard with an almost religious zeal. I watched her bring them to life, design new garden beds, and scour free listings for stones to make paths. My bookish little sister applied every bit of her smarts to turning our tiny patch of grass into a colorful wonderland. And that tenacity is still burning bright, both in how she cares for Eden and how she works to build her career.

"That's so great, Haze!" I say, pulling her into a hug. "I can talk to Ernie about lining up our schedules so I can be home with Eden when you're working."

As if summoned, my niece wakes with a grunt and a squeak that quickly becomes a squall when the sun hits her little eyes. I pull her out of the carrier, bouncing her on my hip.

"Actually, I was thinking Mom could do it," Hazel says, taking the baby from me.

I scoff. "Seriously?"

"Yeah. I mean, she's great with Eden, and you've already rearranged your life so much for us. I want you to be able to have some space." She glances over my shoulder, and I turn to see Owen, the med bag slung over his shoulder, heading our way.

"You sure you can trust her?" The thought of relying on Libby to arrange her schedule in advance, to show up when she's needed, to take care of Eden at all feels like expecting your cat to make you dinner.

Hazel sighs. "Wyatt, you've got to start cutting her some slack. She's doing everything she's supposed to do. She's only got six more months of parole before she's released to probation."

"Assuming she doesn't fuck up before that," I mutter. "I wouldn't take that bet."

"Come on, Wy," Hazel says, a warning in her voice, but I don't have to argue with her, because Owen arrives and slings an arm around me.

"How's my favorite patient?" Owen asks, smiling at Eden. She squeals at him, and Owen and Hazel fall into a conversation about babyproofing. On the surface he's his usual smiling, helpful self. But his fingers are tapping out a near frantic rhythm on my shoulder. When I glance up, I see the flex of his jaw, the effort in his smile.

"Okay, well, Mom and I are going to head home if I can pry

her away from Felix," Hazel says with a not-at-all-annoyed eye roll. "She's asking him about remodeling our kitchen."

"She's not touching that kitchen," I practically growl.

"I think she's just interested in talking to a strapping young McBride boy." Hazel smiles as if this is hilarious and not disgusting.

"Please go rescue him," I beg.

"I'm on it!"

Hazel trots off with the carrier flopping against her back and Eden bouncing on her hip, expertly intercepting Libby.

"She's so good with people," I say, watching as she steers our mother away from Felix and toward the car. "It's weird how attached she is to working with plants."

"Sometimes your strengths and your passions don't quite align," Owen replies. He slips his hand into mine.

"You doing okay?" I ask.

Owen smiles, but his eyebrows are heading toward his hairline. "Yeah, why?"

"Because Betsy took a pretty gnarly cleat to the head and you had to deal with it," I say. "It was a lot."

"It's my job, Wyatt," he says, and even though he's still smiling, his voice sounds low and tight.

"I know. And you're great at it. I've seen you with Eden. You're incredible with kids," I say. "But that doesn't mean scary situations stop being scary."

"I'm fine," he says like he's slamming a door. He starts pulling me toward my truck. "Do you want me to drive to Francie's party this afternoon?"

With all the excitement, I nearly forgot that we're headed to Francie's engagement party in Indianapolis this afternoon.

"Would you rather I drive?" I ask. This conversation suddenly feels like walking through a field of land mines.

"We can do whatever you want, Wyatt," Owen says. He sounds fucking exhausted.

"We could skip it," I offer.

Owen sucks in a breath. "No. I need to go."

"If you're not feeling up to it, you don't have to. I'm sure Francie will understand."

Owen's jaw is set. "I'm going. She's my best friend, she's always been there for me, and I can go to a party for her," he says, and I can't tell if he's trying to convince me or himself. He takes a deep breath and lets it out hard. "I'm fine. It was a tense moment, but everything is fine."

"You keep saying *fine* like that's the best you can be," I say.

"You can drive," he says, ignoring that. "The party's at five, so pick me up at four, okay?"

"Sure," I say as we approach my truck.

He reaches for the door and opens it. "You should lock this," he says, sounding almost exasperated.

"And you should take a nap," I snap, my frustration getting the best of me.

"Yeah" is all he says before shutting the door on me.

And then he's gone.

CHAPTER 31
WYATT

"You don't have to be nervous," Owen says as we approach the grand brick two-story house with hulking white columns, one of the biggest, most impressive homes on an already-grand stretch of North Meridian in Indianapolis.

I want to tell him that it's not the house that's making me nervous or the fact that we're about to walk into the engagement party of his ex-girlfriend. It's the fact that not six hours ago, I watched this man have what looked an awful lot like a panic attack. It's the fact that rather than talking about it, we spent the drive up here listening to one and half Debbie tapes (both from when the relationship was going well, if all the Boyz II Men is to be believed). It's the fact that he's practically pulling muscles trying to smile, to laugh, to pretend that everything is absolutely fine.

As if I wouldn't notice the way he keeps flexing his fingers in his lap, like he can't hold them still. Or the rhythmic tic in his jaw. Or the way he keeps staring off into the middle distance, lost inside a deluge of thoughts he's expending every ounce of energy to hold back.

"I'm fine," I say, and then jump a little when a young guy in black pants and a red vest suddenly appears at my window, his hand out.

"Valet," Owen says.

"Right." I dig through my purse and hand over my keychain, wishing I had time to pull the car key off the ring of keys that open various locks at the Half Pint. But maybe the grandeur of the house *is* getting to me, because I just hand the whole jangly mess over. I get out of the truck, and as the teenage valet hops in, I smooth the ruffled hem of the floral sundress I borrowed from Hazel. "This party seriously has *valet*?"

"Josh's mom is a top executive at a pharmaceutical company, and his dad is a plastic surgeon," Owen says, and hooks my arm into the crook of his elbow. "They were both a little disappointed that Josh decided to be an ER doctor."

"Okay, so give me one more rundown," I say, pausing at the foot of the steps leading up to the door. I can hear the tinkling of a piano that's definitely being played live. The polite hum of chatter floats through the windows. There's a floral arch over the door, spilling blooms and greenery onto the wide porch. For some reason when Owen said "engagement party," I pictured a back-yard barbecue situation: someone's dad standing over a grill, a buffet table with a red-and-white checkered tablecloth.

I did not picture *Bridgerton* meets *Succession*.

"Francie and Josh and I all met in med school. We did our residencies together. Francie and I dated for a couple of years during residency, but we broke up in our third year," he says.

I want to ask why, but that doesn't feel like a casual question when we're seconds from walking into her engagement party. And when Owen is already vibrating at such a high frequency.

"Josh is so obviously the one for her." As he says it, he seems to relax for the first time since this morning. There's a genuine smile pulling at his lips. "And thank god they realized it, because now here we are."

I've never seen a man so sincerely delighted by his ex-girl-friend's happiness.

Someone—a cater waiter? A party planner?—wordlessly opens the door just as we approach, welcoming us into a grand marble-floored foyer filled with even more flowers.

"Most of the people here are probably doctors, I'm sorry to say." Owen guides me through the entrance. "A lot of med school and residency people. Francie and Josh both got full-time jobs at Riley Children's when they finished, so our friend group stayed pretty solid."

But you left? The question is right there on the tip of my tongue, but I bite it back. This party coupled with the scene at the soccer game this morning suddenly has me realizing how little I know about Owen. I thought he was such an open book, but all this time he's kept the attention on me, conveniently avoiding sharing details about his past.

"Owen!" A beautiful, petite Black woman, her hair pulled back in a tight bun, comes rushing through the crowd, arms out, a stunning goldenrod chiffon dress practically floating around her. She engulfs him in a hug so full of warmth and happiness that I feel a frizzle of joy just watching it. "I'm so glad you're here."

Owen sinks into the hug, finally seeming to let out a breath. Then Francie steps back and pivots to me with a wide smile.

"And you must be Wyatt," she says. "I'm a hugger. Can I a hug you?"

"Sure," I tell her, and I've barely gotten the word out before she pulls me in. She hugs me with the same warmth she lavished on Owen, and her embrace actually calms the undercurrent of anxiety I've been feeling all day.

I like her instantly.

"I wish I didn't have to charm a bunch of old white CEOs at this thing, because I'd much rather be in a corner with a margarita learning why this man is so obsessed with you," she says with a wicked grin.

"Francie," Owen warns, but he's smiling too, the tension of this morning melting off of him.

"What? I'm your best friend, that's my job," Francie says.

"Well, I'm happy to give you the bullet points real fast," I tell her. "I'm cool as shit, funny as hell, and I do this thing with my tongue—"

"Oh my god, the two of you together are lethal," Owen groans.

Francie cackles. "We have *got* to arrange a double date," she says to Owen.

A tall, thin white man strides over, and from his confidence and the comfort he seems to have with both Francie and this house, I assume this must be Josh. The man looks like a J.Crew model, all blond and blue-eyed and plaid-shirted. He definitely owns more than a few fleece vests and actually looks good in them.

"Excuse me, folks, but my great-grandmother just arrived," he says, trying for a comical grimace, but he's completely unable to tamp down the wide smile that overtakes his face as he makes eye contact with his future bride. God, Owen was right—it's obvious these two are made for each other. "Unfortunately we have to go genuflect."

"Lemme at her," Francie says with a feisty grin. "Grandparents *love* me."

She pulls Owen into another quick hug and whispers something in his ear that makes him smile. Then she gives me a quick wave and makes me promise we'll hang out soon before disappearing into the crowd with Josh.

———

The party is lovely—the drinks are free-flowing, and the food is next-level—but two hours later, I have to admit I'm tapped out. I've had to delicately remove myself from a man in the over-seventy set who kept trying to touch my tattoos, but mostly it's been doctors. So. Many. Doctors.

And do you know what doctors like to do when they're drinking together?

Tell truly disgusting stories.

I learned about a guy who was brought in by ambulance because he was found bleeding in a grocery store, only for the doctors to cut off his pants and discover they were stuffed with raw steaks. There was a woman who was brought in from the airport because TSA spotted a bomb in her vagina on the X-ray machine. They brought a bomb squad into the operating room, but it turned out it was just a lighter. She was a very dedicated smoker, apparently, and I remain filled with questions.

And people put *so* many things up their asses. I'm not usually one to yuck someone's yum, but oh my god. A whole apple? A light bulb? A fucking *hamster?* Humanity is so much more fucked up than I thought.

And throughout the conversation about ass accoutrements and other emergency room disasters, Owen remains loose. He laughs and smiles, sipping on a series of beers, but he doesn't say much. He tells no horror stories, and honestly, that makes me respect him more. His patients don't deserve to be cocktail party fodder.

A lanky white guy yawns—he works at Cook County Hospital in Chicago and has the most horrific stories of the lot. "You know, Owen," he says, "you were smart to go into private practice. Better hours, much less stress. Way to get out while you could."

Owen nods and gives a little laugh, and I think I'm the only one who notices it's a bit brittle. "Always thinking ahead," he says, then tosses back the rest of his beer. "If you'll excuse me, I'm going to hit the restroom."

He gives my elbow a squeeze, then disappears into the crowd.

"I'm so glad he settled down," the woman next to me says. I think her name is Mira? Maura? When she introduced herself, I was too busy trying not to stare at the bloodred lipstick on her obvious veneers. She's been eyeing me all night, noting every time Owen touches me, her pointed gaze on my tattoos. She leans into me now, talking like she's got a secret, and it's all I can do not to step away from her cloud of sickly sweet perfume. "That thing third year was so wild. We were all so worried he'd, like, quit medicine and go work on an oil rig or something."

Her overdrawn lips curl into a Cheshire Cat grin, her high-lighter catching the glow of the antique chandelier overhead. And I realize this is some kind of power move. Mira can barely control her face as she watches me to see how I'm going to respond. If I'm going to ask, *What thing third year?* And even though I want to, I will not give this bitch the satisfaction.

"He loves his patients," I tell her, which has the benefit of being true. "He's doing great."

But in the back of my mind, a tiny voice says, *But is he really?* His reaction at the soccer field revealed the wear at his seams.

"Well, that's good," Mira says, like she doesn't believe it. Like she wants to coax me into giving her some dirt.

Before she can say anything else, I take a step back. "If you'll excuse me, I'm going to freshen my drink," I say, then place my empty champagne glass on the tray of a passing waiter and melt into the crowd.

I circulate a few times, thinking maybe Owen got drawn into a conversation with one of the silver-haired executives or some other doctors, but I don't find him.

"Excuse me, where's the bathroom?" I ask a waiter, who points me down a hallway.

I turn the corner and run into Francie.

"I'm peopled out," she explains, leaning against a wall beside a painting that looks like it came from a garage sale but is probably worth more than my house.

"I don't blame you. This party is something else," I say.

"The one my parents are throwing up in Gary is going to be much more relaxed," she says. "Their work colleagues are all middle school teachers and bus drivers, and the food will be served in disposable trays. I can't wait."

"Sounds much more my speed," I confess.

"Mine too," she says. "Don't get me wrong, I love Josh's

parents, but they become different people entirely when it comes to stuff like this. I just accept it and move on."

I nod.

"Hey, so I saw you talking to Mina. I should probably do some damage control," Francie says. I realize she means Mira/Maura, she of the gaudy makeup and the fake sympathy. "That witch was always trying to get Owen in an on-call room. I only invited her because she's dating Josh's best friend from undergrad."

I shrug, because Mina/Mira/Maura didn't really get to me. Not in the way she intended, anyway. Mostly she just made me more concerned about Owen.

"Hey, Francie, can I ask you something? What happened during third year?"

Francie sighs. "That's not my story to tell, but Owen lost a patient, and it really fucked with him. Like, beyond what one would expect. There was a minute where I wasn't sure he'd come back from it."

"But he did?"

She nods. "Eventually. He worked through it."

"Oh. Okay."

"That's not to say he's over it. I'm not sure if you ever get over something like that. You just learn to compartmentalize it."

That doesn't sound like a great strategy. And maybe Owen's compartment isn't big enough to hold the enormity of what happened to him. Maybe something about what happened to Betsy this morning made the door to that compartment spring open, and now some not-great stuff is leaking out.

"Keep an eye on him," Francie says. "He puts on this whole persona of the smiling, happy, calming Superman, steady and strong. He wants to do the saving. He doesn't want anyone to have to save him." After a minute, she adds, "I'm not even sure if he would know if he needed saving."

"Thanks, Francie."

"You're welcome. I like you, Wyatt. You seem like a tough, no-nonsense bitch, but because he's my best friend, I'm obligated to say that if you hurt him, I have plenty of ways to take you down and make it look like an accident, okay?"

She winks as she says it, which takes the edge off the menace, and we both laugh. But I know that Francie is *also* a tough, no-nonsense bitch and that the warning has teeth.

"Now, if you'll excuse me, I need to go schmooze the boomer executives my future in-laws insisted on inviting to this shindig. And just a little pro tip from me to you? When Owen needs a break from peopling, you can usually find him hiding in a bathroom somewhere. Bad news for you is that this place has, like, forty-five of them. But I'd start back there." She points down a small hallway that's mostly full of cater waiters passing in and out of the swinging door to the kitchen.

I wander the first floor, peeking into bathrooms, all the while working up my courage to ask Owen some questions. About third year. About the panic attack. About why he feels the need to hide this stuff behind that brittle smile. He doesn't need to hide from me. This wasn't supposed to be a relationship, what we have, but it's obvious that it's become one when we weren't looking. And if we're going to have a relationship, I'd like him to trust me enough to tell me the truth. To show me the whole unvarnished mess of him.

I look in three bathrooms before I find him in a little powder room tucked back by the sunroom. The door is shut, but I take a swing and knock.

"Occupied," he calls through the door.

"Zip up, because I'm coming in," I reply.

The door swings open immediately, because Owen isn't actually *using* the bathroom, just sitting on the toilet lid doing a *New York Times* crossword puzzle.

"You know, we can just leave. You don't need to haunt these people's very ugly bathroom," I say, eyeing the sad-looking French peasants herding sheep on the toile wallpaper.

He laughs, arranging his perfect Owen smile on his face, and it's all I can do not to tell him to cut the shit. I don't need the perfect happy Owen. I just need *Owen*, cracks and all. But the man looks like he's trying so fucking hard to hold on to his sanity, and to take that away from him would probably only wound him further.

"Or we can talk," I say. I glance over my shoulder and see that we're alone in this tiny, tucked-away hall.

I brace for him to blow me off, to say we need to get back to the party, to pretend.

But he surprises me by standing up and wrapping his hand around my wrist, giving me a tug. I tumble into the tiny bathroom with him, landing flush against his chest. He reaches past me, his hand brushing my hip, and pulls the door shut, flipping the lock.

"I have a better idea," he says, and that fake smile suddenly becomes something a whole hell of a lot sexier.

"A bathroom quickie? With all these eighteenth-century peasants watching us?" I nod at the wallpaper.

"Then I better do some of my best work," he says. He ducks his chin and starts peppering the underside of my jaw with soft kisses and swipes of his tongue. Then he spins me around, placing my hands on the marble countertop. I catch sight of him in the mirror, his eyes dark and full of hunger.

"I've been wanting to flip this frilly little dress up since the moment I saw it," he growls into my ear, dragging the gauzy fabric through his fingers.

I wanted to talk, but it's clear Owen doesn't want that. He wants this, and isn't this what I promised him? Wasn't this our agreement? No strings? No relationship?

"Don't threaten me with a good time," I reply, my voice husky with need. Because even amidst my hesitations, I still want him more than should be legal. Does the DEA know about the potent affects of Owen McBride? Do they know what it feels like to want him? Because feeling his hands coast over my hips, gliding down between my thighs and fisting my lace panties so tightly I'm half worried he'll rip them, half desperate for him to…it feels dangerous.

"I want to destroy these," he says, giving the lace a tug. "I want you to walk out of this fancy-ass party wet and bare and defiled."

"What's stopping you?" I ask, eyebrow arched.

His only response is to jerk his hand and the tear the lace. He raises the fabric to his face and inhales, then shoves it in his pocket, never taking his eyes off mine in the mirror. And I'm riveted to his gaze like I'm under a spell, like he's pulling my strings. When he kicks at my heels, I widen my stance. When he presses down between my shoulder blades, I lower myself onto my elbows, tossing my hair back so I don't lose sight of him.

He reaches into his back pocket and pulls out his wallet, dropping it onto the marble countertop.

"Open it," he says, and like I'm in a trance, I flip it open. It's clear to me now that this is what Owen needs: a sense of control. It may not be honesty and conversation, confession and absolution, but it's something only I can give him.

"Find the condom," he says.

"You brought a condom to this party?"

Owen leans down, licking the shell of my ear, before he growls, "Wyatt, do you not understand that I *always* want you? Everywhere? That you're *mine*?"

The words send a wave of heat through my body, and I pull the condom from between some twenty-dollar bills and hold it up to him. I'm breathing hard, my eyelids heavy as the desire for this man overtakes me.

It takes him seconds to sheath himself, and with his eyes still on me, he fists his cock and enters me in one hard, fast thrust.

I drop my head into my hands to stifle my moan.

"Eyes on me, Wyatt." His voice is a low scrape that raises goose bumps along my arms. I lift my head and meet his eyes in the mirror, his gaze pinning me there.

His hands clasp my hips and he goes to work, the rough, hard slide of him drawing me closer and closer to madness. But every time my eyes begin to drift closed, he stills, his hand fisting my hair until I look up, meet his dark gaze.

"Do you want to come?" he asks me, his fingers flexing, the most delicious tug at my roots nearly driving me to orgasm.

"Yes," I moan, beg, plead.

He folds himself over me until he's in my ear again. "Fingers on your clit, Wyatt."

The command is nearly too much, but I do what he asks, reaching down, my fingers slipping over the wetness. I press in soft circles, my lips parted as I careen closer and closer to oblivion.

"That's it, pretty girl," he growls. "Let me watch you. Eyes on me."

There's a split second where I don't think I can do it. I'm not sure I can come while I watch him. Standing there on the edge of an explosive orgasm, my eyes nearly squeeze shut against the explosion of pleasure, but I force myself to maintain eye contact in the mirror. To let him see me.

I *want* him to see me.

And the instant I feel the release, the flood of pleasure coursing through my body, Owen bites my earlobe before he rumbles, "Good girl."

And then he follows me over the edge.

CHAPTER 32

WYATT

I ran into Madeline and Betsy at Pete's this morning. Betsy made the girl who kicked her in the head sign her bruise

In Sharpie

Madeline was thrilled

OWEN

She seemed okay?

WYATT

Madeline said all clear from the ER

I asked Betsy what nine times seven was

I can't be sure if she was correct because truth be told, I don't actually know the answer

OWEN

63

WYATT

Good looks AND brains? I'm a lucky girl

JUNE 8 AT 5:22 PM

OWEN

You're not working tonight, right?

WYATT

Free and clear, my man

OWEN

Wanna come over for dinner?

WYATT

Can we have pizza?

OWEN

Can I put a vegetable on it?

WYATT

In your dreams, McBride

OWEN

You're lucky you're cute

WYATT

YOU'RE lucky I'm cute

OWEN

Ain't that the truth

JUNE 15 AT 7:32 PM

WYATT

Bad news. Jonah's got food poisoning, so I'm staying to close

OWEN

Booo. I wish I could stay up, but the last two on-call nights have kicked my ass. I'm exhausted

There's a key under mat. Just let yourself in
when you're done

WYATT

Quite the fortress of security you guys have there

OWEN

You gonna rob me, Wyatt?

WYATT

You gonna punish me for it?

OWEN

Only if you ask nicely

CHAPTER 33
OWEN

June 29

FRANCIE

I still cannot believe you had a bathroom quickie at my engagement party!

In my future in-laws' house!

I don't know if anyone's ever had sex in that house

OWEN

Haven't you and Josh?

FRANCIE

Fuck no. His mother scares the shit out of me. We sneak out to the pool house like respectable adults

I like Wyatt, by the way

OWEN

Me too

I don't tell anybody about the panic attack. Not Wyatt, not Francie, not Felix. I tell myself that if it happens again, I'll call the therapist I saw when I was in residency, maybe set up a Telehealth appointment or get a referral to someone closer to Cardinal Springs.

But I don't. Betsy is fine, things are smooth at work, and gradually the aftershocks fade.

And anytime I feel the tight fist of anxiety start to squeeze my chest, I call up the image of Wyatt's reflection in that gaudy gold mirror, her cheeks flushed with pleasure, her lips swollen and pink, pressed together to suppress a moan as she came on my cock.

With her eyes open. It was the most beautiful thing I've ever seen.

So I'm fine.

And when I spot her across my dad's backyard, her curls brushing the ink on her bare shoulders, tipping her head back to laugh at some joke my twin brother is telling, I feel better than fine.

I feel fucking fantastic.

The can of pineapple with our hastily scrawled contract sits on the mantel in my living room. If Felix has seen it, he hasn't said anything. Neither has Wyatt, which is interesting, because the "rules" have been evaporated into a mist at this point.

She's melted into my life such that I'm not sure I could extract her if I tried. And she doesn't seem to mind. Most nights when she gets off at work, if she's not needed back at her house to help Hazel with Eden, she lets herself into mine and slides into the bed beside me, folding herself into my body and dragging my arm across her waist. Sometimes I peel down her panties and set about making her moan, but sometimes I just pull her in tight, nestle my nose into the mess of her curls, and fall back asleep to the rhythm of her breaths.

This was supposed to be no strings attached, but there are strings everywhere. And they're getting tangled.

I keep waiting for her to notice, to rear up, to pull back, to drag that pineapple can off the mantel and shake it at me, reminding me of our agreement.

I can't tell if she's forgotten or if she's changed her mind.

I don't dare ask.

Instead, I let myself enjoy the way she lights up when she catches me looking at her. I watch the curl of her lips as her smile turns into a naughty smirk. I relish the sassy sway of her hips as she crosses the yard.

I feel myself fall in love with her when, despite being surrounded by our families and closest friends, she slips her hand into mine.

I am so very much in breach of contract with this woman.

"What are you doing all the way over here, Doc?" she asks.

"Ignoring me, that's for damn sure," Decker grumbles, and it's only then that I remember I'm standing next to my sister's boyfriend. He was telling me something about…fuck, I wasn't listening.

"What's the matter, hometown hero?" I tease him. "Can't handle not being the center of attention?"

My father's postage stamp of a backyard is packed with people balancing paper plates full of deliciousness courtesy of Dad, who's been manning the grill all afternoon. Summer has settled into Cardinal Springs, hot air lying over the town like a wet flannel blanket. Everyone is coated in a sheen of sweat and sunscreen, some cheeks already pink after a morning spent standing on Main Street to watch Decker drive by in a convertible, Grace by his side, the Stanley Cup sitting between them.

Because just last week, Decker led his hockey team to his third Stanley Cup victory, then promptly announced his retirement.

And now that trophy sits on a table in the center of the celebration, a man in white gloves guarding it to make sure nobody does anything untoward with it. Which apparently doesn't include

Decker pouring an entire case of Upland into it and passing out sips like this is some kind of holy jock communion.

That, I was surprised to discover, is perfectly allowed.

"Fuck off," Decker says, but he's grinning. I think he's taking this retirement thing pretty well. "I'm just trying to relay details so I can go stare at *my* girl."

"Is this about Grace's birthday?" Wyatt asks, letting go of my hand and slipping hers into my back pocket. It makes my vision go fuzzy. "Carson was telling me: Indianapolis, cake, karaoke."

Decker nods. "Yeah. I reserved a bunch of hotel rooms for everybody. I just need to know if you guys want to be together or not."

I nearly choke on my beer. Do we want to be *together?*

If you're asking me, absolutely yes.

Do *we* want to be together, though?

I glance down at Wyatt.

"Actually, I told Carson I'd bunk with her," she says. "I don't want her to be alone."

Record scratch.

Fuck.

"Great. Okay. Perfect." Decker blows out a quick, hard breath like he's warming up for Game Seven, not standing in the middle of his victory party. "I don't have to tell you what a big deal this is. Grace has *never* agreed to a real birthday party. I want everything to be perfect."

"You think *I* need this warning? Go talk to Felix. He's much more likely to pick up half a bachelorette party in Indy and cause a scene," I tell Decker.

"Oh, I intend to," Decker says, narrowing his eyes at my brother. "Enjoy the party."

"Congrats, man." I nod at the Stanley Cup, which is currently holding a grinning baby Eden.

Decker smiles. "That's the only prize I care about," he says, pointing across the lawn at where Grace is snapping a photo of Eden in the Cup.

And then he charges across the lawn to claim her.

If he weren't talking about my baby sister, I'd probably melt.

"That's okay, right? If I stay with Carson?" Wyatt asks once we're alone.

No. I hate it. Even if a few bricks have been removed, there's still a wall between us. And I want all of this woman. Every piece. Watching her come with her eyes on me was so very close to everything I need. I just wish that mirror hadn't been between us.

I want her connected to me in every way.

But I signed that pineapple can. I promised her. So I keep all that to myself.

"Of course," I lie. "Just as long as you promise to sneak over for a late-night visit."

She grins the grin that tells me we're going to have a *very* good time, and that takes the edge off the revelation that she's staying with Carson.

"What else is a bad girl gonna do but sneak into the good boy's hotel room?"

CHAPTER 34

OWEN

July 15

"Hey, Owen, can you listen to this cough?"

I'm standing in Wyatt's living room, waiting while she finishes throwing things in a suitcase for Grace's birthday party in Indianapolis. We're only staying one night, but when I peeked into her room, it looked like a bomb had exploded inside a laundry basket, covering the room in soft, cozy shrapnel. I made the mistake of asking her how long she'd be, and the look she gave me made me back away slowly.

Now I'm waiting for her in the living room.

Hazel is standing in the doorway to the kitchen, Eden perched on her hip. The baby's cheeks are rosy, her nosy runny, but the mucus clear.

"What cough?" I ask, and then Eden does me the favor of demonstrating. It's a classic, unmistakable barky cough that I hear over and over in the winter.

"Sounds like croup," I say. "Does she have a fever?"

Hazel shakes her head.

"She eating and drinking okay?

"She's fine. It's just the cough." Eden lets another fit rip, and Hazel cringes. "It sounds so awful."

I nod. "It really does. But if she's in good spirits, she's eating and drinking, and she doesn't have a fever, the only thing to do is manage the cough as best you can. You can turn the shower on as hot as it goes and stand in the steam. It'll help open her airways. Just keep her upright."

Eden coughs again.

"You sure, Doc? Sounds pretty bad," Libby says, padding into the room in slippers, wincing.

"If she gets a fever, manage it with Tylenol or ibuprofen. If anything changes you can call me," I tell them. "She might have a rough time sleeping tonight, but she should be fine."

Wyatt finally emerges, dragging a rolling suitcase with the corner of something sparkly sticking out the side, the zipper not fully zipped.

"Good night, my little Typhoid Mary," Wyatt says, chucking Eden under the chin and planting a kiss on the top of her head. Eden gives her auntie a smile, then launches into another coughing fit.

"I'm off to the shower," Hazel sighs, hoisting Eden higher on her hip.

"I'll make sure we have Tylenol," Libby says.

"Call me if anything changes, okay?" I call after Hazel.

"Will do!"

"I thought Fatima was on call tonight," Wyatt says. "What with you being an hour away, drinking champagne with me."

"She is, but this is the kind of service you get when your sister is boning your pediatrician," I tell Wyatt with a kiss.

"Boning? Is that what this is?" Wyatt laughs.

"Tonight? I fucking hope so." I pull my keys from my pocket and twirl the keychain on my finger. "You ready to go?"

Wyatt smiles, then bats her eyes at me like a cartoon character. "Can I drive? Please? Pretty please?"

I sigh. "At some point we're going to have to discuss your need for control behind the wheel," I say.

"I give you control at other times," she says with a devilish grin and waggle of her eyebrows.

"Damn right," I growl, slapping her ass. "If I get a tape deck installed in my truck, will you let me drive?"

"The Debbie tapes won't sound right without the lo-fi disaster that is my twenty-five-year-old sound system," she says. "You won't get the true depth of his affection or the misery of his heartbreak."

I cock an eyebrow at her. "Your logic is far from sound."

"My logic doesn't need to be sound because my ass is round like a peach," she says with a wink, and *that's* logic that stands.

CHAPTER 35

WYATT

The party has been a smashing success, as evidenced by the perma-grin on my best friend's face. Carson and I have been on high alert so that in case she hit a bad patch, needed a weepy grief moment, we could whisk her off. But her karaoke picks have been nothing but joyful, off-key love songs aimed at the man who reserved a penthouse suite for us to party in.

Now the celebration is winding down, the cake reduced to crumbs on dessert plates scattered around the room. Way too many empty bottles of way-too-expensive champagne litter the suite, and everyone is starting to yawn from the effects of that many bubbles and that much aerobic dancing.

I'm nestled into an oversize leather couch, leaning into Owen, our fingers entwined. His chest is rising and falling in a comforting rhythm, his warm breath shifting the ends of my curls against my neck. My voice is scratchy from belting out "I Will Always Love You" (the Dolly version, obviously), followed by a slew of Destiny's Child hits with Grace and Carson.

"Okay, I think I should probably head to bed," Carson says, rising from an armchair. I watch the way Dan's eyes track the hem of her sparkly tiered skirt, which rises up her thighs as she stretches, but when he catches me looking, his eyes darken and return to the rocks glass clutched in his fist.

And then I remember that I'm supposed to go with her, and my heart sinks. I'm not ready to climb out of Owen's arms yet. But Carson is a little wobbly in her heels, and I'm not about to let her wander through this hotel alone.

"I'm coming with," I say, taking a deep breath like I'm trying to store up the feeling of Owen before I retire to my bed.

Alone.

Fuck.

Being a good friend is fucking hard sometimes.

"Me too!" Grace trills, her voice slippery from the champagne. "I want a girls' good night."

"I'll get everything squared away up here," Decker says. He leans in for a kiss, then nips at her cheek. "Don't be too long."

And on that obviously suggestive note, the party ends. We cram into the elevator, half giddy, half exhausted.

Owen is behind me, his large hands resting on my hips as I lean back into him, my arousal growing right along with his.

"You're going to sneak over for a visit, right?" he whispers, slipping a hotel keycard into the back pocket of my jeans.

"Dear god yes," I say, barely containing a moan.

And then we all tumble out of the elevator and head toward our hotel rooms. The boys each have their own. Carson and I are the only ones sharing, and Grace is hot on our heels as we make our way to the door. I glance over my shoulder to watch Owen key into his room across the hall, tossing me a dangerously smoldering look before he disappears behind the door.

There's a bottle of champagne in a bucket of mostly melted ice, which Decker had waiting for Carson when she arrived. Despite the fact that we're all good and drunk, Grace grabs the neck of the bottle, making surprisingly quick work of the foil and the cage despite her tipsy fingers. Then she pops to cork with a squeal.

"To the birthday girls!" I rasp, my voice well and truly shot.

It's actually Carson's birthday too. For the last twenty-five years, she and Grace have celebrated together; Grace's mother died giving birth to her, and Carson always worked to distract her from the pain and grief the day represented. In the past, the two of them have disappeared for a night of drinking and screaming karaoke, the ensuing hangover allowing Grace to simultaneously hide from her misery and disappear into it.

But this year, now that Decker's by her side and she has finally shared the weight of her grief with her family, she decided to celebrate with everyone she loves.

And while Decker planned this event for Grace, he made sure it still felt like a joint birthday party for the lifelong best friends.

"Okay, let's get down to business," Carson says, knocking back an entire glass of champagne in one swallow. Then she turns to me. "Why the hell is your suitcase in this room?"

"Wait, *what*?" I sputter. I'm buzzed to high heaven, but I'm not trying to get so drunk that I can't sneak into Owen's room and have my way with him.

"There is a man staying across the hall who wants nothing more than to have your suitcase on *his* floor. So why are you *here*?"

"I didn't want you to be alone!" I cry.

She rolls her eyes. "Ah, yes. That doesn't make me feel at all pathetic."

"Hey, don't talk about my best friend like that," Grace slurs.

"I'm just saying, I'm not looking forward to sharing a room with you while you silently pine for that giant hunk of pediatrician across the hall. I'd much rather order the entire room service dessert menu and sample everything while watching HGTV."

"But—"

She holds up her finger in a kindergarten teacher *don't you dare* warning. "No. You're not going to use me as some kind of smoke screen to trick yourself into believing you're not in a relationship with that man."

I look at Grace for support, but she practically turns her back on me. "Hey, I'm with her on this one," she says, then hiccups. "I know you have a whole dark and twisty past that makes you fear relationships that you like to keep secret. And that's fine. We're your friends and will love you irre—I mean, regardless. And we'll be here if you ever want to share it. But we're done pretending when it comes to my brother."

"Go *be* with him," Carson pleads.

But I'm still stuck on the "dark and twisty past."

"I'm not trying to hide things from you guys," I say, the alcohol catching up with me and making me feel a touch of melancholy.

"We know, hon," Grace says.

"We figured you'd tell us about it when you were ready," Carson says.

"We've tried to be patient, but it's hard, okay? Because we love you," Grace adds.

Suddenly we all morph into a pack of stereotypical drunk girls weeping into our champagne.

And I tell them. Everything. About Romy and our adventures in Nashville. About meeting Griffin and how the three of us became a trio. About how things slowly began to change after Griffin and I started dating. How he'd disappear and come home smelling like perfume. How girls would show up at the apartment and he'd say they were crazed fans. How he quit his job so he could pursue music and I supported him emotionally *and* financially while he contributed nothing.

And finally, how the night I got the call about Libby's arrest, I walked in on Griffin kissing Romy on our couch.

"And I think the reason I kept Romy at arm's length, even though I *knew* in my heart that she didn't do anything wrong, was that even being reminded of Nashville made me face my greatest failure," I finish.

Carson's champagne glass hits the bedside table with a heavy thud. "Do not give that man that kind of power," she says, her voice lower than I've ever heard it.

I sigh. "It's not even about him, though. Not really. It's that I should have *known* better. I grew up with Libby Hart. I watched her give her heart to a string of men who were more suited to being gas station dumpsters on a hot July afternoon than halfway decent boyfriends. She picked garden-variety jerks, abusers, leeches who took what little she had, and all of them left her in the end. I watched her cry over those assholes. Real honest-to-god tears. And I told myself I'd never let that happen to me. I'd do better. So I should have seen him coming.

"Instead, I ignored it when Griffin quit his job to take gigs even though it meant I had to pick up extra shifts to cover the rent. I explained it away when he came home from a show with lipstick on him or panties in his pocket. I laughed it off when he borrowed my truck and got it towed, then stuck me with the cost of getting it back. When I finally walked in on him kissing Romy, it hit me. *I* had picked him. *I* was the one making excuses for him. *I* had put myself in this situation. I was no better than Libby."

Grace's eyes are watery, but Carson looks furious.

"Fuck off with that," she says finally.

"Carson!" Grace cries.

"What does *that* mean?" I gasp. "I finally pour out my dark and twisty past and you tell me to fuck off?"

Carson settles back against the headboard and sips on her champagne like she didn't just swear at me. "It means fuck off with *that*. With taking responsibility for men who will under no circumstances take responsibility for themselves. With blaming the victim for the atrocious behavior of men—and that includes your mother, by the way. Fuck *off* with that. You're Wyatt Fucking Hart, and some walking case of syphilis disguised as a drugstore cowboy can't take you down."

There's a beat of silence in the hotel room.

"Damn, Carson," I say.

"What? Are you seriously telling me that Griffin Stone still has so much power over you that you're going to let him keep you from a man so good that he's spent several months letting you pretend this is just a hookup even though he's clearly in love with you?"

I open my mouth to reply, but I have no words.

"Truly, Wyatt. Fuck. Off. With. That."

I let out a surprised breath. "Dang, where did all this piss and vinegar come from?" I ask my sweet little kindergarten teacher best friend.

Carson takes the bottle of champagne by the neck and sloshes more into her glass.

"Well, this champagne is certainly hitting me fast," she says, her cheeks rosy. "But mostly I'm just tired of watching my friends tie their shoelaces together and then act confused about why they keep falling down. Romantically speaking."

"Why do I feel like that's directed at me too?" Grace says.

"Because it is. Or it was, anyway, before you figured out that Decker was the perfect man. And thank god for that, because otherwise we'd be spending tonight in that scuzzy karaoke bar in Broad Ripple again, and I love you, Grace, but holding your hair back while you yarf tequila does not a happy birthday make."

"I love you." Grace lunges at Carson, champagne sloshing onto the floor.

"You too," Carson says into Grace's hair. Then she turns to me. "Just...be in love. Don't try to analyze it or handicap it or hide from it. Don't call it something else. Just *be in love*."

CHAPTER 36

OWEN

I'm trying to come up with the perfect dirty text to send Wyatt to convince her to sneak over sooner rather than later.

For a while there, it felt like Wyatt was the thing that calmed the loud voices in my head. She stilled the low-level vibration that thrummed through me at all times.

But lately it's starting to feel like she's her own vibration, and the level is high. I want her all the time. I *need* her.

And I need to stop pretending this is some casual hookup, because the nights she crawls into my bed, I sleep better than I ever have. I love hearing about her day, watching her toss back the most hideous junk food and sip fountain Cokes the size of her head, listening as she tells me what amazing new thing Eden's done.

I need it.

I need *her*.

The knock at my door drags me out of my attempts at creative smut. The room service I ordered must have arrived.

"Coming!" I call as I delete yet another text draft, wondering if I should just give up and type *I need you* into the little box.

But it's not my burger, fries, and Caesar salad at the door.

It's Wyatt.

And her suitcase.

She's breathing hard like she ran here, but that doesn't make sense because the room she's sharing with Carson is just across the hall.

She opens her mouth, then closes it, pressing her pretty pink lips into a firm line. Her gaze drops to the floor, and everything from the flex of her jaw to the set of her shoulders says she's having a very intense conversation with herself.

I want to take her in my arms, pull her into this room, never let her go. I want her to know that I can be whatever she wants, meet her wherever she is. This doesn't need to be hard.

But she looks so determined, my beautiful, brash, sassy girl. She looks fierce, and something tells me that the debate she's having with herself is important.

So I wait.

I watch her breathe. I watch her close her eyes. I watch her clutch the handle of her suitcase.

I watch her.

And when she gives the smallest nod of her head, like she's finished giving herself a pep talk, she looks up to meet my eyes.

I brace for impact.

"Can I stay with you tonight?" she asks.

"You can stay with me forever," I tell her, the words rushing out before I can weigh them, filter them, approve them for public use.

But I mean it, every word.

Her eyes grow wide, and for a moment I worry she's going to run. This is not what we agreed to when we signed that pineapple can. I worry I'm pushing her too far too fast. I don't want to lose her.

But then she smiles, her teeth catching her full lower lip, and whatever she was struggling with lifts off her right before my eyes.

"You know, everyone thinks you're a good boy, Owen

McBride," Wyatt says, stepping forward, craning her neck to look up at me. She presses her palms into my chest, urging me backward, and I let her push me. She releases her suitcase inside the room, the door slamming behind her. "But I happen to know that you've been *very* bad."

"Why is that?" I ask, my heart pounding beneath her touch.

"Because we had a deal," she says. She marches me backward, this tiny little powerhouse, until the backs of my knees hit the bed. I land with a bounce, unable to take my eyes off her. She climbs up onto the bed, settling her knees on either side of my hips before lowering herself slowly—so slowly—into my lap.

"We had a deal," she says, ducking to brush her lips gently across mine. "But then you went and made me fall in love with you."

The words roll over me slowly, then all at once, like a crashing wave. I grab her hips to still her, catching her gaze with mine.

"Wyatt."

She pauses, a smirk on her lips but a question in her eyes. "Too much?"

I can't hold back the laugh that claws its way up my throat. "Wyatt, I think I started falling in love with you back in that roadside bar on that freezing night in January," I tell her. "To hear you say it now is more than enough."

I kiss her, my lips and tongue sliding across hers.

"It's everything," I whisper into her mouth.

"I love you," she whispers as she presses me back onto the mattress, settling her warm little body over mine.

"I love you," I whisper back as I thread my fingers through her hair, angling her lips so I can sweep my tongue over hers.

"I love you," she says as she fumbles with the button of my jeans, as I shimmy out of them, as she sheds her shirt and her denim skirt.

"I love you," I tell her as I roll her onto her back, wrapping my arms around her and gathering her to me, feeling every inch of her skin pressed against mine.

"I love you," she tells me as she reaches for the condom I left on the bedside table, ready for what I thought would be a sneaky, late-night hotel hookup but has become so much more.

We don't rush. We don't tease. We don't play games.

We consume one another.

As I push into Wyatt, I feel every molecule of her, every hitch of her breath, every nail digging into my back, every slide of her thighs along my hips, her feet pressing into my ass as she urges me closer. We mutter broken declarations of love between kisses and sighs, only separating to breathe and press our foreheads together and *feel*. I memorize this woman I love, this woman who loves me. I *have* her. She's *mine*.

I reach for a pillow and lift her hips, placing it beneath her ass so the angle of my cock and the thrust of my pelvis stroke every sensitive part of her, and I'm rewarded by this beautiful woman tipping her head back, lips parted, and letting out my name on a delicious moan.

"Owen," she cries, and I feel her body approach orgasm, the flood of her heat over my cock and the clench of her muscles around my body.

"Wyatt," I say, part plea, part prayer.

I don't even have to ask.

Just as she falls apart in my arms, she tilts her chin up.

Her eyes are open.

She stays with me.

And I follow her over the cliff.

CHAPTER 37
WYATT

It's a testament to the comfort of being wrapped up naked in Owen's arms that it takes me four rounds before I realize that the buzzing sound interrupting my bliss is my phone on the bedside table.

And the only reason my phone would be buzzing at three a.m. when do not disturb is on is because Hazel is calling me.

And the only reason Hazel would be calling me at three a.m. is because something is wrong.

I jerk out of Owen's arms and snatch my phone off the table, fighting off the remains of sleep to swipe the screen.

"Hazel? What's wrong?"

"Is Owen with you?" She's doing that *I'm trying to remain calm but it's a trial* voice.

"Yeah, why? What's wrong?"

"It's Eden. I did the steamy shower thing, and she stopped coughing and got sleepy, so I put her down. She didn't feel warm or anything, but I just went to check on her, and she's burning up."

"What's going on?" Owen says, rolling over.

"It's Eden. Hazel says she's got a fever."

I put her on speaker.

Owen flips on the light and sits up. "I'm here, Hazel. What's going on?"

"I can't find the thermometer, but she's burning up."

"Is she awake?"

"I picked her up, and she just kind of passed out on my shoulder."

Owen stills.

"So she's not crying?"

"No. She's really tired. I'm not sure if it's because it's three a.m. or—"

"Hazel," Owen says, his voice taking on just a hint of steel. My heart rate climbs. "I need you to try and wake her up. Lay her down and take off her jammies, that usually does it."

I hear Hazel's sharp intake of breath as she processes the seriousness of Owen's tone.

There's a rustling, and I think Hazel has set her phone down. Then I hear her attempt a soothing coo, but there's a wobble to it.

"Hey, baby girl, can you wake up for Mommy?"

Owen's brow is furrowed, his muscles bunched.

"How's she doing?" he asks.

"She's...she's awake but really listless."

Owen closes his eyes, pulls in a deep breath.

"Hazel, I want you to look at her ribs. When she breathes, what does it look like?"

The pause seems to go on forever, but it's probably only a few seconds before Hazel's voice comes back, this time with an edge of brittle fear. "Her chest is sort of...I don't know how to describe it. It's caving in? It doesn't look right. Should I call Fatima on the on call phone?"

"You need to take her to the emergency room. As quick as you can," Owen says, climbing out of bed and fumbling for his pants. "I'll call ahead and let them know you're coming, and I'll head that way. It'll be about an hour, but I'll be there as fast as I can."

"And Wyatt?"

Owen glances up as if he forgot I was in the room, then fumbles for his shirt.

"I'm coming too," I say. I jump out of bed and scramble madly for my clothes.

"Owen, what's happening?" Hazel's voice cracks.

"It's going to be fine. She's probably got a more serious respiratory infection than we thought. She'll need some breathing support and medicine at the hospital, so you need to get her there. *Now*."

The seriousness of his tone sends a shiver up my spine. I'm dressed in record time and reaching for my suitcase to zip it up when Owen says, "Leave it. We need to go."

"But—"

"It's not important, Wyatt," he snaps.

I've never heard him talk like this before. He doesn't look at me. Not even when he holds out his hand and says, "Give me the keys."

"Why?"

"Because I'm driving."

"I can dr—"

"Give me the fucking keys, Wyatt."

I hand them over, my stomach in knots as a merry-go-round of anxious thoughts whirls around in my brain. There's Eden, so tiny and struggling to breathe. There's Hazel, my sweet baby sister trying so hard to hold it together, that watery crack in her voice betraying her fear.

And there's Owen. His jaw clenched, his shoulders too high, his body taut like a rubber band stretched to its limit. That voice is so steely, so remote, with just a hint of desperation.

It takes a silent elevator ride and a sprint through the parking garage before I remember the only other time I've heard him sound like this.

That misty morning on the soccer field.

CHAPTER 38

OWEN

I don't remember the drive to the hospital. I don't remember stoplights or exits or double yellow lines flying past us. There aren't many cars on the road close to four in the morning, which is probably good, because I definitely do not obey the speed limit.

When I pull up to the small county hospital, I park in the first spot I see even though a sign says it's reserved. I know Wyatt is jogging behind me as I race to the emergency room entrance on my long legs, but I don't turn to make sure she catches up.

My body is moving as fast as my mind.

I try to keep myself from panicking as a slew of competing thoughts whirls through my mind. It's absolute pandemonium in there.

But the thought that screams the loudest is *You weren't paying attention*.

It would have taken five minutes to grab a stethoscope and listen to Eden's lungs before we left for Indianapolis. I might have heard fluid or wheezing or some other sign of infection. I could have put her on breathing treatments at home before she go to this point, listless and struggling for air in her mother's arms.

The echo of another mother's screams thrums beneath everything.

The nurse at the desk recognizes me and buzzes me through the restricted doors, and I make a beeline to where this small hospital puts pediatric cases. As I race past curtains, I question whether I should have told Hazel to take Eden to Bloomington, which has a much bigger hospital with a pediatric staff. The desperately underfunded county hospital has only one pediatric specialist, and it's anyone's guess whether or not they'll be available. But I wasn't sure how bad Eden's breathing had gotten, and I didn't want Hazel to risk the longer drive.

The last curtain on the left at the end of the ER hallway is closed. I skid to a stop and swipe it open to find Hazel hunched over a pediatric bed, the metal arms raised. Eden is on her back in the middle, already hooked up to oxygen, a pulse ox monitor, and an IV. Libby is in a chair in the corner chewing on her manicure, and on the other side of the bed is—

"Fatima? What are you doing here?"

She looks up, a white coat thrown over her pink pajamas, a stethoscope around her neck.

"What are *you* doing here? I thought you were in Indianapolis." Her eyes sweep over me, her brow furrowed. I probably look like I got dressed in a tornado, my hair askew, mascara still smeared around my eyes. I'm wearing pants with no underwear and shoes with no socks, and I think my shirt is buttoned wrong, but I haven't paused to check.

"Hazel called me, and I told her to bring Eden here."

"Good," she says slowly, like she's trying to solve a puzzle. "But why are *you* here?"

"Because I—" I start, but I don't have words.

"He drove me," Wyatt says, walking up and taking my hand in hers. It feels foreign and cold, and even though she's right beside me, she feels far away. Everything is simultaneously too loud and oddly muffled.

Fatima nods, then she studies me for a beat longer. "Well, Dr. Anderson is sick, so they called me in to do the workup on Eden."

Dr. Anderson is the pediatric specialist for the county hospital, and while I know he's a good doctor, I'm glad Fatima was the one at Eden's bedside until I could get here. I trust Fatima.

But I reach for the chart at the end of the bed anyway.

And Fatima swats my hand away.

"You're not on duty tonight, Dr. McBride," she says, then eyes me like this is some kind of test.

"Right, but I'm here now, and I'm her doctor."

"Not tonight," she says. "You made sure she got here, and now we're taking care of her."

"Cut the shit, Fatima," I say.

Wyatt's hand tenses in mine.

"Owen, it's fine," Hazel says, her brow furrowed.

That's when I realize that I'm making everyone in the room uncomfortable. Fuck, this is not how things are supposed to go.

"Dr. Adebayo was just telling us that Eden has RSV," Hazel says.

Fatima nods. "We'll admit her for a round of breathing treatments and monitor her fluids and her airway. She doesn't show signs of pneumonia, so I'm guessing she's going to feel a whole lot better in the next twenty-four hours with the oxygen support."

RSV. Fuck. Of course. I missed it because of the croupy cough and because July isn't normally the season for respiratory viruses. But it happens.

And I missed it.

"Right, okay, that all sounds good," Wyatt says, her voice tentative. "That's good news."

"It is," Fatima says, turning to Hazel. "I know it's tough when babies get sick like this because they can't tell you what they're feeling. And seeing your child struggle to breathe is terrifying. But you did exactly the right thing, and she's going to be fine."

"You don't know that."

All eyes turn to me, and it takes me several seconds to realize I said that out loud.

Fatima narrows her dark eyebrows. "Dr. McBride, can I see you in the hall?"

Fatima smiles at Hazel and says something I can't hear over the ringing in my ears. Then she pivots on her heel and strides out of the curtained area. I drop Wyatt's hand and follow her. But she doesn't stop in the hall. She keeps walking past empty beds until she reaches a closed door. She opens it and gestures for me to go into what turns out to be a supply closet, then follows me in and slams the door behind her.

"What the fuck is going on, Owen?"

Her expression is a mixture of pity and scorn, and I can barely look at her. I can barely understand what's happening, how I went from being in bed with Wyatt, happier than I've ever been in my life, to standing in this cold, dark hospital supply closet feeling like I've nearly lost everything.

Eden is fine. I *know* she is. And yet I can't seem to get hold of myself. It's like someone loaded me into a roller coaster car and shoved me down a hill and I'm trying to get out while the thing is still moving.

"I'm sorry, it's just..." But I trail off. I don't know what *it* is. I just know that my brain is too loud and my body feels like it's vibrating too fast. I can't catch my breath, and I feel like my heart is trying to escape from my chest. Everything is spinning, and it's cold but I'm sweating—

"*Owen*," Fatima says, gripping my upper arms. The venom is gone from her voice. She tugs gently on my sleeves, and suddenly I'm sinking down onto a cardboard box in the corner of the room. "Owen, listen to me. I think you're having a panic attack. I need you to take a deep breath, okay?"

I try, but it feels ragged in my chest, and I huff the air out quickly.

"Good, try again. Breathe while I count to four, okay?"

She counts, and I breathe. It takes a few tries before I'm able to slow my breathing down, but once I do, Fatima nods.

"Okay, now I need you to name three things you can see," she says, and when I don't answer right away, she repeats it.

My eyes dart around the small room, unable to land on anything, but Fatima gives my arms a squeeze, and something inside me slows.

"Uh, paper towels," I say, scrambling for words. "Bottles of cleaner. Shelving units."

"Good," Fatima says. "Now give me three sounds you hear."

This one requires more effort, but Fatima is patient. "The air conditioner humming," I say finally. "Someone talking down the hall, probably at the nurses' station. And, uh, does the pounding of my own heart count?"

"I don't think the judges will have a problem with that," Fatima says. "Okay, now I need you to move three parts of your body."

I wiggle my fingers, which are clenched on my thighs, feeling the gentle release of tension in my forearms. Then I slowly roll my neck, breathing with the motion as something in my shoulders cracks. And finally I reach up and swipe at my cheeks, where a trail of tears is making its way down into the collar of my shirt.

"Okay, good," Fatima says, letting out a long breath of her own. "Now, I'm going to take care of Eden, and you are going to go home."

"But—"

"No," she says, her voice kind but firm. It's the voice I hired her for. And I need to remind myself that I hired her for her skills too. "You are going home. Are you safe to drive?"

I remember that I drove here with Wyatt. In her truck. And I have a sudden sinking, miserable thought.

I haven't felt this bad since Dylan Anders. This feels *just* like Dylan Anders. Eden isn't dying. Eden is going to be fine. I know that. I repeat it like a mantra. But that doesn't change my feelings. The feeling of inadequacy. The fear of making a mistake.

I remember the look on Hazel's face. The fear on Wyatt's.

Things didn't go wrong. *This time.*

I walked out of Wyatt's house so sure that I had given the right advice about Eden, and I was wrong.

I was wrong, and I nearly hurt the person I care about most.

I was wrong because I was thinking only about her.

I was wrong, and I can't do this again. I can't.

Wyatt deserves better. My patients deserve better.

I can't do this again. Not *again*.

"I'll get an Uber," I tell Fatima as my stomach curdles.

CHAPTER 39
WYATT

A nurse gets us settled into a room, wheeling a sleeping Eden in her grim little bed. As horrifying as it is to see her there, her chubby limbs connected to tubes and wires, a tiny, faded hospital gown pooling around her, I have to admit that her color has improved just in the short time we've been here.

"This room is nice," Libby says, sitting down on one of two chairs. Hazel takes the recliner beside Eden, her worried eyes never leaving her daughter.

"It's a hospital room. What could possibly be nice about it?" I snap, the exhaustion finally hitting me. I got just a couple of hours of sleep, the drive to the hospital was incredibly tense, and now that the adrenaline is bleeding out of me, I'm starting to unravel. I wrap my arms around myself, missing Owen, who hasn't come back yet.

"I'm just trying to look on the bright side," Libby says. "We could be stuck down in the ER all night like that time you fell down the stairs when you were five and broke your ankle. That was *awful*. There was a drunk in the next bed who moaned for hours and hours and scared the dickens out of you. Neither of us got any sleep."

"You mean the time we were staying at that cheap motel because we got evicted and I slipped on a beer someone spilled in the stairwell and broke my *arm*? That time?"

"Oh, right, it was your arm," she says, like that's the most important part of the memory.

When Fatima walks into Eden's room, I look over her shoulder for Owen.

But he's not there.

"Okay, looks like everyone is settled," Fatima says, reaching for Eden's chart. She peruses the notes and nods. "Her pulse ox is improving, just like we want to see. If everything keeps heading in this direction, I think she'll be discharged by tomorrow night. In the meantime, I think we should give Hazel and Eden some room. It's a tight space. Hazel, that recliner lies flat. I know it's hard, but please try to get some sleep. Eden's not going to get better faster if you stare at her. She's in good hands, and so are you."

"Yeah, you two should go home and sleep," Hazel says to Libby and me. "Wyatt, you can drive Mom."

She sounds authoritative. Like a mother. It takes my breath away.

"I came here with Owen. There's no more room in my truck," I say. I sound like a stubborn teen, and I hate it.

"Where is Owen, anyway?" Libby asks.

"Oh, he went home," Fatima says.

"He what?" The words are out of my mouth—part panicked, part aghast—before I can control my tone. I feel Libby's eyes on me, studying my reaction. "How? I mean, I'm his ride."

I pat my purse, hearing the rattle of my keychain.

"He called an Uber," Fatima says. "There was nothing for him to do here, and he needed sleep. I suggest the two of you get some rest too."

He called an Uber.

The words hit me like a slap.

Not six hours ago, he was telling me he loved me over and

over again. And now he's walked away when my niece is in the hospital? He just…left?

I pull out my phone and check our text thread, but there's nothing from him. No apology, no explanation.

Something isn't right.

"Okay, we'll head out, then," Libby says. She gathers her purse and gives Eden a soft kiss on the cheek, then wraps Hazel in a hug. "Get some sleep, honey, okay? Call us if you need anything. We can bring breakfast in the morning."

"Yeah," I say, giving Hazel a hug, but I'm only halfway present. My brain is grasping for explanations. Anything that will make me stop worrying about Owen's sudden disappearance.

"Thanks for coming," Hazel says, her voice watery.

"I'll always be here for you, Haze."

"I know. I know that with every part of me. But make sure you show up for yourself too, okay?" She squeezes my arms. "Maybe drop Mom off and go to Owen's?"

Yes. Yes, that's exactly what I'll do. Owen's just tired and stressed, rattled from our dark-of-night rush to the hospital. I'll go find him, reassure him that Eden is okay, and maybe we can finally talk about what's been going on with him.

I think back to my conversation with Francie, and I wonder if he even knows.

———

The truck is still in the reserved spot by the door, the tires between the lines but slightly askew. I think back to our arrival, to the way Owen swung the wheel into the parking lot, the way the truck lurched to a halt. I wasn't paying close attention because my thoughts were consumed with worry about Eden and Hazel. But now that Eden is safe and Hazel is resting, I can't escape the memory of how Owen looked: his clenched jaw, his knotted shoulders, the tension that absolutely radiated off him.

"So, you heading over to the good doctor's house?" Libby asks as I pull out of the parking lot.

"What?" I nearly forgot she was beside me, and my hands are clenched around the wheel, my knuckles white. *Something isn't right.* I keep repeating it like a mantra.

Libby *tsks.* "That boy seems like he's got his feelings all in a knot. It's not good, honey bun."

I clench my teeth so tightly my molars ache. "Would you cut it out with the honey bun shit?"

Libby turns to face me. "Wyatt Jean, what is your problem with me?"

Now my hands unclench from the wheel, flying up and smacking the aging fabric on the ceiling of the car. "Are you kidding me right now?"

"I'm not. You're treating me like some evil stepmonster, and I don't like it." She turns back to stare out the windshield, her arms crossed over her chest. "I know I wasn't a great mother—"

I snort. "Understatement."

"But I've always loved you. I took care of you as best I could. I tried to shield you from the worst of things."

"Did you? Really? Did you shield me from Brandon, who would show up at our apartment drunk and backhand you while wearing his fucking class ring?"

"Yes, Wyatt. He slapped me, and then he left. And the next day *we* left."

"Why didn't you call the cops?"

She scoffs. "The cops? Are you kidding? The cops wouldn't have done shit, and if they'd tried, it just would've made things worse. I took us out of that situation, which was the best thing I could do."

"And into what? A string of cheap motels in Alabama? That trailer in Apalachicola that was full of mold?"

"You always had a bed to sleep in and food to eat, and you always had me," she says.

"Until I didn't! Until you left with that guy Jayden or Cayden or Braxton or whatever the fuck and decided taking me with you was too inconvenient. Then you told me to hit the bricks."

"I—" she starts like she's got an argument, but the word dies in her mouth. She sighs. "I'm sorry. All I can say is that at the time, I thought I was doing the right thing. You were old enough to take care of yourself, and I think part of me knew you could do it better than I could. You said it yourself—I could hardly give you consistency. The sooner you got out on your own, the sooner you could start living a better life. And you were so angry with me by that point, it felt like independence was the best gift I could give you."

There's a long stretch of silence between us, the only sound the rush of the warm summer air through the open windows as we drive toward town.

Libby sighs. "I'm sorry, Wyatt. For everything. For not doing better by you, for leaving you behind, for taking Hazel. And then for dumping everything on you when I made yet another stupid decision. You picked up the pieces, and Hazel is who she is because of you. She is smart and brave and strong and an incredible mother to that baby, and *none* of that is because of me. You did that, Wyatt. And you should be proud."

It's not until I pull up to the house and turn off the truck that I realize there are tears pouring down my cheeks. I think about what Carson said about Libby being a victim too. About how I've been blaming her for the actions of the men she chose. Could she have done better? Absolutely. But could she have done worse?

Jut the thought makes me shudder.

"I don't expect you to forgive me. And hell, I definitely don't deserve another chance. But I want you to know that I'm trying. For Hazel and for Eden, but also for you. You deserve that, Wyatt," Libby says. "You've worked so hard, and you deserve at least that."

She gives me a long, sad look, then gathers her purse into her lap.

"Now, you go on after your doctor," Libby says, reaching up

and tucking a curl behind my ear. "But please remember that even though you are the strongest woman I know, that doesn't mean you need to hold up a man, okay? If I've learned anything in this life, it's that a man's gotta hold himself up first."

CHAPTER 40

OWEN

I should be in bed, but I can't sleep. The house is too quiet, and the pounding of my heart is too loud.

Felix is on a fishing trip with some guys from college. I try to call Francie again, but it goes to voicemail. She's probably working at the hospital.

And I can't call Wyatt. Not yet.

It's in moments like these that I realize how small my circle is. Maybe it was growing up in a big family in a small town, but it always felt important to keep things to myself. Our little house was always so busy, and with that came stress. Plus there was the stress of losing Mom. The stress of Dad trying to be a single father to five kids under nine. The stress of trying to minimize everyone else's stress.

I was just a little boy when my mother died. I barely remember her. There wasn't much I could do to ease the burden in my house, but I felt it deeply even in first grade. I watched my dad try to hide his tears. I watched Archer try to step up and help out. I watched Dan withdraw into himself. Felix, my twin, was already showing signs of being an easily distractible, happy-go-lucky wild rumpus, creating messes and making everyone laugh.

I figured out pretty quickly that the best way I could help my family was by following the rules and working hard at everything I tried. It made everyone happy. It made life easier.

And it served me well. It meant I made it to state champs in baseball, then snagged the valedictorian spot. It got me through college, then med school, then residency.

Until the day I wasn't as good as I needed to be.

And somebody died.

I know Eden will be fine.

I *know* it.

But my body doesn't.

My body is back in that emergency room three years ago, listening to a mother wail. My body is in a hospital conference room, answering questions about all the choices I made that led to Dylan Anders's death. My body is sitting across from the chief, hearing her tell me I needed to seek treatment or take a leave of absence.

And I did. I did the therapy. I took the risk management classes. I finished my residency.

I followed the rules, and I succeeded.

And I vowed never to make that kind of mistake again.

Never to let my guard down again.

Never to get distracted again.

I know what I have to do if I want to be the best possible doctor. I know what I need to do to take care of the people I love.

And I love Wyatt. I know that for sure.

But I can't love her the way she deserves. I can't do it all. I just can't.

Back in residency, my therapist told me that I had to learn to notice when I was juggling too many balls. When that happened, I needed to figure out which balls were glass and which balls were plastic. It was okay to let plastic balls drop. They wouldn't break. She told me to focus on juggling the glass balls and pick up the plastic ones when I had space and time again.

Dylan Anders was a glass ball.

My ability to practice medicine? The thinnest glass. I have to focus on that first.

But Wyatt?

Wyatt is the finest crystal.

And she doesn't deserve to be juggled at all. Even knowing how careful I need to be with her, I still risk dropping her.

Shattering her.

All I can do now is set her down gently.

The knock at my door is soft, but it may as well be a gunshot for how I jump at the sound.

And standing on my doorstep is the most precious person in my life. The person I would do anything to protect.

"Why didn't you use the key?" I ask, thinking back to all those nights she slipped into my bed, molding herself around my sleeping body. I can already tell I'm going to be holding those memories close, revisiting them often.

"I wasn't sure if you'd be here," she says. She sounds like she's trying to cajole a frightened dog out from behind a dumpster. There's a little line etched deep between her eyebrows. She's trying to take care of me. I'm just one more person in a long line of people Wyatt has stepped up and tried to take care of. "You left without saying anything."

Right. Just another way my scrambled brain has hurt her.

I hold the door open, and she comes in.

"Sorry," I say, following her into the living room. "I figured you'd want to stay with Hazel and Eden."

She whirls around to face me. "Hazel sent us home to get some sleep." She pauses, studying me. "Eden is doing fine. But Owen… are you?"

"No." The word is out of my mouth so fast it takes me a moment to process that the voice that said it was mine.

And saying it out loud makes me feel…*relief*. Because if I'm not okay, I have a good reason for what I'm about to do. Because I can't be what Wyatt needs. It's all right there in front of her. I just need to make her see it.

"Okay," she says slowly, and the admission seems to calm her too. She nods, swallowing hard. "Okay, well, we should talk about that. Or you should talk about it with somebody else. But I'm here for you no matter what. You can tell me anything."

As I look at her—her hair still mussed, her eyes bloodshot from stress and lack of sleep, her brow furrowed as she tries to solve me like a Rubik's Cube—it all clicks into place. Wyatt is sitting on my couch, ready to take on whatever mess I throw at her. Ready to fix it. To fix *me*.

Just like she took care of Hazel. And Eden. And Libby. And that asshole Griffin Stone.

Everyone but herself.

God, she's so tough. So strong and smart and savvy. It's time for her to turn that awesome power on herself.

It's time I let her go.

CHAPTER 41

WYATT

"I think it's time to stop," he says.

I hear the words, but I don't understand them.

"This was supposed to be no strings attached for a reason," he says, like he's delivering a diagnosis. Like he's listing treatments and their side effects. Dispassionate and scientific—the perfect doctor. "We've gone too far, and we need to stop."

I blink at him like he's spoken a foreign language, my brain whirring.

The last few hours have been an absolute tsunami of stress, but before that, we were in bed. I was curled into the nook of his arm, and he loved me. And I love him. That's why I came here. I knew that because we loved each other, we'd be able to talk about what's going on. We could find help together.

This...this doesn't make any sense.

"What are you talking about?" I ask.

He turns to the mantel and pulls down the pineapple can. "We said if we wanted to reassess, we could do that. Walk away without a fight."

Without a *fight*? He thinks I'm not going to fight him on this?

"No, that's what *you* said because you thought *I'd* want to walk away. But I don't want that," I say, trying to keep my voice even. "I love you."

He has the good grace to flinch.

"It hasn't even been a day since we said that. That we love each other. Not even one fucking *day*." I'm quickly losing the battle to control my tone.

But all he can do is stare down at that fucking pineapple can.

I take a deep breath and try again. It's clear something is very wrong with him, and it's making him react badly. But I can...I mean, *we* can...

"Owen, I know that what happened with Eden freaked you out," I try. "And maybe your brain is telling you that something about it was your fault, but hear me when I say it wasn't. I talked to Dr. Adebayo, and she said croup and RSV often present similarly, and Eden didn't have a fever when we left, and she could have—"

"Stop," he says, his eyes closed like he's in pain.

"No, Owen. I won't stop. Something is going on with you, and you've been hiding it for too long. From me, from your family, maybe even from yourself." My words are rushing out like a desperate tidal wave, the pressure in my chest growing as I watch him breathe, and close his eyes, and pull away. "Please, Owen, listen to me. I don't know what happen during third year, but—"

"*Stop!*" he shouts.

I've never heard Owen McBride shout.

It's loud and stern and—

And it's final.

"Please don't do this, Owen," I whisper, as if I can bring him back to me, to *himself*, with a gentle plea.

"I'm sorry, Wyatt," is all he says, and I can't tell if the apology is for yelling or the fact that he's systematically dismantling me piece by piece. Everything hurts. This *hurts*, and I don't know how to fix it.

He's still holding that goddamn pineapple can like it's proof that this is rational. That this is fair. That it's right.

Nothing about this is right.

"You're sorry?" I force my eyes away from the can with the rules that were supposed to keep us honest, with our childish, hastily scrawled signatures. They land on him.

I didn't want this. The contract was my idea because I didn't want *any* of this. I was trying to make sure I'd never wind up standing in Owen McBride's living room, tears welling in my eyes while I frantically tried to figure out what I'd done wrong and how I could fix it.

I thought that pineapple can would protect me.

Just like always, I thought I knew better.

But once again, I chose wrong.

That goddamn fucking pineapple can.

My tornado of emotions is spinning so fast that I can barely separate them, but fury wins out.

I snatch that pineapple can from those strong, capable hands that used to hold me so gently, like I was precious. Like he could protect me. I feel its weight in my hand, pull my arm back.

And then, like a rubber band snapping, I hurl it.

The can hits the living room window with an unholy clatter, and the glass shatters.

The shock of what I've done lasts all of five seconds before I turn back to him.

"You did this to me. I didn't want this. I tried to stop it. But you made me fall in love with you," I say, sobs forcing their way between my words. "And then you broke my fucking heart."

And then I race for the door before he can take anything more from me.

———

I pull into the driveway just as the sun is rising. After I left Owen's, I drove around, cruising down the rural highways outside of town and praying I wouldn't come across a cop as I tested the speed limit in several counties. I'm exhausted and frayed. My eyes are dry and swollen from crying, my throat raw from screaming along with Debbie's breakup mixtape.

And my heart is well and truly broken.

I climb out of the truck and say a little prayer that Libby's asleep. I don't think I can take her *I told you so* on top of everything else. What I need now is to burrow under the covers and sleep until this doesn't hurt anymore. Or sleep and then pretend this doesn't hurt anymore when I wake up. I'll pretend while my tender shattered heart heals, covers itself in scar tissue until it's strong enough that no one will ever break me again.

It's what I've always done.

It's the one thing I'm good at.

I sling my purse over my shoulder, realizing that I need to text Carson about getting my suitcase from the hotel. Which means I'm going to have to explain everything that transpired over the last few hours. And oh god, Grace—I'm going to have to tell her that things between her brother and me are over.

Fuck. Everything I was afraid of has happened, and it's all so much worse than I thought it would be. Once again I looked at all the evidence, knew in my gut what I should do, and then went and did the exact fucking opposite.

I'm nothing if not predictable.

My shoulders roll forward like my body is ready to fold in on itself as I trudge up the front path. The door is unlocked because Libby doesn't give a shit about safety. And honestly, I'm too miserable to care either. I half hope there's a killer with a chainsaw standing in my living room, ready to cut me to ribbons. It wouldn't hurt worse than this, but at least it would distract me.

The house is quiet. I exhale in relief and start making my way down the hall.

"You okay, honey bun?"

I freeze. Libby's on the couch, a steaming mug of coffee in her hand. She's still wearing her clothes from last night.

"What are you doing up?" I ask.

"I was waiting for you in case you came home."

I search her tone for her trademark sass. She loves to tease. But what I find there is so much worse. It's not pity.

It's empathy.

I thought I was all cried out. I thought I'd need to drink a bathtub's worth of water before my body could form more tears. I thought I was too tired, too broken—hell, too stubborn to cry anymore.

But the tears pour out of me anew, great heaving sobs, and suddenly I'm rushing across the carpet and into Libby's open arms.

"Mom," I cry, the word on my lips nearly as comforting as her hug.

"Oh, sugar, I'm so sorry," she whispers into my hair as I sob on her shoulder, mourning everything I've lost. To Owen. To Griffin. To my own stubbornness.

And to my own hardening heart.

CHAPTER 42

MONDAY, JULY 17 AT 8:22 AM

OWEN

I'm sorry, Wyatt

CHAPTER 43

OWEN

August 4

The long, slow trudge through the rest of the summer begins. The first two weeks of August are usually slow, with kids out of camp and not yet sharing germs at school.

But it doesn't feel slow. Not to me. I keep myself busy, staying late to see extra patients and do follow-ups. I ride so many miles on the Peloton that I think the thing now sighs when I get on it. I offer to help my brother work on the sixty thousand half-finished house projects, even though I have the carpentry skills of hyperactive puppy. I even pick up a few shifts at my dad's hardware store.

Anything to distract myself from the constant low thrum of stress that now exists beneath my skin.

Wyatt's absence is like a wound I have to work not to pick at. I skip drinks with my brothers at the Half Pint. I make sure Fatima does Eden's RSV follow-up.

But mostly I throw myself into work. I refer Avery Madison to an allergist for his persistent sinus infections. I send Kayla

Marshall for a bone scan after two broken legs in six months. I take every open volunteer slot at the after-hours clinic and all the extra on-call shifts Fatima will give me.

And I wait for my life to go back to the way it was before Wyatt, when I filled my days with answering texts and calls from my patients' parents, before I knew how fragile everything was.

Before I knew how destructive I could be.

I'm in my office planning an HPV vaccine clinic when Fatima pops her head in.

"Yo, I'm here to snag the on-call phone," she says.

It's sitting on my desk, the screen already lit up with messages. The office closed only twenty minutes ago, and I've already fielded a call about poison ivy exposure from Joseph Blake's mother. He's had it twice before, and each time it gets a little more gnarly, spreads a little more aggressively, so I told her I'd stay late and she could bring him in for a steroid shot.

"I can just keep it," I say, clenching the phone in my fist. "I don't mind."

Fatima shakes her head. "Nope. You've had it all week, and while I appreciate the break, Daphne wants to watching *2001: A Space Odyssey* this weekend. Do you know how boring that movie is? I'm fighting for my life to stay awake. The on-call phone is my ticket out."

"Come on, that movie's a classic," I try, but I can hear the edge of desperation in my voice. I try a smile, but Fatima frowns.

"Are you okay?"

"I'm fine." I lean back in my chair and try to relax, like I need to prove it to her.

"Right. Fine," she says, but I can tell she doesn't believe me. She holds out her hand. "Give me that phone."

I sigh. "Fine."

"Seriously, what's going on with you? You've been snappish with the front desk staff, and last night I drove by after dinner and your car was still here. And while I appreciate you taking the phone for the entire week of our anniversary, you seem off." She pauses, then grins. "Are you not getting laid anymore?"

"Out," I groan, pointing at the door.

"Try to relax this weekend, okay? Like, for-real relax, not whatever high school theater production version of relaxing you're doing," she says, waving her hand at my slumped form. "Remember, Owen, the body keeps the score."

And fuck, I know that. My body is in knots. I've been sleeping like shit for weeks. Muscles in my back that I didn't even know existed ache. Last night, in a fit of insomnia at three a.m., I decided my pillows were shot and ordered all new ones and a memory foam mattress topper.

I pull out my phone and check the shipping. They should arrive tomorrow, so hopefully a decent night's sleep is only a day away.

Hopefully a decent night's sleep is what I need to get back to normal.

Hopefully there's a normal to get back to.

August 5

It's Saturday night, and my brothers are all at the Half Pint. I told them I needed to work on a medical conference proposal, so now I'm home alone, searching the internet for medical conferences I can attend. Honestly, writing up a conference proposal sounds like a really good distraction.

This is what my life has become.

Is this what normal was before Wyatt? Was I extremely boring? Or am I being punished with this new pathetic normal for thinking I could be what Wyatt needed? Punished for being so wrong that I wrecked her?

I'm deep in the American Medical Association website when my phone lights up with a call from Francie.

A call, not a text.

My breath hitches as I answer. "What's up, Frank?"

"How's Wyatt?" That's her greeting. And from the flatness of her voice, I realize I've been caught.

Francie has been busy with work and wedding planning these last few weeks, so we haven't talked much, and I've been able to keep the truth to myself. I haven't lied, only avoided.

"What?" I ask, the word sticking in my throat.

"How's. Wyatt."

"She's, uh…she's fine."

"I knew it!" Francie cries.

"Knew what?"

"Something happened. I can tell. Your texts have been too careful, and you haven't brought her up at all. Before, it was all *Wyatt this* and *Wyatt that*, and suddenly there's nothing. Something happened, didn't it? Don't you dare lie to me, Owen McBride."

I consider lying, but even though the thought makes my stomach clench. I've been telling so many lies lately, desperately trying to find some sense of normalcy again. So many lies, and not one of them has helped. Each one just feels like another stone in my pocket, weighing me down.

So for once, I go with the truth.

"We're not together anymore."

There's silence on the other end of the line. I brace for the explosion I know is coming.

But Francie's reply is calm. Too calm, maybe.

"Are you at home?"

"Yes."

"Don't move. I'll be there in an hour."

"Francie, you don't—"

But she has already hung up.

———

The first thing she does when she walks through the door is envelop me in a hug. And I really do feel enveloped, even though she's barely five feet tall and her head doesn't even come past by chest. We always called Francie "the tallest women in the world" back in medical school, and this is one of the reasons why. Her presence is *big*.

And this hug is warm and reassuring.

I don't realize how badly I need it until my eyes grow watery.

Without a word, she leads me into the living room and pushes me down on the couch. She's in her pajamas, her hair tucked into a pink silk bonnet, her dark skin shiny and smelling like cocoa butter, like calling me was her last task before bedtime. She settles in beside me, tucks her feet beneath her, and places a throw pillow on her lap.

"Okay, walk me through it," she says.

"Through what?" It's not that I don't know what she's asking. It's that suddenly there's genuinely too much to tell. My emotions feel like a broken spigot, ready to spray in an unexpected direction at any moment.

"What happened with Wyatt?" she asks, patient.

I sigh, slumping back into the couch. "I don't know, Francie. Everything just …" I scramble for words, but they only recede even further into the recesses of my brain. My heart begins to pound, sweat pricks at my temples, and then suddenly the words are there. They're *everywhere*, loud inside my head.

You lost focus. You tried to do too many things. You broke it. You broke her. It's your fault. You messed it up. You need to pay attention. Focus. Try harder next time. Don't—

"Owen."

I realize my hands are in Francie's hands. She's squeezing gently, the pressure pulling me out of my spiral.

And then I'm talking. About Eden and that night in the hospital. About what happened in the hotel room before that, how Wyatt finally said she loved me. About her history and how we exposed that clown Griffin Stone for the phony he is. About walking into the bar that night in January when I was supposed to meet Francie for a drink but instead my life changed.

I tell her about how Wyatt protects her people so fiercely, always takes care of them.

And about how I couldn't do the same.

Francie listens to all of it, nodding and *hmmm*-ing but otherwise not saying a word. And when I finally stop, she waits to see if there's more before she speaks.

"Did you ever tell Wyatt about Dylan Anders?"

My stomach curdles. "No," I say, but then the memory surfaces of her begging me to talk about it right here in this room, asking about third year like she had any idea. And I *yelled* at her.

I feel like I'm being run over by a truck repeatedly, by bones being ground to dust, my insides flattened into a noxious goo.

"Well, she asked me about it at the engagement party. Apparently that witch Mina mentioned it but didn't spill the details. So Wyatt asked me."

"What did you tell her?"

"I said it wasn't my story to tell," she answers, her eyes sad. "But I saw how close you were, how much you cared for her. I assumed you'd tell her eventually."

"I didn't," I say, then shift uncomfortably. "It wouldn't have made a difference."

"Why not?"

"I guess it would have helped her understand why I ended things with her, why I can't be in a relationship."

Francie nods. "Say more about that."

I shrug. "Well, you know. You were there when everything went to hell. I tried to be a good boyfriend to you and a good doctor and a good student all at the same time, but it was too much. I couldn't focus on everything. I made mistakes. I killed Dylan Anders."

Francie's eyes go wide, then narrow. "First of all, no you did not. You did *not*. He had a freak accident at a playground, and any doctor in the hospital would've ordered the same treatment you did. You're holding yourself to a standard you can never, ever reach and then punishing yourself for it, just like you did then."

"I—"

Francie holds up her hand. "No, I'm not done." She breathes in and out, a long, calming breath. "I already knew that was an awful time for you, but hearing you tell it now, I realize it was even worse than I thought. Because in your toxic stew of memories, you've gotten one crucial detail wrong."

"What?" I ask.

She waits for me to see it, but I don't.

"We broke up *before* Dylan Anders," she says.

I rear back, trying to make sense of that.

"What? No. I—"

"Yes. Your brain has reordered events to fit the faulty narrative you've been telling about yourself. That you failed at everything that night in the ER. That Dylan Anders was the inciting incident, that your anxiety came from that." She squeezes my hands. "But you were struggling well before that, Owen. You weren't sleeping, you were barely eating, you were working way too much. You were vibrating at a frequency so high it's a wonder you didn't achieve liftoff. And I tried to talk to you about it, but every time you'd just plaster on a smile and say everything was fine. We drifted apart because I didn't want to be in a relationship with someone who couldn't be honest with himself, much less with me, and that was that. Josh and I had our first date the night before Dylan Anders died."

"How is that possible?" I say, wracking my brain for information that will make everything fall into place.

"You told yourself your anxiety was a result of what happened with Dylan, but I don't think that's it. I think you were anxious well before that," she says. "Maybe even the whole time."

Something inside of me cracks, and tears stream down my face.

"God, I'm such a fucking wreck," I say, shocked to hear sobs between my words.

Francie pulls me to her, wrapping me up in another hug, and I sink my face into her shoulder as I cry.

"You're not. You just need help, Owen. You need to let yourself be a little bit broken for a while and not try to handle everything alone," Francie says, her voice catching. "*Please*. Let me help you."

CHAPTER 44

WYATT

September 3

It's been more than a month since I walked out of Owen's house heartbroken and fell sobbing into my mother's arms.

Like I hoped it would, my heart has slowly knitted itself back together, but I'm still working on filling in the cracks. Some days the pain hits me out of nowhere and takes my breath away, but those days are growing fewer and further between.

On the whole, I'm able to maintain a stiff upper lip. It's what I do. I make things work. I clean up messes.

And I guess I'm thankful that Owen spared me the trouble of having to clean up his too.

It's Sunday night, and we're preparing for our newest Hart family tradition. Well, our *only* Hart family tradition, but it's a start.

Sunday night family dinner began just after everything went to hell with Owen. I was spending most of my time huddled under the covers, trying to sleep off my heartbreak. I called in sick to work a few nights, terrified I'd see Owen or one of his brothers at the bar and start sobbing like a sap into a pint of beer. Libby, who'd been gentle with me in a way I had never experienced, finally burst into my room, trailing the smell of pepperoni.

"Get up, my little misery princess," she trilled. "I have pizza, and you're gonna eat it."

And all four of us—Libby, Hazel, Eden, and me—crowded around the tiny kitchen table and finished off two large pies, though Eden mostly played with the cheese and chomped on left-over crusts.

From there, it became a tradition. At first we got takeout, but soon Hazel started perusing the *New York Times* cooking app, claiming we needed more vegetables in our life.

Now that Jonah knows what he's doing at the bar, there's been more stability in my work schedule. I can always take Sunday nights off to eat with my family. And now that I have fewer night shifts, I've been able to start helping Ernie with management duties. And what has the old man done with his newfound free time? He's gone and gotten himself a Harley. I keep telling him I'm not heaving kegs for him if he gets himself smeared across the highway, but he just laughs, because he knows I will.

"Do we want the bagged Caesar or the bagged Mediter-ranean?" Libby asks. Just because we're home cooking doesn't mean we chop like peasants, as she said the first time she came home with a bagged salad.

"Mediterranean," Hazel says. She pulls a bubbling baked ziti with perfectly browned cheese from the oven, the kitchen filling with the delicious smell of tomatoes and mozzarella and oregano. "It goes with the theme."

"These dinners are themed now?" I ask as I act as Eden's personal sheepdog, steering her away from electrical cords and the drawer with the kitchen knives. She's been a tiny terror ever since she started crawling. I can't believe she turns one next month.

"I got cannoli for dessert. I picked it up from Don Diono's," Libby says.

And there it is, another memory that feels like a paper cut on my heart: Owen calling up Don Diono's and paying the tab for the worst date of my life.

But I take a deep breath, and the hurt ebbs, the wound scabbing over again.

"Hear that, baby girl? It's Italian night." I scoop Eden up and blow raspberries on her belly, eliciting the most delicious baby giggles. It shocks me that at this time last year, this whole-ass person didn't exist.

Now I can't imagine my life without her.

"Okay, Auntie Wy, time to settle down for dinner." Hazel pulls Eden out of my arms and puts her in her high chair, sprinkling ziti across the tray along with some lettuce from the salad. Within seconds, Eden's smeared in marina as she smashes ziti into her little face.

I'm two bites into the most delicious baked ziti I've ever eaten in my life when I realize that Hazel hasn't reached for her fork yet. "What's up, Haze?" I ask.

She takes a deep breath. "I have an announcement."

I still.

"I heard back from my advisor today with some great news," she says, a wide smile on her face. "Eden got a spot in the childcare program they run out of the medical school. It's this incredible developmentally focused daycare that starts early childhood education when they're the age she is now."

"Well, that's great, honey!" Libby says, holding up a forkful of ziti like a toast.

"Wait, where is this program?" I ask.

"It's right on campus," she says, then pauses. "At Cornell."

Libby's fork freezes. She's caught up with me.

"I'm going back to campus for the spring semester. I'm subletting a studio from my old roommate who's doing an internship in San Francisco. It's pretty cheap, and my financial aid should cover it. I'll leave after New Year's. That'll get me the last credits I need for my degree. I'll graduate on time, and in May you can come out and celebrate with us!"

I blink, taking it all in. Hazel—and Eden—are leaving.

Across the table, Libby's mouth is hanging open.

"You guys, this is great news! I'm going to graduate on time. I had a baby, and I'm going to graduate *on time*," she says.

"That's amazing," I whisper, because it is. My baby sister is a wonder, and she's worked her ass off for this.

But still…she's leaving.

"Then what?" Libby asks. "What will you do after you graduate?"

Hazel shrugs. "I'm not sure yet. Maybe I'll come back here and work for the parks department for a little while. But I have some time to figure that out. Right now my priority is getting my diploma, and with Eden in this incredible program—which is *free*, by the way—I'm going to be able to do that."

My eyes are welling up, and I tell myself I'm just proud of my sister for the way she set her mind to a seemingly impossible task and slayed it. Just like she always does.

Libby and I wrap her in hugs. We toast her with our sodas and laugh when Eden holds up a noodle to mimic us. We enjoy our dinner and talk about Hazel's plans. I offer to drive boxes up to Ithaca in my truck and help her move into the apartment.

I pretend I'm not hurting.

But inside I feel like I'm being torn apart.

CHAPTER 45

WYATT

September 4

"Hazel's leaving," I say as soon as I shove through the door of Grace's bookstore. It only just opened for the day, and it's still empty save for Grace and Carson, who are digging through a box of early copies of forthcoming books sent by publishers.

"What are you doing here?" I ask Carson. "Aren't you supposed to be teaching kindergarteners?"

"It's Labor Day," Carson says, pulling the new Emily Henry from the box and clutching it like it's the Holy Grail. "They're at home terrorizing their parents."

"Oh," I say. I didn't even realize it was Monday, much less a holiday. My brain isn't exactly firing on all cylinders.

"What do you mean, Hazel's leaving?" Grace asks, leaning over the counter by the register.

"She's going back to Cornell for the spring semester. Her advisor helped her get Eden into this highly coveted campus daycare program for baby geniuses, she found a good sublet, and she's leaving. Right at the beginning of January."

"Wow," Grace says.

"Yeah," I reply.

"And how do you feel about that?" she asks.

I smile. "It's great."

Grace rolls her eyes. "You know 'it's great' isn't a feeling, right?"

I groan.

"How do you *really* feel?"

I think about this for a moment. I do feel happy for Hazel, and proud beyond measure. I've always known she can do anything, and the fact that she stayed on track with her degree at an Ivy League school while growing and birthing and raising the most badass little ankle biter I know is frankly incredible.

But the fact that she's going to put that baby in the back seat of her car and drive away? That makes me feel sad. And…

"Lost," I finally say.

"Oh, Wyatt," Grace says, her brows knitted together, before rushing around the counter and pulling me into a hug. Carson joins her, and the three of us cling to each other until we're a teary, rocking mass.

When we finally pull apart, we sit down on the overstuffed chairs Grace has set up for shoppers browsing books.

"Okay, talk," Grace says.

"I don't know, you guys. It's just weird. I came here because Hazel needed me. And after she went to college, I stayed so she'd have a place to land, you know? I didn't want her to be stuck in the dorms over breaks because she didn't have a home. But this time, she's leaving more permanently. She's starting her life, and I won't be in it. Which leaves me in this house that isn't mine with a mother I'm trying to maintain a tentative peace with for the first time. And that feels weird, to be thirty years old and living with my mother in *her* house. I feel…extraneous."

"You're not extraneous, Wyatt," Grace says gently.

"You have us," Carson says. "And the Half Pint. Ernie can't run that place without you, you know."

"So, what, Libby and I become roommates?"

"You and I could become roommates," Carson says. "I'm still trying to get out of my parents' house. And if you're not moving in with Owen—"

Grace makes a *tsk*ing sound, and Carson presses her lips shut, eyes wide.

For weeks I've avoided spilling the whole sad story to my friends, partially because it's humiliating and partially because Owen is Grace's brother. It's not fair to make her listen to me bitch and moan about someone she loves. I figured they'd notice we had stopped seeing each other and just assume the fling had ended naturally.

"Sorry," Carson says.

I shrug, and nobody says anything for a long beat.

"But also if you want to tell us what happened between you and Owen, that would be great," Carson finally says, the words bursting out of her.

I bark out a laugh, because nosy Carson is maybe my favorite Carson. And the laugh helps cover the twinge just below my left lung that always pinches when the subject of Owen comes up.

"I told you. It was never serious. We had this incredible fling, and it ran its course." Am I gritting my teeth while I'm talking? Because it feels like I'm gritting my teeth.

"Bullshit!" Carson yells. Like, *yells*, so loud that I flinch.

"*Carson*," Grace admonishes, shooting her a look.

"What? No. This worked last time. So I'm trying it again." Carson clears her throat like she's preparing to deliver a proclamation, then shouts, "*Bullshit!*" again.

My hands fly to my ears, suddenly remembering that Carson's voice is fine-tuned to make a room full of five-year-olds snap to attention.

"Okay, you have to stop doing that," I say, pulling my hands away.

"Well then, tell me what I *should* do, because trying to walk you through your emotions about Owen McBride is like trying to get kindergarteners to recite Shakespeare. I'm fucking exhausted, Wyatt," Carson says.

"*You're* exhausted?" I scoff. "Why is this any of your business?"

"Because we love you!" Carson exclaims. "For god's sake, we love you to the moon and back, and it's killing us to watch you do this to yourself."

"Do what?"

"Pretend you're not hurting," she says.

"She's right," Grace adds. "We've been going along with this charade for more than a month, and I'm getting it from both ends. Owen has been an absolute vault, but he's back to his old workaholic demon ways. His phone is always attached to his hand, and his mind is only on his patients. Or so he says, when he says anything at all."

My body reacts to this tiny dispatch from Owen Land like I've been starving on a deserted island for months. I've tried my best to avoid him, to not think about him, but this little reminder that he's just walking around town *existing* makes my mouth water. Like I can taste the information.

And I'm terrified by how delicious it is.

Until the reality of it leaves a bitter taste on my tongue.

Because if Grace is telling the truth, then Owen isn't doing any better than he was when I last saw him. And while it would be easy to revel in the fact that he's just as miserable as he's made me, instead I just ache for him. As heartbroken and hurt as I am by what he did to me, I know it all came from a place of deep sadness. Owen was hurting before me, he was hurting while he was with me, and he's still hurting.

I've been hoping that the one silver lining of this whole mess is that maybe Owen would start to feel better. That maybe he'd deal with whatever was plaguing him.

But I guess not.

"Do you want him back?" Grace asks carefully.

"That's not up to me," I tell her. And it's not a question I know how to answer. Do I miss Owen? Like a phantom limb. Sometimes he's still there, and sometimes I feel his absence like real physical pain.

But I'm not going to beg. All I can do now is try to heal.

"Okay, back to you feeling extraneous," Grace says, leaning back in her chair. "Here's the thing: you've been taking care of other people for years. Maybe even for your whole life. And there's still somebody you need to take care of now."

"Carson?" I ask.

"Hey!" Carson cries.

"What? You've been trying to get out of your parents' house for months."

"Stop changing the subject," Carson grumbles. "We're talking about *your* life disasters, not mine."

"Okay, then who are we talking about?" I ask, because I have now thoroughly lost the plot.

"Yourself," Grace says. "You've been taking care of everyone else your whole life, and now it's time to take care of *you*. Figure out what *you* want. Go where *you* want. Make *your* life happen."

———

I think about Grace's words for the rest of the day. What do *I* want? It hasn't even occurred to me to wonder, but I consider it as I work my shift at the bar, pulling pints and heaving kegs. As I drive home, a Debbie tape in the cassette player. As I wash my face and crawl into my bed, ready for another night of trying not to remember what it was like to fall asleep in Owen's arms.

As I do all that, I think about it.

And just before I drift off, it comes to me.

I pull out my phone and open the text thread I've had going with Romy since she left Indianapolis. Last month she got word that her own tour was a go: twenty-two cities, headlining small clubs and theaters, starting in New York and ending in Los Angeles.

ROMY

> You know you're welcome to join me on any leg you want. I can't pay you, but you can bunk with me in every hotel. It'll be like a sleepover, like old times.

That text is from a week ago, just after I told her the whole sad, sordid story about Owen. Back then the plan seemed ludicrous. I had Hazel and Eden to worry about.

But now a tour sounds like a good idea.

CHAPTER 46

OWEN

September 9

When the plywood finally comes off the living room window after two months and the sunlight pours in, I nearly gasp. It's been covered up ever since the pineapple can sailed through it, and I forgot what it was like to have light in the living room.

After Wyatt fled my house, I taped some cardboard over the jagged glass. I swept up all the tiny broken pieces. I waited for Felix to come home and ask me how the window broke. But he just took one look at me, then set about replacing my sad, falling-off cardboard with plywood.

"I've always wanted to learn how to repair historic wooden windows," was all he said.

That was two months ago.

And to my surprise, despite the laundry list of unfinished projects in our house, he did.

The window—stripped, glazed, and holding a shiny new pane of glass—is lying on the living room carpet.

"Okay, I'm going to place the window, and then you'll hold it while I secure it," Felix says.

I was skeptical when he told me he needed me to assist on this job, but he assured me I'd be wielding no tools, so I agreed. And my therapist has been encouraging me to try and be social again, so I figured I'd start at home alone with my brother.

Felix lifts the window into its spot, then nods for me to take his place. Once I'm holding it, he steps back.

"So how's therapy going?" he asks, and it's not lost on me that he lobs this question as soon as he knows I'm trapped. My stomach clenches like it always does when therapy comes up. I'm not used to letting my wounds show.

The night I cried all over Francie, finally recognizing what a disaster I was, she helped me reach out to therapists. I visited four potential providers over the next week, finally settling on a guy about my age who has a disconcerting penchant for boat shoes but not a trace of condescension in his voice.

Dr. Berry is a psychiatrist whom I've been seeing twice a week for three weeks. He knows about that night with Eden and what happened with Wyatt. He knows about Dylan Anders. He knows about my mother dying when I was just six. He has diagnosed me with generalized anxiety disorder, and I've started an antianxiety medication.

And on his advice, I've told my family about all of this.

"Therapy's good," I say, and I can practically hear Dr. Berry's voice in my head: *Say more about that.* "It's hard. I'm learning a lot about myself, but I leave exhausted. It's going to be a long process."

"But you're going to keep doing it?" Felix asks as he roots through his toolbox.

"I'm going to keep doing it," I confirm, and just saying it actually does feel good. It feels weird, since I've spent my whole life making sure nobody knew I had trouble with anything ever, but it feels good.

"Excellent," Felix says. "Glad to have another fuckup in the family."

He laughs.

And I laugh.

And even though my life is far from perfect, I feel okay.

"So has this therapist told you to pull your head out of your ass and fix things with Wyatt yet?" Felix asks.

I nearly drop the window.

"We haven't gotten that far," I say, swallowing hard.

It's true. I told Dr. Berry about the night I rejected her, about our relationship, about the pineapple can, about meeting her in the bar back in January and how she was wary of me. How I pushed her and cajoled and convinced her to trust me, only to smash her to bits.

Dr. Berry told me I needed to apologize to her, but he made it sound like something we'd tackle down the road. I'm still working on getting through a therapy session without crying.

And I don't think any amount of therapy is going to help me come to terms with what I did to her. I'm finally starting to understand that Dylan Anders's death wasn't my fault. I didn't do anything wrong. But Wyatt? What I did to her was wrong, and it was absolutely my choice.

I sigh. "I don't know if I even *could* fix things," I confess to Felix, giving voice to one of the intrusive thoughts that's been swirling in my brain. Another thing I've learned in therapy? If you say something out loud, you take some of its power away. "I hurt her pretty bad. I don't know if she'll ever trust me again."

"Yeah," Felix says, "but are you really not even going to try? I mean, this window? Everything about this window said *don't even try*. Decades of paint, some of it lead. Glazing that had degraded, water in the panes, rot taking hold. The sashes were a wreck, and one of the weights was missing. Most people would have taken one look at all the wear and said, 'I'm better off just tossing it, replacing it with something new.' But you know what? Historic windows, even ones that have been through shit, will last you longer than some new bullshit you buy at Home Depot."

The whole time my brother is talking, he's systematically nailing the window into the frame with precise movements, protecting the glass and the sash, making sure everything is placed perfectly.

"But I like the hard work. I think it's worth it," he says. Then he turns to me. "I think you do too."

I feel my eyes watering, a side effect of all the therapy. Turns out that when you start acknowledging your feelings, you have to let them escape however they want. I'm discovering that for me, that involves a whole hell of a lot of crying.

Thankfully, my brother is unfazed.

"You love that girl. I saw you two together. She was good for you, and you were good for her. Don't walk away from that," he says.

I drop my gaze to my feet, because this much eye contact with my twin is a lot. We don't really do this. In fact, it's only my foray into therapy that has us talking about real shit at all. I'm learning that my whole family avoids the hard stuff by focusing on the good. And while positivity is great, there comes a point at which it's more toxic than helpful. This kind of conversation—like every-thing else in my life right now—is new. And like I said, it's weird, but it feels good.

Still, I have to cut the tension with a joke. "When did you become Dr. Phil?"

"Dr. Phil is a con man," Felix shoots back. "I'm just your brother. And I'm telling you to sit down and use that big brain of yours to figure out a way to fix things. Show Wyatt that you love her, that you're sorry, and that you want another shot."

CHAPTER 47

WYATT

September 15

GRACE

I have something for you. Any chance you can
come by the store when you get off?

It's Friday, and Jonah is closing, which means I actually get to
leave the bar with enough energy to enjoy a hot bubble bath and a
glass of wine when I get home. But I can swing by Grace's bookstore first to see what she's got for me.

It's probably another romance novel. She's been trying to get
me into them ever since I told her all about what happened with
Owen. I assume she thinks reading about love will heal my
broken heart, but mostly it just makes me angry. Things always
work out at the ends of those books, but that has not been my
experience.

I pull up to the old camera store where Dog-Eared Books is
housed. It's after nine, and the shop has been closed since seven,

but it's lit up and warm on this oddly crisp late summer evening. I park my truck and knock on the door of the shop. Grace pops up from behind the counter, a manic-looking grin on her face. She hustles over and unlocks the door.

"I'm glad you're here. I want to run down to Pete's and grab a milkshake. Would you mind holding down the fort for me? Thank you so much!" Grace practically yanks me into the store. "Lock it behind me, okay?" she says, then runs out and pulls the door shut.

"Can't you just—" I start, wondering why she can't lock up the shop herself and go get a freaking milkshake. The store is closed for the night. There's no need to bring me into this.

But she's already trotting down the street toward the diner.

I sigh, flipping the lock, then trudge into the store. I smell like beer and French fries, and I *really* want that bath. Why couldn't she just give me whatever book she's trying to get me to read and let me leave?

I'm making my way toward the overstuffed chairs when my toe connects with a cardboard box. As I walk around it, I glance down and see the words scrawled in messy Sharpie:

OPEN ME, WYATT HART

My heart leaps into my throat, because I recognize that messy scrawl.

I haven't heard from Owen since that text the morning after I ran out of his house, that sad, weak apology. I've managed to avoid him completely, and in a small town like Cardinal Springs, that has practically been a second full-time job. I am *tired*.

And now here he is—or his handwriting, anyway.

I consider walking out, but my feet are rooted to the floor, my curiosity getting the best of me. I lower myself down to my knees.

I open the box and find…

Tapes.

Piles of tapes.

Each one is numbered and has songs listed on the small lined cover in the same messy scrawl.

I pick up tape number one and read the track list, only to burst out laughing when I realize it's "Hurts So Good" by John Mellencamp ten times. The same song over and over, just like that first night at Sorry Charlie's.

I reach for tape number two. This one is a more straightforward mixtape with lots of different songs, but the references become clear pretty quickly. "Scenes from an Italian Restaurant" and "My Funny Valentine" and "Let The Circle Be Unbroken." Each one is a little wink to a moment I shared with Owen. I laugh when I see The Pina Colada Song on the next tape. There's a whole tape full of eighties hits that played at the dance marathon. There's one called "Bro Country Sucks" that's just the greatest outlaw country of all time interspersed with Romy's songs. There's an entire tape full of songs about pickup trucks.

My breath catches when I get to tape number fifteen: a copy of Debbie's breakup tape. I laugh only to realize that I'm crying.

And then I reach for tape sixteen, the only one left in the box.

"Sorry Seems to Be the Hardest Word" by Elton John
"If I Could Turn Back Time" by Cher
"Emily I'm Sorry" by boygenius
"Apologize" by Timbaland (feat. One Republic)
"Let Her Go" by Passenger
"Somebody That I Used to Know" by Gotye (feat.
*   Kimbra)*
"Back to December" by Taylor Swift
"making the bed" by Olivia Rodrigo
"Say Something" by A Great Big World and Christina
*   Aguilera*
"Jealous Guy" by John Lennon

And at the bottom of the box is a note.

.   .   .

To be continued…

I gasp, then look up to see Owen standing in the warm light of the bookstore. He's smiling, but the deep line between his eyebrows betrays his nerves. His dark, thick hair is pushed back, and his sharp jawline is covered by a shadow several hours past five o'clock.

"Sorry for all the subterfuge," he says with a shrug, another box in his hand.

"It's okay," I whisper, my voice watery. After so many weeks of avoiding him, I feel his presence in every part of my body. My hips ache for the feel of his large hands. My neck longs for his lips. I feel a phantom tug at the curls at the nape of my neck, an echo of meetings past. All this time Owen's been haunting me, no more than now, when he's standing right in front of me.

I can't move.

"I spent weeks trying to figure out how to show you how much I love you," he says, and my chest swells sharply. "And how sorry I am for wrecking everything."

"Yeah," is all I can say.

"I'm working on getting all the words right," he says. "In therapy."

My eyebrows rise. "Therapy?" It's one of the sweeter things he could say to me.

"Yeah. Turns out I have an anxiety disorder." He half laughs and gives a lazy shrug, but then he presses his lips together, his eyes worried. "That's not the reason why I hope you'll forgive me, but I figured I should let you know that I'm trying to get better. For you, but also for me. Maybe that helps to hear."

I look down at the sixteen tapes laid out on the floor around me.

"To be continued?" I ask, my eyes dropping to the box in his hand.

"Oh, right!" He sort of jumps, like he'd forgotten this next part, and I laugh. Fuck, he's so cute. He crosses the floor and hands me the box he's holding. I pull the lid open to find more tapes.

Dozens and dozens of tapes.

All of them blank.

"We were in the process of recording this building love story, Wyatt," Owen says. "We made all these memories in just a few months. And then I fucked it all up. I hurt you because I thought pulling away now would protect you from getting hurt even more later. And I'm working on that shit in therapy, but just know that I realize how messed up it was. I see that now."

He pauses, sucking in a long breath, steeling himself. "If you want tape sixteen to be the end, I completely understand. I don't deserve forgiveness for breaking your heart."

He reaches down and grasps my elbows, tugging me off the floor.

"But I'd like to earn it, Wyatt. If you'll let me, I'll spend every day trying to earn your forgiveness. I want to spend the rest of my life filling these tapes with memories we make together. And when we run out, I'll buy more. When I'm old and gray, I want to stare at a shelf filled with tapes, my messy handwriting and your brash script on the liner notes, each one a diary of our adventures together. Each one a chronicle of how much I fucking love you.

"Please make mixtapes with me, Wyatt."

There's so much to say. So much to talk about. So much hurt to mend, both mine *and* his.

But I desperately want to press play.

I suck in a breath, then reach up, threading my fingers into the hair at his nape.

"I fucking love you too," I tell him, then rise up on my toes and kiss him. "I will absolutely make mixtapes with you."

EPILOGUE

WYATT

October 14

The birthday girl is wearing her cake. As a birthday girl should when she turns one year old and her mother places a cake decorated to look like a botanical garden in front of her.

"Don't worry, this is just the smash cake!" Hazel says to the crowd, laughing as Eden shoves green frosting up her nose. "I have a whole cake that's just for eating."

"I wish smearing frosting all over your face was socially acceptable for adults, because that looks fucking fun," I say to Owen, who is standing behind me, his arms around my waist, his fingers hooked through my belt loops.

"Wyatt, you can smear frosting anywhere you want," he says, his voice low and delicious in my ear. "I'll happily help clean you up."

"Don't threaten me with a good time," I reply.

"Last time you said that, we ended up fucking in a bathroom during a party," he replies.

"I'd hate to break tradition."

I'm just starting to drag him toward my room when Carson comes skidding over, holding up her phone.

"What do you think this means?" she asks, shoving a text message in my face. I have to grab her wrist and physically restrain her so I can make out what she's trying to show me. It's a photo of a Florida lottery ticket, and beneath it, it simply says *We won.*

"It looks like a scam," I tell her.

"It's from my *parents*," she says. "They're down in Boca visiting my aunt. I called my mom, but when she answered she was drunk. *Drunk*, Wyatt. I'm, like, freaking out. I looked up the numbers, and if this is real, my parents just won *fourteen million dollars.*"

"Holy shit."

"Seriously," she gasps. "They're supposed to come home next week, but now I have no idea what the hell is going on."

"Whatever it is, it sounds like it's going to be wild!" I tell her, patting her on the back. Then I sink back into Owen's arms, my head pressed back into his chest, happy that my wild times are behind me.

Unless you count the rapidly stiffening erection in my boyfriend's jeans. Feels like there are some wild times happening *literally* behind me.

"You know, if your family is about to come into some cash, I know who you should talk to," I tell her.

"Who?"

I point at the broody finance bro in the corner. Hazel is handing Dan a plate holding a comically large slice of bright green cake, and he's looking at it like it might try to steal his money.

Carson's cheeks flush.

"C'mon, don't be scared, Carson! I'm sure he doesn't bite." I lean in and wink. "Unless you're lucky."

"Have you been drinking?" she asks.

"Just happy," I reply, gazing up at Owen.

"Ugh, you guys are gross," she grumbles, then stomps away, probably to find Grace and shove the text in her face.

"Are we gross?" I ask Owen.

"Well, we spent this morning making a mixtape of songs about sex and then seeing if I could make you come once for every track, so...maybe?"

It's been a month since I found that box of tapes in Grace's bookstore. ("Dog-Eared Books is now officially the site of the grand gesture—I should put that in an ad!" she told me when I talked to her about the scheme.) Since then, we've filled four more tapes. I have a feeling Owen is going to be ordering a new case of them before the year is out.

I've decided to join Romy for two weeks of her tour in the spring, and Owen will take a week of vacation to come along for half of it. When I return, Carson and I are going to look for an apartment together. Owen asked if I wanted to move in with him, but I worried it might be a little too soon. Therapy and medication are doing wonders for him, but healing is a long journey, especially when you've been dealing with anxiety for your whole life. I want him to keep focusing on that.

But I do use the key under the mat to slip into his bed most nights.

"Grammy's incoming with the wipes!"

Libby flies through the crowd, a package of baby wipes held aloft. She pulls Eden from her high chair and begins to wipe her down.

"You know, this is called a whore's bath," Libby whispers with a wink.

"Mom!" Hazel cries. "Can we not?"

"In front of the baby or in front of your friends?" Libby asks innocently.

"In front of *anyone*," Hazel admonishes.

Things with Libby have improved a little. She still makes me want to roll my eyes most of the time, but I'm working on trying to see her less as a villain in my story and more as a character with flaws. Flaws she's actively trying to overcome, I often have to remind myself, because her flashy clothes and garish makeup and sass mouth and just general *Libbyness* sometimes make it easy to forget.

The doorbell rings, and Libby cries, "Who the hell is ringing the doorbell? This is a party!" Then she shouts, "Get on in here!"

I roll my eyes and answer the door, unprepared for the four men in suits and dark sunglasses standing on our stoop.

"Can I help you?" I ask.

"We're looking for Daniel McBride," the one in front with the thick mustache says.

"Uh, who are you?"

"Securities and Exchange Commission," he says, holding up a gold badge that makes my mouth go dry. "Is he here?"

"Right here."

I turn and see Dan standing behind me, glowering.

"Dan? What the hell is going on?" Owen appears behind him, a deep line etched between his brows. Felix and Archer are next, crowding around the door to stare down the suits.

"Daniel McBride, we need to talk to you," the man with the mustache says. "Can you come with us, please?"

"Fucking finally," Dan mutters.

ACKNOWLEDGMENTS

First and foremost, I need to thank every reader and reviewer who joined me on this journey to Cardinal Springs. *More Than A Feeling* was a book that came from my deep love of romance, so having romance readers embrace that book has been one of the high points of my career.

Big thanks go to my agent, Kate Testerman, and the team at KT Literary. There has been no greater jolt to my career than signing with Kate. She's the reason you get to *listen* to the Cardinal Springs series!

Thank you to Alison Cherry, as always, for her incredible copy editing. I thought I was pretty good at grammar, and then Alison came along.

Thank you to Sarah Hansen at OK Creations for her incredible cover design and redesign. She's so good at interpreting my weird ideas and canvas mock-ups into something truly spectacular.

Thanks, as always, to Tiffany Schmidt, my homegirl, my ride-or-die, my road trip bestie. You saved me *big time* this year. I'm so lucky to have your encouragement, support, and keen eye for story.

Big, colorful hugs to Hannah Slaughter, my breakfast bestie who talks smutty books, cheers me on, and asks the perfect questions at the perfect time. I'm so glad you manifested our friendship. I'd be lost without it.

All the love to my book club, which is still too cool to have a name. Getting together with you each month to shout about butt stuff and tropes we hate and books we love is my favorite thing. You all were the very first readers to embrace *More Than A Feeling*.

Pretty sure most of my readers are because you guys wouldn't shut up about your love for it. I'll make you guys bacon-wrapped lil smokies for as long as you'll have me!

Big shout out to the Carrot Cake Hype Squad! Sarvanez Tash, Lauren Magaziner, Rebecca Behrens, and Jessica Spotswood have let me join their kidlit retreats to write two smutty books. And thanks to the Highlights Foundation for the cozy cabins and the carrot cake. Sorry for all the dirty words I wrote on your property.

For my boys. I hope you never read this.

For Poptart, who snored at my feet beneath my desk while I wrote.

And to Adam. For everything. Always. Forever.

ABOUT THE AUTHOR

Lauren Morrill is the author of spicy adult and sweet YA romance. She lives in Knoxville, TN with her husband, YouTuber Adam Ragusea, their two sons, and Poptart the pup. You can find her online at instagram.com/laurenmorrill (and while you're there, please tell her to stop scrolling).

ALSO BY LAUREN MORRILL

Cardinal Springs Series

More Than A Feeling

Caught Up In You

Just What I Needed (coming Fall 2025)

Standalones

Sister of the Bride

Young Adult

Meant to Be

Being Sloane Jacobs

The Trouble With Destiny

Better Than the Best Plan

It's Kind of a Cheesy Love Story